18528

D0458332

DATE DUE

JAN 2 2 2000	NOV 1 9 2009	DP
JUL 0 5 2000	SEP 1 9 2011	
SEP 1 2000	FEB - 4 2012	
SEP 2 0 2000	JUN 2 6 2013	
AUG. 1 2 2002		
JUL 3 0 2003		
OCT 0 6 2003		
NOV. 0 1 2004		
APR. 2 5 2005		
NOV 2 9 2005		
FEB 1 0 2007		
JAN 2 1 2008		

Grant Public Library
Grant, NE 69140

WITHDRAWN

TUMBLEWEEDS

FRONTIER STORIES

Also by Will Henry
in Large Print:

The Brass Command
Return of the Tall Man
The Tall Men

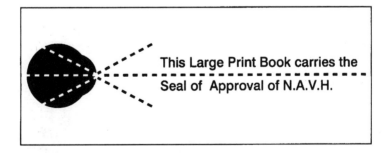

This Large Print Book carries the
Seal of Approval of N.A.V.H.

TUMBLEWEEDS

FRONTIER STORIES

Grant Public Library
Grant, NE 69140

Will Henry

Thorndike Press • Thorndike, Maine

Copyright © 1999 by Dorothy H. Allen

All rights reserved.

Acknowledgments may be found on page 378.

Published in 2000 by arrangement with
Golden West Literary Agency

Thorndike Large Print ® Western Series.

The tree indicium is a trademark of Thorndike Press.

The text of this Large Print edition is unabridged.
Other aspects of the book may vary from the original edition.

Set in 16 pt. Plantin by Rick Gundberg.

Printed in the United States on permanent paper.

Library of Congress Cataloging-in-Publication Data

Henry, Will, 1912–
    Tumbleweeds : frontier stories / Will Henry.
        p.   cm.
    ISBN 0-7862-1337-X (lg. print : hc : alk. paper)
    1. Frontier and pioneer life — West (U.S.) — Fiction.
    2. Western stories. 3. Large type books. I. Title.
    PS3551.L393 T86   2000
    813'.54—dc21   99-046981

18528

*One Last Ride — for My Children
Valerie and Christopher*

Table of Contents

Foreword

Tumbleweeds are born to wander. So with these tales of the Old West. No pattern of the planting is followed. The roots go down along strange fencelines. The incredible documentation of Cole Younger's fifteen-hundred mile ride on the great Northfield Raid may lodge beside a blue norther of an old cowboy's lie conjured up between blizzards in the snowbound bunkhouse of the Tumbleweed Land & Cattle Company, or the hijinks of a windy about a boy's "capture" of Sam Bass.

The final inquest of the coroner's jury into the identity of the man who murdered Jesse James finds itself brought up against the same bottom wire of fate with the legend of the Indian who became *el presidente*. But that is the way that it is with tumbleweeds. They know not where they begin or where they shall come to rest. They only roll on forever.

Like young gunman Johnny McComas, hunted by the Pale One through the death-still streets of Laredo. Or the American kid, tracking the most dangerous game into the towering grasslands of far Africa. Or Bass Cooper and his experience of when the number five was a bad medicine number in one sense and a passport in another.

Their stories unfold, never pausing, carried on the keening of the western wind, caught in the glint of the sun off lance blade and carbine barrel. The great and famous pass over the same buffalo grass with the nameless waifs and strays from nowhere. Out there it is all the same. All are the tumbleweeds of life. At the last fenceline, they lie as brothers.

For the waifs and strays
of every range . . .
Will Henry

The Skinning of Black Coyote

Tracy eased the little line-back dun out of her shuffle-walk and put her to a stiff lope. Ahead of him, three miles, the Big Bend of the Arkansas glinted dull silver in the brassy noon sun. Behind him, six miles off across a country flat as a spinster's chest and near as uninteresting, crawled the snaking line of Conestogas he was trail-guiding to Bent's Fort.

Tracy swept the wide valley of the Arkansas with constant, quick-swinging glances as he let the mare take her own gait toward the river. A big man, Tracy Higgins, lean as a weather-split hickory post and near onto as hard. About the same color, too. Tracy would allow his pedigree was as white as they came — but his history was something else again.

Snatched out of a burning log fortress up on the Medicine Road, when he was a rising six-year-old, he'd been reared up by the same Ogalala Bad Face band of Sioux that had put the flame to the frontier trading post of which his father had been chief clerk. Later, as a teen-age young one, looking a sight more the Ogalala Bad Face he'd been reared than the Ohio Irish he'd been born, he'd taken to guiding wagon outfits from Independence and Kansas City to Bridger's Fort up by Salt Lake. With the booming of the Santa Fé trade, he'd switched trails and gone to work for Bent and St. Vrain, guiding freight outfits on the Santa Fé.

Right off he'd liked the New Mexico Trail a heap better than the old Medicine Road. The country was all new to him, and the outfits were mostly small professional freight trains, like the one he had behind him right now. And the Santa Fé Trail had been a good one for Tracy. In three short seasons, he'd made stake enough to buy and load the bright new Conestoga that rumbled along in the train behind him.

Right now, though, Tracy was about as unhappy as he'd been in a long spell. Let a man tie up his whole savings in a wagon-load of goods, like he had his tied up in the last wagon of that train back there, and he was bound to run into a sign that would read unhappy to him. Only yesterday, where they'd been mired in at Cow Creek, Tracy had picked up that sign. It was just a little thing, and mostly a scout wouldn't have paid any heed. After all, when you're in Indian country, it sure isn't anything to find an old, worn-out moccasin lying around a heavily used crossing like Cow Creek. Hell, the country from Turkey Creek on was crawling with Kiowas and Comanches. Only trouble was, this wasn't any Comanche or Kiowa moccasin. It was Arapaho.

Tracy had been just as unsettled by that as if he'd spied a Comanche arrow broke off in a Powder River buffalo carcass. An Arapaho moccasin was that much out of place on Cow Creek in Kansas Territory. And it wasn't only the moccasin; looking around, he'd found other signs.

First off, there'd been a mess of them — upward of two hundred, 'way too many for just a hunting party. Then, the ashes of their cook fires hadn't cooled clear out at the time he'd dug into them. So they were a big bunch, and they were close. That much was plain. But something else that he saw made his backbone bust out with pimply flesh high enough to hang your hat on. This something else had a whale of a lot less right being smack-dab in the middle of an Arapaho campsite than the old moccasin.

It was a clean print of a big foot, the edges of the impression sharp-cut in the damp earth, the square toe and cross-cutting heel mark taking away all question of Indian origin. That print was as plainly white as the crude cowhide boot that'd put it there. And the only set of boots with that peculiar toe that Tracy knew to be any-where within a hundred miles of Cow Creek were around the size-twelve stomp-ers of Big Tate Barker.

The little additional thought that struck Tracy with such a peedinger of a wallop was that Big Tate just *happened* to be wagon-bossing the train that was following him right now! What Big Tate had been doing in the Arapaho camp and how he had managed to get there without Tracy's knowing about it were the questions that turned on the restless spit of the scout's mind as he swung down off the dun mare and let her muzzle-out into the milky wa-ters of the Big Arkansas.

The night before Cow Creek, they had camped at the Little Arkansas. It must have been sometime during that night when Big Tate had slipped out of camp and night-ridden to Cow Creek. Since it

14

was a round trip of thirty-five miles, it must have taken the wagon boss the best part of the night. How in tarnation had he managed it without anybody wising up? What was he up to?

Crooking his mouth, Tracy made a sound in his throat that only an Indian or another frog could have detected from the dry *r-r-rack-rack! rack-rack!* of the little spotted frog found in any prairie wet spot bigger than a bucket.

Out of the stream, belly-deep in the five-mile current, the barrel-ribbed little mare left off her sucking at the opaque water, raised her keg-sized head, muzzle dripping, to stare at the talented six-foot croaker on the shore.

"Ho! Ye, Knaska! Come on outta thar. Ye've had yer gutful, and we got ourse'fs some Arapaho to run down."

Knaska was the Sioux word for frog, and truly no horse could have been more aptly called. The dun mare was no more then thirteen hands, rib-sprung and bench-legged as a bulldog in front, broad-beamed and cow-hocked as a Holstein behind. She was unquestionably the ugliest mare ever foaled — and the fastest.

Swinging aboard her, the scout headed due west, up the right bank of the Arkansas. It was eight miles to Walnut Creek, their camp for that night. Tracy meant to scout every mile of the eight, up and back, before Big Tate got the wagons past the Arkansas.

The valley along Tracy's side of the river was broad and open, spotted here and there with a lone snaggle of a cottonwood, slashed occasionally by the low ridges of red clay and yellow sandstone. Otherwise, the two-inch buffalo grass was the only obstruction to limitless vision.

The other side of the stream was another story. Across there, the ridges became considerable bluffs, high and frequent enough to have hidden ten thousand Arapahoes. It was these bluffs that the scout's worried gaze searched for the next two hours of his journey. But he didn't see so much as the wisp of a feather tip, or the sun-glance off a lance blade.

By the time he reached the fork where Walnut Creek spilled into the Arkansas, he was beginning to wonder if he'd plumb lost his "Injun sniffer." And judging from his next actions, his smeller wasn't all he'd lost. Any man who'd been Ogalala-raised that would go for a swim in mid-afternoon in the wide-open gut of hostile Indian country must have had a head as mushy as a scalped settler's. But give a boy — be he two, twenty, or three times twenty — a long, dusty ride ahead of where a pretty creek fork rambles into a fine wide river, the mixed waters running cold and chuckling over a clean sand bottom, and you've got yourself a swimming party.

It took Tracy maybe ten seconds to shuck out of his buckskins, crotch his Hawkens in a convenient cottonwood, turn the mare loose to graze, and splatter his hide into the Arkansas. The first idea Tracy had that he wasn't the only human within shouting distance of the Arkansas was when a chance glance to check Knaska's whereabouts showed him the little mare standing tense and prick-eared.

Tracy made a great show of resuming his splashing and wallowing, but he threw one eye-corner look at the bank behind him. Instantly, every nerve in his body went catgut tight. The bank off which he'd plunged was about six feet high. Atop it grew the cottonwood whereon he'd so neatly draped his skins and hung his Hawkens. Two minutes before that cussed cottonwood had been the loneliest tree in Kansas Territory. When he looked at it now, it was no longer so.

Sitting their shaggy ponies, utterly motionless, gravely studying the antics of the naked white idiot in the Arkansas, were two dozen Arapaho braves. Those red sons were no friendlies! Their gargoyle faces were smeared black with charcoal grease paint. Blazing bands of ocher and vermilion slashed across their broad cheekbones, zebra-striped their low foreheads, cornered their wide mouths. They were in full head-dress — lances, bows, ponies, and persons decked and hung with war feathers. A hunting party would be plain-shirted, un-feathered.

One man stood out over all the rest. He was tall and angular, sun-blacked, with a great, flat-boned face, a tremendous jaw, and an ear-to-ear knife slash of a mouth — the whole adding up to about the roughest-looking redskin Tracy had ever seen. And Tracy knew he had seen him before.

This beauty was no subchief, no local nabob. The snow flash of bonnet feathers, cascading down his back and foaming across his pony's flank, trailed almost to the ground — seven feet of them, a hundred coup claims at least, maybe more. Where, oh where in the hell had he seen that face before? For one detail and one alone, Tracy thanked his trained eye: there hadn't been a gun visible in the passel of them.

Tracy had one chance. He took it.

In the midst of the porpoise snorts and buffalo bellows issuing from the white maniac in the river now came a series of spotted frog croaks. *"R-r-r-rack, rack-rack. R-r-r-rack, rack-rack."*

The slit-eyed watchers on the shore nodded, the one to the other. Very good imitation. Very creditable. As skilled, almost, as an Indian's. They paid little heed to the frog-headed pony ambling into the stream, splashing through the hock-deep shallows toward her master. This was a good situation. Cut just to size for the red man's love of the dramatic. Just wait till this fool turned shoreward to retrieve his gun and dress skins. *Aii-ee!* That would be the time. Let him turn and look. Wait till then. Don't shoot now. Let his eyeballs pop out along his cheekbones in terror. That was it. Hold the arrows till he turned around. Gently now, the mare is close to him. Don't hit her when he turns to see us. Be careful of the mare. We want her. So, so. Gently, now.

The minute Knaska came within hand's reach, Tracy went aboard like a painter crawling an orphan colt. His heels pistoned into her ribs, and the panther scream of the Ogalala Sioux exploded in her pinned-back ears.

"Hiii-eee-hahhh!"

Ahead of Tracy, if he were to cross it, lay three-quarters of a mile of the Arkansas — shallow, it was true, but as deep as four feet in places. And four feet was plenty deep to slow up Knaska enough to let the red scuts plumage up his back with arrow feathers. His best chance was downstream, and he took it. Swinging the mare hard left, he sent her buck-jumping down the shallows along the shelving bank.

He was in luck. All the Indians but one had plunged their ponies into the stream after him, and they could make no more speed than he. But that one, the snow-feathered chief, had sent his gaudy paint stud horse pounding down the bank to cut Tracy off, when he came out of the stream. He was fully abreast of Tracy as the latter kicked Knaska in toward the bank.

As he came showering out of the water, Tracy got a split-second's relief from the fact that the chief's bow was not unslung. In its stead, the tall Arapaho brandished a polished hardwood skull cracker — a toy that was four feet long and crotched a six-pound cannon ball in its forked end.

Tracy had no course but to ride out and into the Arapaho, one way or another. He came out at an oblique angle, sheering

20

away from the Indian's charging mount as though in panic. The paint stud was nose-close to Knaska's rump in two jumps.

With both ponies going at a yellow-lather clip, the scout threw every ounce of his weight backward against Knaska's hackamore, literally pulling the mare's forehoofs off the ground, haunch-sliding her to a stop that took half the skin off her hocks. The paint stud couldn't match it. His sliding stop carried him ten feet past Knaska, leaving him off balance for all the time Tracy needed.

Before either chief or stud horse could recover and wheel, the scout drove Knaska crashing into the Indian pony's rump. It was a jarring, twisting impact, Knaska's right shoulder smashing into the stud's left haunch, sending the Indian pony hock-over-fetlock down the adjacent shelf bank of the Arkansas. Horse and chief cascaded into the swirling waters in a tangle of thrashing hoofs and wildly scrambling rider.

Arrows were whistling close around Tracy, when, in response to his inspired Sioux yelling, Knaska flattened out and belly-skinned the short gamma grass.

When the fall-off in the drum fire of the barefoot pony hoofs behind him and the

21

increasing arc of the trajectory of the passing arrows let him know that Knaska had opened up breathing space between himself and his pursuers, he turned and shouted insults after the Indian fashion.

"*Wa klure! Wa klure!* Loafers! Loafers! *Nohetto, keyokas!* There you are, you clowns! *Canniyasa!* You are failures, all of you!"

The Arapahoes set up a yammer of return coin for these insults, and Tracy sent them a parting gesture as readily translatable in the hand language of the *Shacun* as in that of their white brothers, the *Wasicum*. With the gesture, he gave out a last yell of defiance: "Remember who has done this to you, you dog-eaters. It is I, To-Ke-Ya, the Ogalala. *Wagh!*"

It is the natural fortune of the Trail for those hardy souls assigned to ride the head of a line of Santa Fé freighters — in this case the brooding giant, Tate Barker — to ride up on many a strange sight.

"Fer the luvva Gawd," muttered Big Tate, reining in his horse and waving the wagons behind him to a halt. "That damned son of a Sioux must've go'd crazy."

There were grounds for the wagon boss's

22

doubt of Tracy's sanity. Six feet, two of heel-hammering white scout, aboard a bandy-legged yellow mare, belly-stretching to a flat gallop, with nothing between the two of them and the afternoon sunshine but a horsehair hackamore and a saddle — it was enough to give the oldest prairie hand a pause.

"Whut in the name of hell happened to ye?" Big Tate shouted as Tracy haunch-slid the dun mare to a dirt-showering stop.

"I got jumped by a party of Arapahoes. Up by Walnut Fork." Tracy talked fast. "I wuz takin' a swim jest below the Fork, when they rode up on me. Lucky fer me I got this mare call-broke. I played dumb like I ain't seed them yet, whistled the mare up, and clumb aboard. They give me a run fer a space, but I had the most hoss under me."

"Wall, ye fer sure air a spectacle 'thout yer skins on. How many of the red scuts wuz thar?"

" 'Bout twenty braves . . . one real salty chief," Tracy answered.

"Whut'd the chief look like?"

Tracy noted Big Tate's sudden interest. He watched him narrowly, as he said: "Big devil. Tall for an Injun. Broad, bony face. Biggest jaw I ever seen. White heron-

23

feather bonnet trailin' nigh into the dust. *Woyuonihan!* He was a real chief. *Wagh!*"

"Never heard of him." Big Tate's denial was short, but Tracy saw the quick shift of the pig eyes. "And quit gruntin' like a damn' Sioux. I don't cotton to Injuns, and I don't savvy their lingo."

Tracy had it in mind to call him a liar right there, but he hadn't lived with the Sioux for ten years without he'd learned to run all the tracks out before he hollered his hand. Right now he had only two cards on Tate. He didn't aim to tip his mitt before the deal was done. "I 'low ye know enough of 'em to know thet a scout band in black grease and feathers totes up to trouble."

"How ye figger to be so sartin they wuz a scout band? Mebbe thet wuz all thar war of 'em."

Tracy's mouth, wide as any Ogalala's, clamped down tight. "As I come out'n the valley, I seen a cloud of riders headin' in toward Walnut Fork. Thar wuz a passel of 'em. I figger 'em fer the main bunch . . . two, maybe three hundred of 'em, I'd say. Leastways enough so's we'll hafta corral-up at Big Bend 'stead of goin' to Walnut Crick."

"The hell you say!"

"The hell I don't. Ye roll this train an

24

axle-turn past Big Bend, and ye'll roll her ag'in' my report."

"Wall, git out'n the way, then, mister." Big Tate's face stiffened. " 'Cause I'm rollin' 'er!"

"Hold up a minute, Barker. I reckon ye didn't hear me. I said thar wuz a couple hundred hostiles foggin' around behind Big Bend."

"I heered ye. We're makin' Walnut Crick tonight."

"There ain't time. It'll darken on ye 'fore ye kin git camped."

"Whut of it? Ye ain't afeered of Injuns, be ye?"

"Ye damn' betcha. How 'bout ye?"

"Me, I'm tellin' ye we're makin' the crick tonight. I got a schedule."

Tracy looked at him long enough to wear down a lesser he-bear than Big Tate Barker. "I 'low ye have," he said, "but I reckon it ain't the one Bent and Saint Vrain give ye."

The big man went stiff all over. "Ye peep one word 'bout them Injuns to the 'skinners, and I'll gut-shoot ye. I aim to git up to Walnut Crick tonight, and I don't mean to have ye gittin' my drivers all jumped up 'bout a war party trailin' us. Ye understand thet, damn ye?"

Tracy felt the anger in him well up, but, when he spoke, his drawl was as pleasant as a May breeze. "I 'low I do, Mister Barker. Mebbe so a lot better than ye think."

He saw Tate flinch as the hook went into him, and he knew that he'd declared a war that could end just one way — with one of them no longer enjoying the privilege of sucking good air into live lungs.

They made Walnut Fork a good hour after dark. Big Tate said not a word to the company about the hostiles, letting a normal camp be set up, including carelessly bright cook fires and just the regular two-hour guard shifts.

The camp got quiet about ten, the fires going to pinpoint coals about eleven. Half an hour later, Tate rolled out of his blankets, listened intently, came noiselessly to his feet, and drifted out toward the loose herd of saddle stock.

Behind him, Tracy Higgins glided on a pair of feet that had learned to step quiet where a noise as big as a mouse's breathing might mean the difference between whether a man's hair was worn or torn.

At the edge of the horse herd, Big Tate paused, whistling low and easy in as perfect an imitation of a sleepy whippoorwill as Tracy had ever heard. When he heard the horse's answering whicker, the scout knew how Tate had worked the Cow Creek slip — and knew, also, he had a very scratchy customer to accompany. He let Tate mount up and get a start before following him, dogtrotting on moccasins that hit the earth as loud as fat snowflakes.

After ten minutes of powder-footed going, Tracy had worked in to where he was a bare twenty yards behind the sound he trailed — the muffled *plop-plop* of a shod horse going in deep dust. For another five minutes the sound continued, then stopped. Tracy waited a dozen slow breaths, then started working in closer. Finding a proper gully, he slid into it and poked his eyes above the lip. Beyond there, easily seen in the starlight, Big Tate sat his horse, waiting. This must be the place of the meeting — if there was going to be one.

A bullbat twittered harshly out on the prairie. Big Tate answered it, his nighthawk imitation being the equal of his whippoorwill. Ear to the ground, Tracy picked up the shuffle-walking approach of several barefoot ponies. In another few seconds, their shadows bulked up out of the darkness and halted some yards out from the waiting wagon boss.

A single shadow detached itself and drifted up to Tate. Tracy recognized the rider. It was the chief he'd dumped in the river.

"*Ha-a-u*," called the Arapaho softly, his tone as deep and guttural as a muttering bear's. "We meet again."

That voice! Once heard a voice like that was remembered. Watan-goa, the Black Coyote. Tracy had seen him in a dozen boyhood war camps. *Aiieee!* A man would almost rather have any hostile on his hands than this one. *Woyuonihan. A-ah!* Respect this one. Look out for him.

"*Ha-a-u*," answered Big Tate. "Is your heart good?"

"Our hearts are good. Watan-goa's heart is good. We are ready. When we talked of the Creek of the Cows, you told us that one god-dam in your train carried big medicine for Watan-goa."

In his gully, Tracy had to smile at that "god-dam." It was the Plains Indians' name for the Conestogas, taken from the favorite word of their cursing white drivers.

"I told ye right," growled Big Tate. "Thet god-dam is totin' the biggest medicine that is."

"How big?" grunted the Arapaho in impatient tones.

"*Mazawakan,*" snapped Big Tate. "Plenty *mazawakan.*"

Tracy's hair lifted again. *Mazawakan.* Holy irons. Rifles. God Almighty! Guns! So Big Tate was running guns. But where were they? Tracy knew the goods in that caravan. He'd seen the loading in Independence. There wasn't a gun set aboard any of the wagons, to his knowledge. Where the hell did Tate have them, then?

"How many?" Watan-goa's question came hard and hoarse.

"We have dealt before," answered Big Tate. "Our hearts are good. Ye will do as I say with the *mazawakan?*"

"*Ha-a-u.* I will do it."

"Ten, fer ye."

"How many all *mazawakan?*"

Tracy sensed Big Tate's hesitation and, knowing Indians, appreciated it. They were harder to hold to a deal than an axle-greased eel. "A hundred," said the wagon boss finally.

"Good. What does Watan-goa do?"

"Ye take the guns to Pawnee Rock. I'll meet ye thar in three suns, and we'll make the divvy. Ten *mazawakan,* ye. The rest, me."

"It is agreed. Where *mazawakan* now?"

Tracy thought the chief's assent came too fast and wondered how Big Tate had the guts to try a deal like this with Watangoa. Apparently the wagon boss knew the Black Coyote better than Tracy did. He himself wouldn't trust the slit-eyed devil any farther than he could pitch a bull buffalo.

"Ye know thet big god-dam with the red wheels? The bright blue one? The spankin' new one?"

Tracy's hair was getting used to standing up. His Conestoga was the only *new* one in the caravan. Its wheels were as red as saddle sores, its bed as blue as a summer sky.

"*Ha-a-u.* The one that eats the dust?"

"Ye got it. Thet's the one. The last one in the line. Wal, it's loaded with five thousand pounds of bolt calico" — Tracy silently amended the boss's figure. Five thousand, two hundred and fifty pounds. He ought to know, by God. He'd paid for every pound. — "but it's carryin' six thousand pounds, now. That's a hundred ten-pound rifles in thar, as wasn't when she rolled from Independence."

"*Ha-a-u! Ha-a-u!*"

"Me and the 'skinner whut's drivin' thet god-dam loaded 'em in at Council Grove.

30

Now, air ye all straight on whut ye do tomorry?"

"Watan-goa remembers well, but would hear once more."

"All right. In the mornin' we cross the crick early. The new god-dam will cross first, 'stead of last. I'll be drivin' the second god-dam, and I'll mire her in the middle of the crick. Soon's ye see me stuck, ye jump the first god-dam, grab the guns, and ske-daddle. Ye got thet, now?"

"*Ha-a-u.* It is clear."

"All right, then. Ev'eything's all set?"

"No." The chief's disagreement was quick and blunt.

"Whut the hell's the matter?"

"The scout. The *Wasicum* who calls him-self To-Ke-Ya, the Fox, and who speaks with the tongue of the Cut-Throat People. What of him? He is a warrior. What of this one?"

"Don't worry 'bout thet Sioux cub. He's goin' to git his 'fore we roll in the mornin'."

"How will this happen?"

"In the mornin' I'll accuse him of dealin' with the Injuns to jump the train. The boys'll buy the bluff on account of him comin' in naked yestiddy with thet yarn 'bout bein' jumped by a war party. When

31

he talks back, I'll gut-shoot him. Thet satisfy ye?"

"*Ha-a-u,*" growled Black Coyote. "Good hunting."

Tracy had heard plenty more than enough. Even as the Arapahoes faded back into the darkness out of which they'd come and Tate headed his horse around, he was legging it for camp as fast as his long limbs would take him.

When Big Tate snuck back into the darkened camp, he found Tracy rolled in his blankets tight as a tick in a dog's tail. Weary from his own two nights of night riding, the big man lost no time getting into his own bedroll. In seconds, he was snoring fit to shake the lice out of his blankets.

Trace waited a full hour, and, when, at last, he rolled out of his blankets, midnight was far past. When he went cat-footing it through the dark toward Big Tate's bedding ground, he carried three objects of tangible value. Item One: a beltful of buckskin laces, three feet long and strong as a boar grizzly's gut. Item Two: two small squares of soft, mending doeskin. Item Three: a short-barreled Ames Navy Pistol, model of 1843, just the thing for sapping hard heads on dark nights.

Big Tate was breathing a little rough, when Tracy moved in over him, but following the soft *tunk* of the pistol barrel behind his ear he relaxed into a rhythm as nice and easy as a breast-fed baby's. In twenty seconds, the scout had gagged and trussed him neat as a suckling pig ready for the roaster.

With the remaining scrap of doeskin and the unused laces, Tracy faded away toward his own wagon. Taos McFarland, the 'breed muleskinner he'd hired on to drive his wagon, was ventilating his tonsils as thunderously as Tate had been. Tracy had to grin as he thought back to how he'd asked the wagon boss to recommend a 'skinner, and Big Tate had steered him onto Taos McFarland. Perhaps the memory sped the pistol hand, for the swinging barrel of the Ames cracked into the side of the sleeping teamster's skull with a smack that nigh knocked him clear out of his blankets. For a bad minute Tracy thought he'd killed him, but Taos started to breathe again after a spell, and the scout stuffed the doeskin in his mouth and tied him, hard.

Slinging the inert form over his shoulder, Tracy started back toward Tate.

"Whut the hell's goin' on 'round h'yar?"

Tracy recognized the complaining voice, testy with years, as that of old Dan Masters, dean of the Bent and St. Vrain teamsters. "Sounds like a couple of buffalo wuz breedin' or suthin'."

"It's me, Dan." Tracy's voice was low. "Tracy Higgins."

"Wal, what the tarnal hell ye doin'? Holdin' a war stomp?"

"Dan, lissen. We got big trouble. Git the rest of the boys and meet me over by Tate's bedroll. No lights and no noise. And move fast."

"Whut's up?" Too long on the South Trail, Dan Masters had been, to be stampeded by a cub wagon scout.

"We got a couple hundred Injuns layin' fer us to cross Walnut Crick in the mornin'."

"What Injuns?"

"Arapahoes."

" 'Rapahoes? The hell ye say. Who's headin' 'em?"

"Black Coyote."

"I'll git the boys," was all the old man said, and Tracy, nodding, carried Taos's body on over to dump it alongside Tate's.

In ten minutes the 'skinners had all come up. Tracy let them have it, short. "Boys, I got Tate and Taos trussed up h'yar, and I 'low ye're all hankerin' to know whut in tunket's goin' on. This bearbrain, Tate, him and this yaller 'breed, Taos, wuz fixin' to let us get our scalps lifted."

"The hell!"

"The hell, yes. Lissen. Last night Tate snuck ahaid up to Cow Creek to palaver with a big bunch of Arapahoes thet war camped thar. Then he snuck back into camp 'thout ennybody seed him. Wal, tonight he snuck out and palavered with the same bunch ag'in. I follered Tate and heered him talk to the chief. It war the same redskin I knocked into the river this afternoon. I didn't remember him then, but, soon's I heered his voice tonight, I did."

"Yeah? Who wuz it? Whut chief?" The interruption came from one of the teamsters.

"Watan-goa," snapped Tracy.

"Black Coyote."

"The one and only. Now, git this. Tate and this h'yar Taos snuck in a hundred rifles at Council Grove. They loaded 'em in my wagon. Tonight I heered Tate dealin' with Watan-goa to turn them guns over to him."

Short and sweet, then, he gave them the whole dirty deal.

"Whut ye aim to do 'bout it, Tracy?" Old Dan acted as spokesman for the teamsters.

"I got a leetle scheme that might pollute Black Coyote's taste fer free guns fer some spell to come. But first I gotta know whether all of ye believe my side. Tate's gonna claim I'm the nigger in this red woodpile, not him. Jest like I told ye he done told Black Coyote he wuz fixin' to do. Tate's woke up now from thet tap I give him. I'm gonna cut his mouth loose and let him talk."

"Hold up, thar." Old Dan's voice was quick. "Iffen ye free his flap, he's jest as apt to yell out to his red friends. Me, fer one, I buy yer yarn. Happen I warn't sleepin' well thet night back thar at the Leetle Arkansaw, afore Cow Creek. I seen Tate ride out, and I seen him ride back. He war gone most of the night."

The old man's support was enough for the others. One after another they spoke up.

"Yeah, the hell with it. Leave his yap stuffed."

"Sure, leave him be the way he is."

"He ought to be kilt outright."

"No," Tracy broke in. "I 'low we ain't gonna kill him. We'll let the Arapahoes do thet."

"Whut ye mean? How's yer idee work?" Old Dan was questioning again.

"Wall, she shapes up thisaway. As long as them Injuns know 'bout them guns, they'll come after us, Tate er no Tate. Ye'll see it thetaway?"

A chorus of quick agreement ran around the invisible ring of listeners.

"All right, then. I figger it like this. Long as Tate and Taos was fixin' to delivery them guns, I reckon we'll let 'em. After all, Black Coyote's bin give the white man's word on the deal, and we gotta make good on it. Let's put thet first wagon over the crick and stick the second one in the crossin', jest like Tate promised them. We'll have them guns in thet first wagon, accordin' to the agreement. When old Watan-goa shows up to claim 'em, why we'll jest let 'em have 'em, thet's all. Is thet clear 'nough?"

"It's beginnin' to be!" Old Dan's dry chuckle was picked up and spread quickly among the other muleskinners. "And I 'low, if we delivery them holy irons like ye aim to delivery 'em, we got a mort of wagon reloadin' to do 'fore daylight."

"Yeah." Tracy's assent was laconic. "And we ain't got more'n a hour of plumb dark left to us."

"Ye and the boys go to it. I'll set h'yar and wet-nurse these infants fer ye." Old Dan's tones were as easy as Tracy's. "Ye'd best leave me thet Iron Medicine ye give 'em 'fore mornin'."

By 4:30 A.M., the last of the reloading was done. The ghost-gray of pre-dawn was putting its sick tinge along the rim of the prairie, as Tracy and Dan Masters squatted by the off-wheel of the lead wagon. The Conestogas still stood in their hollow square, tongues out like they'd been parked the night before. Nothing had been moved, with one peculiar exception. Every wagon stood team-hitched, its three span of patient mules full-harnessed, ready to roll. A mighty close eye, given broad daylight, could have seen one other thing: the lead team in each hitch was picketed down, hard and fast.

It was the one rut in the smooth track of Tracy's plan, but there was no way around it. The mule drivers who would ordinarily have been wheeling those twenty-three Conestogas had something tougher than a mule to skin that morning. They had a coyote. A black one. Name of Watan-goa.

The minutes were crawling after one another so slow you could almost hear

38

them sucking their feet out of the mud after that last half hour. The start had to be just right: enough light to see an Arapaho across an iron sight, not enough for an Arapaho to see tie ropes and picket pins across a creek.

"I 'low we wuz all-fired lucky to git onto Tate 'fore he let them red sons down on top of us." Old Dan's whisper jumped a little with understandable Indian-nerves. "Onct they had them guns, they'd never hold up at jest runnin' off with 'em. Not with all thet powder and shot we found Tate had cached in yer wagon along with 'em. Them Injuns would've had 'nough ammunition to smoke us deeper than a Mizzouri ham."

"They won't hold up, ennyways, even *not* knowin' 'bout the powder and slugs. Bow and errer Injuns'll do ennything to git a gun. We wuz lucky, all right, to git on top of Tate. But we'll be a damn' sight luckier, if we git out from under Watan-goa." Then Tracy was silent a long minute, listening intently.

"Whut'd ye hear?" asked Dan tensely.

"Shet up!" whispered the scout. "I thought I heered Injuns talkin'."

In answer to his statement, a fox barked sharply about three hundred yards up the creek. Its mate yapped back from an equal distance downstream. Out on the plains, directly across the little stream, the sleepy *pee-weet, pee-weet* of a prairie plover made known its owner's awakening. The querulous whirring chuckle of a disturbed prairie hen answered the plover.

"It's light enough," Tracy's announcement came abruptly. "Let's roll."

The two figures arose, slipping along the sides of the wagons, away from the creek. At the third Conestoga, Old Dan climbed up and took the reins. "All set, Tracy."

"Ye got it straight, now?"

"I'm to wait till the second wagon starts into the crick, then come on along like I wuz leadin' off the remainin' wagons."

"Thet's right. Don't stall too long 'fore ye start, er happen they'll smell a mouse."

Leaving the old man, Tracy returned to the second Conestoga. On the seat, bolt upright, by virtue of a four-foot Hawkens' barrel planted in his kidneys, sat Big Tate Barker. The owner of the Hawkens crouched under the canvas sheeting of the wagon cover, just back of the driver's seat, hidden from all but the most inquiring eye.

"All set, h'yar?"

The rifleman nodded as Tracy loomed up.

"Good." The scout's answering nod was

40

hurried. Flicking his gray eyes from the hidden rifleman to the ramrod figure on the driver's seat, he went on. "Now remember, Tate, yer feet air strapped onto thet brake-bar, and ye've got a Hawkens set in yer back ready to separate yer spine, if ye even breathe wrong. Ye drive this wagon spang into the middle of the crick and hold her up thar, exactly like ye told Black Coyote ye would. Thet's all ye do. Not another damn' thing. Ye got it?"

The glowering wagon boss licked his lips and muttered thickly. "I got it, Higgins, but lissen. I ain't got a chanct settin' up h'yar like a damn' pigeon. They'll. . . ."

"Hey! Ye, in the wagon, thar. . . ." Tracy ignored Tate.

"Yes, sir, ye betchy!"

"One eyewink out'n this overgrowed slob on the seat and ye leave him have it 'tween the liver-lights and the kidneys."

"I gotchy."

"All right," snapped Tracy, "we're goin' acrost."

At the lead wagon, his own bright Conestoga, Taos was sharing Tate's rôle, feet lashed to the brake-bar, a rifle barrel from inside the covered wagon none too gently nudging the backside of his pelvis. "Ye know whut to do now, Taos? Jest drive her

41

acrost and up onto the flat over thar. Ye foul up in enny way, and ye'll git yer bottom blowed off."

The fear-sick 'breed, too miserable to find his tongue, nodded like a dumb thing that didn't have any. Stepping up on the near wheel, Tracy leaned into the interior of the wagon, talking through the puckered hole in the Osnaburg sheeting just back of the seat. "Ye all set in thar?"

"All set in h'yar, Mister Higgins." The answer came cheerily from the man holding the Hawkens in Taos's back.

"Wal, then, h'yar goes to delivery them hundred guns to brother Watan-goa."

The Conestoga took off with a hangle of trace chains that was all but drowned out by Tracy's roar to the rest of the wagons: "All set! All set! Stretch out! Stretch out! Hooray fer Santy Fee!"

Tate's wagon lumbered into motion, following the track of the one driven by Taos. By the time Old Dan was shouting and lash-popping his teams into their collars, the 'breed's wagon was lurching and hulking up the far bank of the creek. Behind it, Tate was just carefully heading his mules into the water. In the sand hills beyond the crossing, not a noise louder than a grass sparrow's chirrup was heard. The whole prairie lay as still and as peaceful-looking as a clear lake bottom on a quiet day.

Now! Tate had his teams in midstream. Taos was already a hundred yards out on the prairie beyond the crossing.

Tracy put his heels into Knaska's ribs fit to knock the wind out of her. The clay-colored mare shot into the creek and alongside Tate's stalled wagon. As if on signal, the sand hills beyond began puking out more Arapahoes than there were wheel spokes in the whole caravan.

The hostiles were up on top of Taos and Tracy's beautiful new Conestoga where the canvas top got itself shed-off faster than water off a wet dog's back. And all around the edge of the pretty blue bed, gorgeous black blossoms with stabbing orange centers began bursting into riotous and noisy bloom.

Even as he jumped for the wagon seat of Tate's Conestoga, Tracy couldn't help admiring the effect of that bright garden over there around his Conestoga. It had become especially effective with its new border of quiet red bodies.

Seizing the reins from Tate, Tracy put the mules hammering up the bank. "*Hee-yah!* Hiddy-ap thar! Up ye go! *Hee-yah-hhhh!*"

With the help of the Ogalala panther scream, the scout had the surprised mules on the dead run for the other wagon before the Arapahoes could rally for their second charge. The scout slid Tate's wagon to a stop alongside the first freighter, just as the hostiles came yammering back.

Their second try was better than the first, half a dozen of them actually scrambling into the wagon bed. But twenty salt-tanned muleskinners, with a hundred new rifles stacked and loaded to hand, could down a sinful lot of redskins, especially when they had them so close they could practically spit them to death.

With a brevity of decision that spoke well for his reputation as a field commander, Watan-goa suddenly remembered a previous engagement elsewhere, and he led his surviving followers in a retreat that was aimed at piling up as many sand hills as possible back of the flying heels of the last pony.

There were five injured mules and three still-crawling savages left over. These were quietly singled out and humanely shot — the mules first, as befitted their prior places in the hearts of the 'skinners. Taos McFarland had got himself gut-shot with four arrows, and he was dumped into the empty Conestoga to wait for the end that had come with so much more mercy to the seventeen red brothers sprawled on the ground around the lead wagon. Then the 'skinners waded the creek to drive the rest of the wagons over before gathering around Tracy's Conestoga to hold a trail court over Big Tate Barker.

Tracy made the winning proposal. "I 'low," he announced soberly, "we ain't none of us got no right to set ourse'fs up to votin' no man's life away in cold blood. If we go to blowin' the back of Tate's haid off, it'd be jest plain murder. Ain't no other name fer it. And me, I won't take a hand in no sech a deal. Ner will I set still fer nobody else tryin' it. We've give Tate a fair trial, and I 'low we're goin' to give him a fair sentence."

"Whut ye aim to do, Tracy?" Old Dan sounded anxious. "Ye cain't jest turn a hydrophoby skunk like Tate loose."

"Thet's precisely whut I aim to do, Dan'el."

"By God, Tracy, ye ain't a gonna do it. We won't stand fer it. Tate's gotta git whut's comin' to 'im!"

Several of the others were alongside the old man, muttering rough assent to his demurrer.

Tracy's interruption stopped the muttering. "Look over thar on thet sand hill," he said quietly. "Thet low, red 'un, past thet yeller saddleback. . . ."

The men, following the scout's pointed arm, exploded in a running fire of oaths.

Lining the crest of the sandstone ridge, black against the morning sun, the Arapahoes sat their ponies, not even the stir of a prairie breeze to ruffle the hardcut profile of their motionlessness. Even at the distance, the tall figure and seven-foot warbonnet of Watan-goa picked him out from his fellows.

"Dad-blame my hide!" cried Dan. "I thought them red scuts would be in Wyomin' by now!"

"No, they ain't gone, and they won't be, till we trail into Bent's Fort." Tracy's answering drawl was slow with thought. "In the meantime they ain't gonna hit us ag'in. Ye kin tie on thet. But whut they'll do is foller us . . . they'll foller us all the way . . . every step."

"Wal, whut's that got to do with Tate?"

Tracy let his eyes wander along the distant ridge. "Oh, nothin' in particular. I wuz jest thinkin' mebbeso Watan-goa might have a few questions to ask Tate 'bout what went wrong with the gun delivery. Seein's how Tate set the deal up with the chief in the first place, I wuz figgerin' the fairest thing we could do for him would be to give him the chanct to explain the sitchyashun to Watan-goa. The best way to arrange thet is jest to turn Tate loose."

For a long minute there was silence. Finally Old Dan spoke up, his narrowed eyes watching Tracy, his tones caustic. "I thought ye was against murder."

"It ain't murder," said the young scout quietly, "so long as we don't pull the trigger."

Old Dan nodded thoughtfully. "I 'low ye got a point, Tracy. Fer a minute thar, I thought ye'd gone soft."

"Like a mule's mouth," said a dark-bearded Texas 'skinner. "Whut'd'ye say, boys? Shall we let Higgins talk us into showin' Tate the Christian mercy of turnin' him loose? I'm fer it. Me, personal, I cain't stand to do no cold-blood harm to a feller white man."

A grunted chorus of agreement was the Texan's answer, and, as soon as it came, Tracy stood up.

"If thet's the way you vote it, boys, thet's the way it's gonna be. Let's get set and stretch the hell out of h'yar. I wanta hear

47

blacksnakes crackin' and smell mulehide smokin' afore I'm done talkin' to ye. We got nineteen miles to roll to Ash Creek, and I aim to boil my coffee thar tonight!"

Not Wanted Dead or Alive

The gang had split up from a job and are drifting home by different routes. Jesse, Cole, and Frank are returning to the hideout caves above the Little Blue River. But as the three comrades approach the limestone bluffs which house the honeycomb of caverns, they spot something very peculiar — a handsome harness pony and shiny cart tethered in the bottomland brush.

There is no sign of a driver or passenger. It is plainly a child's rig, and a rich child's, at that. What the devil is it doing *here?*

The wary outlaws look over the outfit. They open the baggage boot of the fancy buggy. Within are a veritable manhunter's welter of the tools of the trade — ropes, leg-irons, handcuffs, giant caps, blasting powder, fuse, even a rusted old monster of a bear trap, and a dog-eared, lurid paperback book entitled HOW TO BE A BOUNTY HUNTER.

The three bandits eye one another uneasily, and close in cautiously on the entrance to the main cavern. Here they see a
huge spindle of towline spinning off a reel
and disappearing into *their* cave. They
watch the rope-line ravel out, as whoever is
inside goes deeper and deeper into their
sacred limestone hole-in-the-ground.

Suddenly big Cole — a burly giant of a
man — nods and scowls and motions
Frank and Jesse, finger on lips, to sneak up
and take cover flanking the entrance to the
cave. As they do, Cole picks up the gliding
rope carefully. He lets it play out through
his hands, feeling like a trailing fisherman
for just the right nuance of "touch." Of a
sudden he has it. He rears back and "sets
the hook" and begins "reeling in" the line
as fast as he can and hand over hand.

Out of the cavern, kicking and spitting
dirt and cussing a blue streak comes a red-
headed and pint-sized kid in a Little Lord
Fauntleroy suit. Around his waist the rope
is tied after the manner of spelunkers to
avoid getting lost underground.

Seeing Cole, but not Frank and Jesse
who are still hidden, he storms at the big
outlaw to know what in the devil he thinks
he is doing, pulling him out of the cave.
Cole replies by demanding to know what

in the heck the kid thinks he is doing *in the cave.*

The kid looks around apprehensively. Then beckons Cole to him with an imperious gesture of the head. The big outlaw first scowls, then leers into a grin, nods, and slides over to the kid's side. Winking broadly, he inquires: "What's up, pal?"

{*Note: Cole is played as a grand cross between the Pancho Villa of Wallace Beery and the Long John Silver of Robert Newton, the irresistibly wicked — yet irresistible — villain, all wise and all gullible at once.*}

The kid lays finger to lips and informs Jesse's chief lieutenant that he is looking for the James boys "and that this figures to be their cave," according to his information.

Cole wants to know about the source of that information, of course, but the kid is wise. He shakes him off, winking broadly back at Cole. "Somebody close to the governor," he mutters knowingly.

"Oh, sure," says Cole. "You bet." The big outlaw is overplaying everything for the benefit of the hidden Frank and Jesse. What dumb luck for this smart-acre city kid to run off out into the woods and stumble right onto the secret cave of the most wanted men in Missouri. It tickles

51

the outlaw's sense of humor, and Cole wants Frank and Jesse to enjoy it all. "What else did you get from them sources, kid?" he booms out. "You ain't showed me nothing yet to prove you're really after the Jameses. Phsaw! you wouldn't know them, if they was to jump out of them there rocks this minute!"

"Oh, wouldn't I, Fatso?" says the kid, as Cole scowls indignantly and pulls in his paunch. "Take a look at this!"

From inside his voluminous coat he whips a Wanted flyer on Frank and Jesse James, with pictures reputed to be of the fugitive brothers, plus a screaming box-lettered caption of **$10,000 DEAD OR ALIVE**.

Cole is shook a trifle. He side-eyes the rocks which hide Frank and Jesse. Clears his throat. "Mercy me," he announces, "all that money for them two poor little old outlaws which ain't never really did a wrong nor sinful thing in all of their hounded lives? Tch, tch!"

Cole leers, grins, smacks his lips. He ogles, struts, postures, winks, scowls ferociously, and butters a smile.

"Now come along, sonny. You ain't serious about that reward?"

"I am," announces the kid flatly. "And

52

I mean to collect it."

"Why," says Cole, "you don't appear to need money, now. Whatever are you thinking of?"

"Of running away from home, Fatty. And I need the money to finance the trip."

"I see," says Cole, nodding at what he thinks is the old, old story of the runaway kid who will skedaddle for home the minute it gets dark. "And you allowed you'd turn poor old Jesse in to get that there blood money for him, eh? Now what wrong has the boys ever done you?"

"They've never done me any right. Now quit stalling, Fatso. You want in on the job, or are you going to stand in my path?"

Cole scowls with sudden black temper {a la Wallace Beery}. He raises a hand and strides toward the kid as though he would obliterate him with one magnificent swat.

The kid, incredibly, produces from beneath the same baggy coat a tremendous, old, rusted, horse pistol. The muzzle hole looks as big as the cave to Cole. And the kid takes a two-handed aim and brace as though he intends to touch the ancient weapon off, point-blank. Cole wavers and folds, and raises his hands. "Tut, tut, sonny!" The oleaginous grin is oiling his broad face ear to ear. "Just a little test to

53

see if you was fit to trust. I'm in the outlaw trade myself, you know."

"Never heard of you," snaps the kid. "Talk fast."

Cole suggests a fifty/fifty split on the reward for taking the James brothers. The kid demurs. Says it will be twenty-five/seventy-five, with twenty-five for Frank and seventy-five for Jesse, and Cole taking Frank.

Cole would like to kill the kid, but he stalls. "Lemme see, now," he fingers his chin, frowning at the higher mathematics. "That'll be twenty-five hundred dollars for old Frank and seventy-five hundred dollars for Jesse. Frank ain't going to like that, boy."

The kid shoves the horse pistol into its sidelocks in the overhang of Cole's paunch. The big man grunts and sucks.

"Never mind *Frank*," says the kid warily, stepping back and keeping the gun on Cole. "You in or out? Take it or leave it lay." He cocks the big outside hammers of the pistol.

Cole tries to schnooker him. He begins to talk and to sidle toward him. But the kid still has the rope around his waist, and he sees a loop of the rope trailing around Cole's leg. Seizing the rope, he jerks hard

54

on it, dumping the big outlaw on his fundament. Before he can recover, the kid has whanged him across the hat with the butt of the horse pistol and stretched him flat. Next instant he is putting the muzzle of the weapon to the woozy outlaw's head, evidently meaning to blow his brains out then and there. Frank and Jesse jump out and take him from behind and disarm him. Frank casually discharges the gun up into air. Cole screams, grabs his heart, and falls back to the ground.

Frank bends over and taps him with the smoking gun. "You ain't been touched," he says. "Get up and introduce us to your partner."

Sheepishly, Cole obeys. Or starts to. But the kid is ahead of him.

"What are you two doing, declaring yourselves in?" he demands. "You know these two tramps, Fatty? They friends of yours?"

"You might say they was. They're Frank and Jesse James."

"Oh, sure," nods the kid. "And you're Cole Younger."

"As ever was, sonny," bows Cole, sweeping off his hat. But in replacing the hat, he hits the bump the kid gave him, and his leering grimace is replaced by a black

55

scowl. "Jess," he pleads, "lemme peel him out alive and hang his pelt on the cornfield pole to scare off the crows! *Please!*"

Of a sudden the sharp city kid is seeing the truth. These really are the James brothers and Cole Younger. In the same moment of clear sight, he understands that the $10,000 is up the chimney — and maybeso himself with it.

Jesse and Frank begin to grill him about his manhunt for them to collect the reward money. They are half in fun and half deadly serious. The kid begins to back water. They bluff him with a gruesome fake about the "Swahili Mongolian anthill and honey stakeout" for informers and traitors, and the kid breaks.

"Hold on!" he declares, "you dassn't harm me! I'm Peabody Crutchfield the Third!"

"You're *who?*" demands Frank.

"*Governor* Crutchfield's boy?" echoes Jesse unbelievingly.

"Yes," charges the kid. "And you'd best give me back my rope and my gun and leave me go, too, by jings!"

Jesse looks at Frank, and both nod with vast regret. Yes, the kid's right. Too bad. What a chance!

But crafty Cole, the great thinker, is not

so easily defeated. "Wait up," he says, the Beery look invading his homely face. "Wasn't this here kid out to take you in for reward money? How's come we don't just turn around and take him in for . . . er . . . uh . . . well, you know . . . reward money?"

Frank and Jesse whistle in unison, low and intent.

"Yeah, sure," leers Cole. "Why not? Turnabout's fair play, ain't it?"

The James *frères* nod slowly, still thinking but agreeing.

"I'll make out the . . . er . . . uh . . . document," grins Cole. "I know all about drawing up such deals."

"Better let Frank draw it up," counters Jesse. "He can write."

Cole scowls, but stands aside.

Jesse says: "Better put Peabody under guard while me and Frank are gone to deliver the . . . uh . . . message to the governor. We wouldn't want anything to happen to him before we can collect the *reward* for his capture, now, would we?" He stares at Peabody, who stares right back at him. "How much *reward* you figure you ought to fetch, Peabody?"

"As much as you!" declared the kid, eyeing the brothers.

"But there's two of us," says Frank.

"That's even odds," says the kid coolly. "Get going."

Frank and Jesse start to laugh, then scowl, eyeing Peabody Crutchfield III with some doubt, but then mount up and leave.

Cole and the kid settle down — which means that the kid immediately goes into creating a private little hell for burly Cole Younger in regard to the simple matter of keeping him from getting away and at the same time keeping Cole from getting killed in the process.

{The kid has all the props from his pony cart to work with in this sequence.}

By the time Frank and Jesse return from having delivered their message to the governor, Cole is about to be blown up by Peabody, and only the arrival of the James boys saves him from dismemberment via blasting powder and sputtering fuse. Frank and Jesse now declare Cole incompetent and decide they will take over the guard on young Crutchfield, while Cole rides back to get the governor's reply to the reward claim which they have delivered. They tell Cole the governor's answer will be found in the "old spunk-wood stump near the Widder Gatchly's gate post."

Cole sets out, and the kid commences to work on Jesse and Frank.

{*Sequence takes up where it left off on poor Cole.*}

Cole returns with the governor's note. All crowd around to read it. The contents:

If they insist on returning Peabody to his rightful home, they must pay over to Peabody's father, Governor Homer Crutchfield, the same $10,000 which they had suggested as a suitable reward for his son's safe return. If they decide to keep Peabody, the governor agrees to sign over to them the legal adoption papers and to pay them, in addition, a bonus of $5,000 earnest money, plus amnesty to leave the state, and first-class RR tickets to any point in the U. S. . . . .

Hell is now "officially" to pay, and the pay hinges on how to dump the kid back on his father without further bloodshed, while Peabody, stung by his father's rejection, plus a liking for his first day of running away and the cave life of hunted outlaws of the woods, has decided he *doesn't want to leave.*

It takes all three of his "captors" to hogtie and transport him in the dead of night

59

to the governor's mansion, through the picket lines of deputies and state troopers strung around his excellency's home. And when they do finally get the little s. o. b. into the house and into his father's darkened offices, the lights flare up, and there is Marshal Sam Corbett, covering them with his gun — a sawed-off Twelve-Gauge of mean and convincing ugliness.

"Sorry, boys," he says. "But all's fair in our game, eh?"

The kid glares at Corbett and demands angrily: "Who's *he?*"

Jesse, also angrily, snaps back at him: "Ask your Uncle Cole. He's the genius who thought up this whole thing."

Cole, first flabbergasted, gets a last inspiration just as Corbett is about to identify himself. Raising his voice, Cole stabs an outraged finger at the marshal and shouts indignantly — "How dare you put a gun on decent folks, *Sam Bass!* . . . and in the governor's own offices, mercy sakes. It ain't like you, *Sam Bass,* you foul outlaw and notorious Texas train robber! Heavens alive. And you with a price on your head, too, oh, dear me. . . ."

"A *price?*" cries Peabody. "How much?"

"Fifty thousand dollars dead or alive," swears Cole, big-eyed. "Ain't you never heard of Sam Bass?"

"All right, this has gone far enough, boys." Corbett waves the shotgun at them. "Son," he says to the kid, "I'm Sam. . . ."

"Yeah," says the kid, "I know . . . you're Sam Bass. Stick 'em high, Sam. Grab for the rafters!" And with the order, he whips out the old horse pistol from beneath his coat, cracks Marshal Corbett across the knuckles with the barrel, and, as the lawman cries out and drops the shotgun, he shoves the muzzle of the horse pistol into the marshal's middle and concludes, high-voiced: "R-r-r-r each!"

Cole grins and tells Peabody not to flinch but to hold the legendary Sam Bass, Texas bandit king, right there, while he and Frank and Jesse go and fetch the legal law and likewise, of course, fetch back to Peabody Crutchfield III the reward money for his heroic capture of the Texas fiend.

"Sure," says Peabody. "You can trust me, boys. Hold still there, Sam, or I'll drill you a new hole for your belt buckle!"

"Yeah, *Sam*," grins Jesse, last man out and holding open the door. "And he'll do it, too." He waves to the enraged Marshal Corbett, fluttering his fingers. "Nighty-night, Sam . . . ," and exits with a close of the door and dialing-up of Brahms's "Lullaby."

61

The Great Northfield Raid

The big man sat on the porch of his mother's farmhouse outside Lees Summit. He watched the evening breeze stir among the dead stalks of August corn. He heard the first nighthawk make its hunting sound and, looking up, saw the bird's blunt-headed form launch itself from a far fence post. Across the barnyard an owl hooted softly, ruffled its plumage, glided out from its hayloft hiding place. A-wing, it hooted again, dolefully, keeningly.

The big man moved uneasily, sighed heavily.

He and his two brothers had come in from Texas four days ago — or was it four years? They had come at night, staking their horses out in the wood lot, not daring to stable them in the barn, or to leave them on graze in the open. They had hung to the house during the day, one of them always near the front window, watching the

Lees Summit Road. Each evening they had emerged at twilight, sitting on the porch and talking the moon down. Then, following it, shortly, into the timber, they had bedded down near their saddled mounts.

A long, weary time had gone since the last job at Lamine River. With that time, somehow, had gone their shares of the Lamine River loot. Gone, too, with that time and its misspent gain was something else. Something not to be replaced by another long ride and another armed robbery.

The big outlaw on the porch was thirty-one years old.

Boyhood lay far behind, lost forever in the haze of happy memory. Youth and the first, best part of the man-grown years had fallen away in swift turn. Ahead stretched God alone knew what.

God and Cole Younger.

The little ranch in Texas that he and Dingus James had talked of since the barefoot school days? Their boys' fine dream for the both of them to live it out together somewhere down yonder where the sun was warm and the fat grass stretched from the Sabine to the Pecos? His own private dream of being "Uncle Cole" to Dingus's young ones? Of teaching them to set a hot-blood bolt over a high pile of split rails? Or to throw down a Navy pistol on a cottontail before it cleared three jumps? Or to mend a saddle proper, or trim a hoof, treat a quarter-crack, or fit a set of racing plates?

Just dreams. Sweet as the simple hopes which had built them. Empty as the bitter years which had torn them down. There never could have been one in the first place. Not with Dingus James, or with his kind.

Cole knew that now.

He knew something else now, too.

It was something he had not known before — or, better, that he had not let himself know before. It was about him, Cole. And it unsettled a man. It unsettled him bad.

In the end it was not just Dingus James. It was you, too. In the end, you *were* Dingus. And he was you.

You were of a kind.

Somewhere back across the years there had been a place to stop. To take off the Colts, to hang the carbines up. To forget the rush of the night wind, the flicker of the campfire, the shrill cry of the Rebel guerrilla yell, the spill and clink of the yellow gold into the Missouri wheat sack. To lay aside the maps, the plans, the grins, the curses, the long, careful rides, the sudden thunder of gunfire outside the banks, the crash of railway coach windows shattered by wild shots a-horseback.

But a man could no longer see that far across the years.

Where had he ridden past the place? What hour, what minute, what day would have been the right spot to wheel on Jesse James and declare: "By damn, Dingus, I'm done. From here you ride it alone."

Looking now across the lonely rustle of the cornfield, Cole knew the answer. There never had been such a day or hour or minute. Or such a place. For him and Dingus that time would come only with a posse man's or a Pinkerton's bullet. And the place would be where they were when that bullet struck them down. As long as a man had it in him to be bad, had it 'way deep in his blood and his bones and his will, he could laugh and grin and crack jokes about it and be as breezy over it as he had a mind to be.

He was fooling no one but himself.

When the sun went down and the night wind whistled in the cornstalks, he would know where he was.

Bob, the baby brother, came out of the house just before the last daylight went. He sat down by Cole. Neither of them said anything. Presently, Jim came up through the dusk, walking from the direction of the timber, leading the horses.

"We'd best be going," he said. "Jesse wanted us there by nine o'clock."

Cole nodded and got up.

He took his horse from Jim, climbed wearily into the saddle. Bob looked at him, then looked at Jim. The latter returned the stare, and both of the younger brothers shrugged. They rode quickly out of the farmyard, north along the Lees Summit Road. Three hours later, with the pinpoint of the Samuels' front window lamp pricking at them across the distant fields, Cole still had not spoken.

Turning for the Samuels' barn, Bob, looking at him anxiously, could bear the silence no longer.

"Cole," he said, "what the Sam Hill is eating you?"

Cole came around with a start, squinting his gray eyes as though to pull his mind back from a long way off.

"I dunno, boy," he answered at last. "Maybe it's that I didn't say good bye to Ma. I ain't never forgot before."

"Bushway," laughed Jim. "You just got the fantods."

"Sure," grinned young Bob. "I didn't say good bye to Ma my own self. Shucks, it ain't like we're not coming back."

Cole failed to return the good-natured family grin.

He only nodded and asked low-voiced: "Ain't it, boy?"

Twenty-four hours after the conference in the Samuels' barn, the shadows of Cole's premonitions took form at Fort Osage Township in Jackson County, an easy night's ride from the Kearney farm of Jesse's stepfather, Dr. Reuben Samuel. The substance of those shadows was divided by eight: Frank and Jesse James, Clell Miller, Charlie Pitts, Bill Chadwell, Bob, Jim, and Cole Younger.

Once met — the rendezvous was at the All Souls churchyard on the St. Joe Road — the eight horsemen exchanged only the tersest of travel greetings, then swung their mounts due north away from Fort Osage.

The days of planning, the hours of map-tracing and route-laying had all been done by Jesse weeks before the past night's gathering in his stepfather's barn. Now, as he guided the gang carefully around Kansas City, Lees Summit, and Kearney, bearing ever northward, he continued to keep his own counsel. All that the others knew lay in the six words of instruction he had allowed them: "A bank job somewhere in Minnesota."

But Cole knew him better than any of them. He knew him better than he knew himself. Dingus was worried.

With the instincts of the born pack leader he had seemed to sense that the old gang was getting away from him. Those same instincts had suggested to him what he must do to preserve it — and himself as its head. He must lay out and lead them on a last great job. One which would let them do what they had always talked of doing. Quit and split up with enough money to live on for the rest of their natural lives. It was clear as glass to Cole that Dingus had these kinds of ideas about the Minnesota job. Something else was clear to him as well. Dingus knew where his real trouble lay in the gang, and with which man. It wasn't with his brother Frank. Or with Cole's brothers, Bob and Jim. Or with any of the three new boys. It was with Cole.

Cole wanted to quit. He had wanted to quit since before Lamine River. And Dingus knew that. But this night of August 16, 1876 was a little late in the game for any man to be quitting. And Cole knew *that*.

Riding along, he looked around him at his fellows and thought of the parable of the bad apple. It wasn't just him any more. Frank and Jim had begun to side with him about getting out. Like him they had begun to get harder and harder to talk into going on a job, and harder and harder to handle on one, once they had started. That was precisely why Dingus had brought in those three new men. It was to give him some better grip on things. A man got uneasy when he felt his left hand slipping at the same time he had already lost hold of his right. Cole shook his head, not liking to think he had done that to Dingus.

He peered ahead, through the dark, to where he could see the bearded, bolt upright figure of his best friend, sitting his black Thoroughbred as cocky as though he hadn't a care in the world, and he had to shake his head again, this time in pure admiration. You had to hand it to Dingus. He had more guts than a government mule. And maybe he was right. Maybe this last job would be the one. He had sure planned it that way.

As usual with a big raid involving new men, he had furnished the operating capital himself. No books were kept. The men just drew on him for whatever they needed in cash or equipment, with the advances being held out of their cuts of the job money. If there were no cuts, the pleasure was all Dingus's, and no questions or recriminations ever thought of. In the present case, no expense had been spared, no detail left to chance.

Dingus had each of the boys superbly mounted, each well dressed and rehearsed for the part he would play along the road, and each amply heeled with the pocket cash to back up his rôle. Bill Chadwell and Charlie Pitts, the gang's illiterates, were cattle buyers as was Clell Miller. The three Youngers, most affable at public relations, were railroad men. Dingus and Buck — Frank, that was — the best-spoken of the lot, were graduate civil engineers. Each man, no matter his rôle, carried a carbine slung to his saddle, each was additionally armed with two late-model revolvers. All wore long linen dusters of the anonymous type used by cross-country travelers on horseback of any and all honest callings.

The advance was neatly scheduled as a railway timetable. North through Missouri, meandering eastward, and then north again through Iowa. Once in Minnesota, boxing the horseback compass, circling west, riding north to St. Paul, east and then south to Red Wing, and finally angling back west again into the selected general area of southeastern Minnesota. Deliberately, Dingus had announced no exact town or bank. The choice would be made at the last minute. This time there would be no failures, no leaks of advance information. This time Dingus would pick the victim just twenty-four hours ahead of the strike.

With these thoughts Cole squinted again through the darkness toward Jesse James. As he did, he stiffened. Dingus was watching him. He had been watching him all the time. He broke his glance away, wondering what was going on in that strange, twisted mind which had changed so since the hooky-playing days of Centerville and the Pleasant Grove School. It was as well for him that he could not read the answer to his uneasy question.

Jesse, after a long minute of staring back at Cole, turned again to the road ahead. He kneed the black into a lope, nodding a feeling of purely professional satisfaction.

He had this job figured.

His crew back there was seven-eighths sound. His routes of approach and retreat were worked out in perfect guerrilla detail. There was not a green hand or a weak one riding behind him. He had, in young Bill Chadwell, a native guide born in southwestern Minnesota — a guide who knew every lake, creek, back-road hamlet, bridge, highway settlement, railroad line, wilderness hiding place, and abandoned farm house in the territory.

Nodding again, Jesse smiled the old, quirky wolf smile.

He had this job where it couldn't get away from him. He had nothing but old Cole to worry about, and he could still handle that big muttonhead when the time came. He always had handled him, hadn't he?

As to controlling Cole, who worshipped him, perhaps Jesse was right.

As to the big outlaw being his only worry, he was wrong to the extent of one up and coming little Minnesota city he had never heard of — a happy, prosperous, obscure center of farming and local industry on the banks of the Cannon River. It had been overlooked in the first grand drawing of the master plan for the last big raid, but it had not been passed over by the gathering rush of a history now closing with unseen, deadly swiftness upon Jesse Woodson James.

Its name?

A humble, simple name. A name standing quietly along the banks of the Cannon for nearly fifty years, awaiting only the coming gunfire of the man from Missouri to burn its ten letters into frontier legend for all time.

Northfield.

The gang had been riding in Minnesota two weeks. Behind them, now, lay the way points of St. Peter, Lake Crystal, St. James, Garden City, Waterville, and Madelia. Ahead lay Mankato and Cannon and Millersburg. Beyond them crouched Northfield.

Challenging fate, Jesse first selected Mankato, not Northfield. Bill Chadwell had lived just outside it. He knew the First National Bank there to be as rich as sin. He knew, too, a half dozen back-road ways to get out of the big bend of the Minnesota River in which the town lay.

The day was set, the date agreed upon.

Fate checked her own calendar against that of Jesse James, smiled, and sat back to wait.

On the stroke of nine, Saturday morning, September 2nd, five linen-dustered horsemen rode into Mankato. They tied their fine horses in front of Simm's Restaurant, went in and enjoyed a good breakfast. Returning to the sidewalk, they visited Anderson's Pharmacy and Luscombe's General Merchandise, making several trivial purchases of a kind natural to respectable gentlemen traveling by horseback. Shortly, they found themselves at the bank.

Here their leader entered to seek change for a five-dollar bill. It was furnished him, and he left immediately. At this precise moment an ex-Missourian, now a resident of Mankato, came toward the bank door. The newcomer stood aside for the traveling gentleman in the linen duster to exit. As they passed, the ex-Missourian took one popping-eyed look at the bearded horseman, then turned his own face away so that the latter would not recognize it in dangerous turn.

Subsequently, he went straight through the bank, out its rear door, broke into a dead run down the back alley for the sheriff's office. There he blurted out news of some small sectional and official import.

"Jesse James is in town!" he gasped. "He was just in the bank and went away. There were four others waiting for him outside."

"*Jesse James!*"

It was a far piece from Mankato, Minnesota to Clay County, Missouri, and every mile of it was mirrored in the sheriff's incredulous exclamation.

"By Tophet!" snapped the other. "I tell you I know him, Sheriff! I lived for years in Kearney and Lees Summit. If I seen him once, I seen him twenty times. It's him and his gang, and they've got their eyes on the First National sure as that's a star pinned to your shirt!"

"Let's get to the bank . . . !" The sheriff was already out the door. "They'll pull none of their damned Missouri tricks in my town!"

The sheriff was right.

At the bank, he and a well-hidden posse of townsmen waited the day through. Nothing happened. Jesse James and his men — if it had been them — had disappeared.

All the following day, Sunday, the town remained alerted. That night, two of the suspected men returned, drank quietly for a few hours in a cross-river saloon, and rode peacefully back away into the nowhere from whence they had come.

The sheriff of Mankato advised his ex-Missouri informer to have his spectacles checked, called it a bad day, and went to bed.

At noon, Monday, the eight-man gang reëntered Mankato.

It was the dinner hour, carefully selected because at that time the bank population, staff and customer alike, would be at its daily low. The alien horsemen rode directly down Main Street, keeping their mounts bunched, making no attempt to cover their presence. In the lead Jesse sat his black. Clell Miller sided him. Behind them, Cole and Frank were lost in the body of the pack.

It was the first time in the memory of any of the gang that Cole had not had his bay at the side of Jesse's black, and big Cole was worried. But that was the way Dingus had ordered it, and nobody said a word, or apparently thought anything was wrong. Of them all, only Frank had exchanged a look of hard-eyed doubt with Cole over the last-minute change. And Frank had never had the nerve to buck Dingus.

Now, suddenly, Jesse straightened in his saddle, pale blue eyes sweeping past the bank. Cole stiffened, too.

Just beyond the bank building a crowd of perhaps forty townsfolk stood gathered across the sidewalk. This could be trouble. Bad trouble.

"What the hell are those jaspers looking at?" said Clell Miller tensely, his eyes but a second slower than Jesse's.

"Damned if I know," muttered the latter. "We'll soon see, though."

They saw — or thought they saw — quicker even than that. One of the men in the crowd pointed suddenly at Jesse.

"By god," said Jesse, "the son-of-a-bitch has spotted me!"

"Damn," said Clell. "You certain sure, Jess?"

"Look at the bastard," grated Jesse.

Clell looked. The man who had pointed at Jesse was gesturing and talking to his companions excitedly. In turn, they were staring hard, and not just at Jesse. The whole gang was getting a going over.

"Damnation, what'll we do, Jess?"

"Ride straight on. Don't even look back at the sons-of-bitches. Make out like nothing is wrong. Just ride right on by them and out of town. Pass the word back to the boys."

Clell nodded, dropped his horse back, relayed the order.

While the crowd continued to stare, the gang kept going straight out and away from Mankato, Minnesota — and straight out and away from $55,000 sitting in the opened vault of the Mankato First National Bank — a fortune which could have been theirs for the simple long-barreled request of a loaded Colt revolver and waiting Missouri wheat sack.

The ominous crowd on the sidewalk beyond the bank? It was watching a construction crew working on a building out of sight of the gang's line of approach. The man who had pointed at Jesse James was only calling attention to his superb black Thoroughbred, and the following regards and excited comments of his fellow townsmen had been directed solely at the beautiful horseflesh which carried the rest of the Missouri raiders.

The duly constituted guardian of the law?

Tired out by two days of profitless surveillance and convinced the James gang had never been nearer Minnesota than the June, '73 robbery of the C. R. I. & P. at Adair, Iowa, the sheriff of Mankato was sound asleep in the warm September sunshine in front of his office three blocks away. He didn't even have a deputy on duty at high noon on Monday, September 4th, 1876.

The first stop out of Mankato was made

that night, six hours and eighteen miles north. Jesse took one look at the town's name on the roadside sign, nodded to Clell Miller, by now his steady traveling mate.

"Here's my hometown. She ought to do."

It was Jamesville, Minnesota.

As was their custom, the gang split up, entering the town in the pairings Jesse had ordered all along the line of march: he and Frank, the three Youngers, Pitts, Chadwell, and Clell Miller.

After dark, in the hotel, he and Frank studied the map for three hours. If a decision were reached, it was not announced.

The following day they rode slowly north by west, reaching the town of Cardova, another eighteen miles removed from Mankato. Here they rested their horses, swung wide of the settlement, turned yet more west and pushed on hard. Long after supper, they arrived outside Millersburg.

They did not go at once into town, but made camp beside a wooded stream where there was good grass for the horses and heavy cover for their riders. They ate a cold saddlebag meal, prepared to sleep on the ground. It was September 5th.

Shortly, by the light of a small fire, the

map came out again. This time Bill Chadwell, the Minnesotan, was called into the consultation. Cole, catching Frank James's eye across the fire, stared him down. Frank returned the look, shrugged helplessly. Cole nodded, understanding.

Dingus, weak eyes watering, sandy lids blinking rapidly after the manner of his affliction, made a series of swift finger paintings on the map. He was rising into his high, wild mood. Frank and Cole could sense it far ahead of the others, and it had been the reason for Frank's helpless gesture to Cole. But the latter's understanding nod had not meant that Cole understood Jesse, but only that he understood Frank's bad place in the middle of things.

As to Dingus, somewhere north of yesterday and south of tonight, Cole had lost him. And somehow — crouching now with Frank and Chadwell over that campfire there — Dingus looked suddenly too far away ever for a man to find him again.

The big outlaw shook as if to a passing chill in the night wind. He looked long at the pale-eyed man who had been the friend of his heart in the boyhood dreams, and the ache in his throat came up dull and heavy, and he could not swallow it away.

After what seemed an eternity, but was only an hour of low-voiced conversation, it was apparent to Cole, where he watched and waited alone beyond the perimeter of the fire's dying light, that an agreement had been reached.

And it had. Jesse spoke a word of final approval to Bill Chadwell, waved the rest of them forward.

They came up, squatting behind him, gaunt from three weeks of riding, nerve-strung with the lack of sleep, and with the growing strain of their leader's unwonted secrecy. But the time of waiting was past. The master plan was ready to be revealed. Voice high, the old blink watering his red-rimmed eyes, Jesse laid it out for them.

"This here town we're at is Millersburg," he said, indicating the site on the map. "Now angling up yonder here, ten miles or so, is Cannon City. On north and east here, close to eleven miles, is Northfield and Dundas. The bank we're going to take is the First National. Bill tells me it's the richest in the south part of the state and that it's nothing for them to have a quarter million on hand about this time of year. That's for paying off on the fall harvests and tending to the payrolls of all them little river sawmills we seen along the streams."

He paused, letting them all study the map and think. He still hadn't named his town outright, but only the bank. He watched Cole through the stillness.

"Now, tomorrow, along about noon," he continued, "me and Charlie and Bob will move on through Millersburg without putting up. We'll stay the night at Cannon City."

Again he paused, again went on.

"About four o'clock, Frank and the rest of you will ride on into Millersburg and put up at the hotel. Frank will take you on from there next day and give you the final layout tomorrow night. Any questions?"

Bob Younger and Charlie Pitts, clearly flattered by the honor apportioned them, had none. Chadwell and Clell Miller evidently already knew the plan, as did Frank. That left Jim and Cole Younger, looking at one another.

And Jesse James looking at Cole.

The tall highwayman returned the look, quiet-eyed. He spat into the fire and stood up, his voice soft and easy as the movements of his powerful body.

"Who did you say would ride with you, Dingus?"

"You heard me . . . Bob and Charlie."

"Mind saying why? Bob's pretty green.

83

He ain't never fronted a big job. What's the idea, Dingus?"

"It's the plan," said Jesse, eyes tightening.

The plan, thought Cole. God Almighty, always the plan. Since Pleasant Grove School and their first watermelon raid together — the one where Dingus had killed old Man Pettis's coon dog to keep him from trailing them — it had forever been the plan. What was that poor, addlepated, friendly hound's name? Old Hickory, that was it. A man remembered it as well as he remembered his horror at Dingus, blowing his poor old head off with the shotgun and then laughing: "All right, Hick, let's see you sniff out our tracks now!" Yes, Dingus had always had a plan, even down to murdering a poor old dog. And with him it was always just that simple — the plan — with no damned explanations or excuses or anything. Dingus had a plan. If you wanted to throw in with it, that was fine. If you didn't, you might get the same medicine he'd given Old Hickory. In fact, you sure would get it.

"All right, Ding," he said at last, bobbing his big head at Jesse. "It's the plan."

But even as he said it, he knew it was not all right, and that there was something be-

tween him and Dingus which had never
been there before. A man could feel it,
taste it, smell it. And he could see it in the
uncertain blink of those pale blue eyes
across the fire.

Dingus was afraid of him.

"All right, Cole," echoed Jesse, not taking the blink off him. "Any more questions?"

"I reckon. That is, if it ain't too much to
ask."

"Cole, god dammit, don't you get funny
with me!"

Cole looked at him, something inside of
him squeezing in hard and hurtful, like it
had that years-gone day in the Widow
Bowman's shack outside Lexington, when
he had held Jesse, shot almost to death by
the Union pickets, to his breast and willed
him not to die. He could almost feel again
the desperate grip of Dingus's white hand
on his arm, the rack and spasm of his
bullet-torn lungs, rasping the life out of
him.

"I ain't never felt less funny in my life,
Dingus," he said softly. "I reckon you
know that, boy."

"Now don't give me none of that, you
big bastard."

Jesse said it sharply, showing an edge of

awkwardness in it. All at once feeling *something* across the fire between him and Cole. When the outsized galoot looked at a man like that, it made him think of the Little Blue River and headmaster Peabody and that damned Pleasant Grove School and a whole host of such-like childish things which did not make any difference any more.

"Don't *boy* me, god dammit!" he finished angrily. "You got something to say, say it and be done!"

Cole stared him back until Jesse had to drop his eyes. Then the big man nodded, voice still soft. "You mind telling us where we're going, Ding?"

Jesse brought his eyes back up, blinking furiously.

"*Northfield!*" he snapped. "That all right with you?"

"It ain't mine to say no more," murmured Cole Younger, and turned away from him.

They came from the west. It was 2:00 P.M., and Northfield drowsed in the after-dinner quiet. There were only three of them. If anyone noticed them, it was only because of the fine horses they rode, two blooded bays and a lean, race-bred black.

They crossed over the railroad tracks west of the bridge, the ironshod hoofs of their mounts clinking momentarily over the gravel roadbed. They were on the bridge, then, the hoof noises changing to the muffled fall of caulked iron on worn wooden planking.

Directly, they were into Bridge Square, and still the horses walked, not hurrying, not nervous, but firm and steady under the experienced hands which held them down. Across the square lay Division Street, Northfield's main path of business establishments. On the southwest corner of Division Street, to their right, flanked by the mercantile houses of Lee & Hitchcock and H. Scriver & Co., stood the First National Bank of Northfield. Due ahead lay the hardware stores of J. S. Allen and A. E. Manning. To their left was Wheeler & Blackman's Drugstore.

Bringing his mount free of the square and turning him toward the bank, the man on the breedy-looking black made sweeping mental note of these stores and their related locations. Inclining his head to his companions, he guided the black up to the bank's hitching rail. Dismounting, the three tied their horses, walked casually away from the bank.

At Lee & Hitchcock's, they selected seats on the sidewalk line of drygoods boxes provided for idlers. One of them dug a Bowie knife from beneath his linen duster, picked up a piece of wood, and began to whittle and whistle as though he had ridden eight hundred miles for no other purpose. The other two fell into a close-mouthed conversation, their eyes darting continually to the street that entered the square beyond the bank, from the east.

Shortly, the smaller of the two straightened. "Yonder they come, Bob," he said. "Let's go."

Bob Younger looked up, saw Cole and Clell Miller slowly jogging their horses into Division Street from the east road. He nodded swiftly and passed the word to the third man. "Look sharp, Charlie. We're moving."

The whittler put away his knife, trailed off his monotonous whistle. "I'm right behind you," said Charlie Pitts. "Here goes nothing."

The three men walked to the bank, entered it without looking again at the approaching horsemen.

Clell Miller turned his mount in at the bank's hitching rail, tying him alongside the first three. He moved to the bank door, peered in, turned, and waved at his companion. Cole waved back, swung off his tall bay in mid-street, began cussing and tugging at a saddle girth which was in perfectly good working order.

Clell stood squarely in front of the bank doors. There was no hurry in the way he unbuttoned the linen duster.

Jesse's big plan was running slick as gun oil through a smooth-bore musket.

At least it was *outside* the bank.

Inside, the oil was hitting a few rust pits.

Hard at work, as Jesse and his two henchmen entered the building, were Joseph Lee Heywood, bookkeeper and acting cashier, A. E. Bunker, teller, and F. J. Wilcox, assistant bookkeeper. Heywood, new to his job and overanxious to please, moved unctuously from his desk to meet the strangers. His eager smile ended in a startled gasp.

The Colt passbooks had come out.

"Throw up your hands," ordered Jesse quietly, "and don't holler out. I've got forty men outside this bank. You're the cashier, ain't you?"

Heywood denied it haltingly.

Jesse turned to Wilcox and Bunker in turn. Each shook his head.

Jesse said nothing. When he looked back

again to Heywood, he was beginning to blink.

"I know a cashier, when I see one," he said. "Open that god-damn' safe, or I'll blow your head off."

"I can't open it," the cashier pleaded. "It's got a Bearden timelock on it."

Jesse stepped back, waving to Pitts and Bob Younger.

They seized Heywood, Pitts slashing him across the face with his pistol barrel, Bob hurling him bodily against the vault and jamming his Colt into his belly.

"You still got a Bearden timelock on that safe?" asked Jesse.

Heywood answered stubbornly that he had.

Pitts moved in, shoved his Colt an inch from the cashier's cheek. The powder blast tore open Heywood's face, ripped away his right ear.

"How about that timelock?" said James.

Heywood shook his lacerated head.

"Work on him," Jesse told Pitts. "Come on, Bob, let's get the other two."

In fearful order, Bunker and Wilcox had nothing to say. The bandits pistol-whipped them to their knees. The answer was still the same. The safe was timelocked.

"Keep working on yours," Jesse called to

Pitts. "We'll get an answer somewheres here."

At the precise moment of his instruction to Charlie Pitts inside the bank, history was moving in on Jesse James along Division Street, outside the bank.

Henry M. Wheeler was a nineteen-year-old college student, home on summer vacation from Michigan University. At the moment Cole Younger got down off his bay to begin fussing with his saddle girth, Wheeler was talking with J. S. Allen in front of the latter's hardware store. Fatefully, Henry Wheeler was quick of both eye and curiosity.

"Now why the heck," he asked Allen, "do you suppose that man yonder is making such a to-do about that saddle strap? He'd ought to know better than to stop right in the middle of Division Street. But, say . . ." — for the first time he noticed Clell Miller — "lookit yonder! There's another of them standing by the bank door. Same long duster and all. Now that *is* funny."

"Henry, my boy" — Allen had noticed Jesse, Bob, and Pitts ride up moments before — "it sure is! There's more going on here than looks to be. You set tight and look sharp." With the order, Allen moved down the street toward the bank. Coming along the sidewalk unhurriedly, he turned in at the bank as though to enter on business. Clell Miller grabbed him, spun him into the wall, jammed a Colt into his stomach.

"Hold still and keep your god-damn' mouth shut," he advised.

J. S. Allen was no college youth, and no coward. He got a knee into Clell's groin, leaped away, and raced back up the walk. "They're robbing the bank, boys!" he yelled. "Get your guns! Get your guns!"

At the warning, young Wheeler was off across the square. He was a two-letter trackman at the university and had the lungs to go with the legs that proved it.

"Robbery! Robbery at the bank! They're at the bank! They're robbing the bank!"

At his post in the center of Division Street, Cole watched the boy go. He had a clear shot at him but did not move to take it. There would never be any Old Hickory for Cole Younger. He could no more shoot an unarmed kid than he could a friendly dog. That was Dingus's department.

Cole legged up on his bay, deliberately swinging the animal to block Clell Miller's fire as the latter began to cut down on the fleeing boy. Wheeler thus made it safely away, and in the confusion of his escape Allen had made it back to his hardware store.

Business now grew brisk along Division Street. Until this moment there had been only five outlaws on the scene. Now, in seeming answer to the gunfire, three more linen-dustered horsemen raced their mounts out of a side street and toward the bank. As they did so, Clell and Cole began wheeling their horses up and down Division Street, raking the storefronts with carbine and Colt slugs, Cole's huge voice bellowing to the stunned civilians: "Get in! Get in! Get off the street, god dammit!"

On the echoes of his yell, Frank James, Bill Chadwell, and Jim Younger came up with a rush, adding the dreaded Missouri yelps and their own revolver fire to the crash of store-front glass and bedlam of citizen outcries already rupturing the afternoon stillness of Northfield's main street.

The walls of the First National Bank were no more soundproof than the nerves of the three desperadoes caught within them.

Charlie Pitts spun about wildly. "Jesus Christ!" he shouted. "They're onto the boys outside!"

With the words, he slashed Heywood

93

across the face with his Colt barrel, knocking him senseless, then leaped to join Bob Younger and Jesse where they had Bunker and Wilcox jammed up against the teller's counter.

At the breaking of the outer gunfire, Jesse kicked the kneeling Wilcox in the genitals, rasping at Bob: "This here bastard don't know nothing. How about yours?"

Bob seized Bunker, lifting him to his feet. "All right, mister. Last time around. Where's the cashier's till?"

Bunker gestured toward the cash drawer.

Bob, pulling a wheat sack from beneath his coat, ripped the drawer open. In it were less than a hundred dollars. He scooped the thin flutter of bills into the sack, whirled on Bunker "This ain't the cashier's till, you bastard. There's more money. Where the hell is it?"

He leaped at the teller before he could answer.

"Get back down on your knees, god damn you! Who told you to stand up?" The revolver barrel flashed, and Bunker collapsed. Bob had him by the shirt front before he hit the floor, the big Colt stabbing into his battered face. "Show me that till, you son-of-a-bitch, or I'll kill you!"

94

Watching them, Jesse suddenly said: "Leave go of the bastard . . . we'll find it ourselves."

They had no sooner turned away than Bunker, hysterical with pain, leaped to his feet and ran for the rear door of the bank. Pitts fired and missed, and ran cussing after him. He fired again, down the outer alley. The bullet smashed through Bunker's shoulder but did not drop him. The bookkeeper staggered clear of the bank corner and around it to safety.

Pitts ran back through the bank shouting: "The son-of-a-bitch has got clean away. Let's go!"

At the front door he leaped back as a rifle slug smashed a doorpane and ricocheted into the bank ceiling.

"Pull out, Jess . . . for God's sake pull out!" he yelled at the motionless Jesse. "They're killing our boys outside!" With this warning, he ducked and ran through the door into the street, both revolvers blasting.

"I'm going after him, Jess." Bob Younger's nod went to the still unmoving Jesse. "They'll have us all treed in another two minutes." He vaulted the teller's counter, slid out his second Colt, and shot his way into the street, following Pitts.

Jesse came slowly around the counter. He started toward the door, stopped halfway, and stared around the bank as though bewildered. At the base of the vault, to his left, something stirred, caught his watery-eyed gaze. It was Heywood, dazedly recovering consciousness.

Staggering blindly to his feet, the cashier started weaving unsteadily toward the door. Jesse was after him like an animal. The single shot, fired from a range of inches, struck behind the cashier's right ear, exited above his left eye, blowing away his face. There was no human word in the snarl with which his murderer shoved his lifeless body aside and ran, stumbling, for the door.

Outside, Jesse stepped into a hell's cauldron of citizen gunfire.

Allen's Hardware was Northfield's principal gun store. From the moment of his escape from Clell Miller, its cool-headed owner had begun issuing new rifles and boxed ammunition to all comers. By the time Jesse reached the street, no less than thirty aroused townsmen were firing at his trapped followers. And those thirty native riflemen had had ten precious minutes in which to pick their hidden firing points within half a dozen nearby buildings. Their withering fusillade now forced the first break in the bandit retreat.

As Jesse burst from the bank, an unarmed farm worker tried to run across Division Street to his parked wagon. Badly rattled, Pitts, Clell Miller, and Bill Chadwell cut down on him, their bullets literally tearing him apart. The senseless execution was the spark that blew up Northfield.

Enraged, a townsman ran out of Allen's hardware and blasted a shotgun charge, point-blank, into Clell Miller. Clell now mounted up with Charlie Pitts, guarding Jesse's and Bob Younger's horses, reeled in the saddle. The charge had struck him full in the chest and face. Spraying blood, he fought to stay on the horse, and for the moment succeeded. The next instant Jesse and Bob were clear of the bank, crouching behind their tied mounts, fighting at the knotted reins.

In the interim, death struck right and left among the Missouri raiders. Bill Chadwell, riding between Frank James and Jim Younger, took a .44-40 Winchester slug through the heart. He slid out of the saddle so quietly his companions did not know he had been hit until his riderless horse galloped past them.

Clell Miller, still streaming blood from the pock blast of birdshot, kicked his horse away from the bank's hitching rail, abandoning Bob and Jesse to the closing crowd. A Civil War Spencer boomed from the window of Allen's Hardware. The big .50-caliber ball passed through both lungs, severing Clell's pulmonary artery. Clell struck the dirt of Division Street, flopped around like a wrung-neck chicken, and died right there in front of the bank.

Frank James took a .38 Smith & Wesson slug through the right calf. Cole was swaying in the saddle, shot in shoulder and thigh with rifle bullets. Both were still mounted, when Jesse, at last freeing his black from the rail, hammered up to them on the gallop.

At the hitching rail, Bob, desperately wounded, right arm shattered from wrist to elbow by two Spencer balls, his horse shot dead in his tracks, shouted after his leader.

"Wait up, Jesse, wait up! They got my horse!"

His plea drew no response from Jesse, and only heavier fire from the advancing citizens. Drawing his left-hand Colt, Bob ran back into the shelter of the bank entrance.

Across the street from the bank now,

Pitts and Jim Younger raced their horses up to join Cole and Frank. Pitts was not wounded. Jim was sacked in the saddle from a belly-to-back shot which had just missed his kidneys. The next moment, Jesse had his neighing black among them.

"It's no use, boys!" he cried. "We got to get out, or they'll kill us all."

"All right," shouted Frank. "Which way do we go?"

"The way we come. It's the only way we know, now that Bill's gone. West, over the bridge. Back to Millersburg."

Watching him, seeing the white paste of his face beneath the water of his running eyes, hearing the shrill hysteria rising in his high voice, Cole Younger's expression went blank. He drove his bay forward, shouldering him into the black. As he did so, the last of the thin thread stretching across the years to boyhood loyalties snapped.

"Hold up, Dingus," he said flatly. "How about Bob?"

"The hell with Bob!" The hysteria was plain now. "He's done for anyways. He's bad hit, and we cain't get to him nohow. Besides, there ain't no horse for him. Come on!"

Cole reined the bay around, stared back at Jesse.

"You bastard," he said quietly.

He drove the bay away from them, then, straight toward the bank, standing in the stirrups and roaring to his brother: "Run out, Bob, run out!"

He was hit twice more through the body before he slid his mount up to the bank. They saw his big back twist and buck to the slugs as they tore into him. And they saw him reach the staggering Bob, seize him, and swing him up behind him.

The powerful bay, lurching under the nearly four hundred pounds of the double load, drove back across Division Street toward the bunched bandit riders. The handicap slowed him too much. Another rifle bullet cut into Cole, his fifth wound in as many minutes. Still he would not fall. He was upright in the saddle, when he brought the bay up in front of Jesse James.

"All right," he growled to the white-faced outlaw. "*Now* let's go. Bob's got a horse."

They rode south, keeping to the main road, knowing no other route, each of their minds turning helplessly on the same thought. The one thing that could have occurred to upset the master plan, the one thing Jesse had failed to foresee and figure against, had happened. Bill Chadwell, their Minnesota guide, was gone. The one man upon whom their leader's involved plan of retreat had depended lay staring-eyed dead in the dust of Division Street. And dead with him lay the last, best chance of any member of the James gang keeping himself alive. The thought sawed at them constantly, never letting them rest, setting their jaws, chaining their tongues, driving them onward in heavily building silence.

They were in a strange and enemy land. All roads looked alike. It was a deadly, flat country, thickly timbered, cross-cut by a dozen small streams, blind-trapped by a hundred uncharted lakes. No least elevation was to be gained from which to route a course or determine the proximity of pursuit.

Posse behind, ambush ahead? Armed farmer to the right, enraged villager to the left? Who could tell them now? Who was left to say which way to go? Who among them any longer knew right from left, or north from south? Or road from road?

Chadwell! thought Cole Younger. *Chadwell knew. Dingus's precious little Bill Chadwell from Minnesota, he knew. But Chadwell was dead!*

101

The big outlaw laughed aloud. The strange sound swung the frightened eyes of the others toward him. He laughed again, into their startled faces. They looked away. None of them asked Cole why he laughed. None of them cared to ask him . . . or dared to.

The village of Dundas, three miles south of Northfield, loomed ahead. They rode through it, their five horses abreast, their carbines naked in the afternoon sun, the blood-soaked Bob Younger still mounted double behind Cole. A few people gawked curiously. No one challenged the cavalcade.

Incredible luck had ridden ahead of the fleeing bandits to explain this apathy. The news of the Northfield raid was already chattering the key of the Dundas telegraph, as they rode into the town. But the key chattered alone. The telegrapher was away, absent from his board on a half-hour errand!

In Millersburg, reached at 4:00 P.M., the preposterous luck held. The regular telegrapher was at home, sick. His assistant had locked the key open and gone down to the Little Cañon River to try for an autumn walleye. More curious gaped; more good citizens stared. And, again, no more than that happened. Not a hand was raised or a question called against the bullet-riddled gang.

South of Millersburg now. One mile. Two. Nearly five. No sign of pursuit. And the incalculable luck of the damned was still theirs.

They encountered a farmer, and Cole relieved him of a stout work horse. A second mounted traveler was taken into custody and lightened of the load of his fine saddle. Bob Younger was mounted again. For the first time since leaving Northfield, there were sound horses all around.

Twilight came on quickly. Ahead lay twelve hours of darkness. Twelve hours which, with any reasonable extension of their unbelievable luck, could take them fifty miles and more toward freedom. Tired muscles relaxed; jawlines eased. A little talk began.

But luck was done with them.

Six miles from Millersburg, Bob Younger's borrowed saddle parted its girth. The tall youth fell heavily. He crushed his injured arm beneath him and fainted from shock.

Cole took him up in his arms, carrying him, unconscious, before him. A mile farther along, a turn of the Madelia Road —

their one known route — was missed in the darkness. 2:00 A.M. found them in a trackless tangle of second-growth pine. No moonlight penetrated the matted timber. The only sounds they heard were those of the suck and pull of their horses' hoofs, floundering to move ahead through the pothole bogland their riders had blundered them into. Within the hour, the fine drizzle which had been falling since dusk built into a driving downpour. The air turned suddenly frost-cold.

Men and mounts had had enough. The former fell from their saddles into the muck of mud and swamp grass, not moving from where they dropped. The horses stood, heads down, rumps to the hammering slant of the rain. The storm closed in, the wind crying aloud in buffeting blasts. Soon even the bulking forms of the horses grew indistinct and shortly were blotted out altogether.

It was 3:00 A.M., Friday, September 8th. The Great Northfield Raid was twelve hours old. Jesse James and his men had ridden an incredible sixty-five miles since thundering out of Division Street and across the Cannon River bridge, the last forty miles of it at a staggering gallop through the pitchblind night. And the pothole swamp where their shivering mounts now stood over them, awaiting the first dripping gray of coming daylight, it lay exactly *fourteen* miles south of Northfield, Minnesota. They had ridden the classic circle of the lost.

By nightfall of the 7th, two hundred men were in the field against the gang. And the complexion of these pursuers was altering swiftly from the disorganized rabble of embattled townsfolk and shotgun-armed farmers which had taken up the chase in its first hours. The police chiefs of Minneapolis and St. Paul, accompanied by squads of city detectives, were *en route* to the scene by train. Every county sheriff in southeastern Minnesota was out, backed by his regular deputies and scores of sworn-in civilians. From St. Paul, Omaha, and Chicago the Pinkerton operatives swarmed in. Robert Pinkerton took personal command, with brother William co-ordinating the campaign from the Chicago headquarters.

The gang had been positively identified within the hour of the robbery, as soon as the telegraph key clicked southward to Mankato. The Mankato sheriff woke with a belated start, realized what he had slept through, and wired the St. Paul police the details of his dereliction of duty the morning of the 2nd.

The startling dispatch sparked every telegraph wire in the southern part of the state:

It is the James gang. The Jameses and the Youngers. Track them down. Shoot on sight. Block all the roads. They must not escape. Minnesota must not become Missouri.

With the end of the second day, September 8th, there were no less than five hundred armed peace officers and organized civilians combing the back roads for the fleeing bandits. By the end of that day, pickets were posted at all bridges, river fords, county-road and state-highway intersections. All known back trails and local cow paths were watched. A sprawling semi-circle stretching twenty miles south, and fifty miles east and west of Northfield, was under armed surveillance. Missouri was sealed off.

Or was it? Since the last report from outside Millersburg, the gang had vanished without a trace.

Then at noon on the 8th came a report from a picket post on the Little Cannon

River, outside Watersville. Some hours earlier, the bandits had approached the ford near the picket station. The pickets had fired; the bandits fled back into the woods. The pickets then charged into the timber after them — precisely what the fugitives wanted them to do. The gang doubled back and went over the abandoned ford unmolested.

These Minnesota farmers had something to learn about treeing the wily Missouri coon. The Northfield surround had been broken through before it was well set up, and the Clay County killers were across the Little Cannon and headed home. But the farmers were learning.

The Northfield area was cleared out and a new line established fifty miles to the south, this second line extending nearly a hundred miles, point to point.

Then electric news again.

Late Friday afternoon, the fugitives had invaded a farm house north of German Lake, had taken fresh horses, pounded on their way. At once, a score of posses closed in on the area. They had the Missouri devils now. This time they *were* sealed off from their home state. They knew where they had been within the hour. It would be impossible for six horsemen to break through the German Lake surround.

Night fell before the gathering trap could be sprung. Confidently the pursuers bivouacked in barns and farm houses throughout the quarantined area.

Thirty-six hours of rain, an incessant fall since Thursday evening, would have every road and trail an impassable morass for men on horseback before dawn of the 9th. Throughout the region, the streams were on the rise, becoming unfordable by the hour. Come daylight, the chase would be over. At least, so reckoned the excited posse leaders stationed that night at German Lake.

They reckoned without Jesse James.

The outlaw camp was in a tangled, brackish lowland, six miles east of German Lake. Its conditions were a far, lonely cry from what his followers had come to expect of Jesse's charmed leadership. There were no cheery campfires here. No rough guffaws and backhouse jokes over the division of the loot. No fresh, highly trained Missouri Thoroughbreds, munching their nosebag oats on the picket line, waiting to carry their dashing riders away from the cloddish mounts of some half-hearted posse of fellow Missourians. There were no booming laughs from Cole. No dry-blinded, acid humor from Jesse. No scholarly bit of Shakespeare or the Scriptures from Frank, the company intellectual. Here was no canopy of warm Clay County stars, no couch of dry wool horse blanket, no well-known road stretching across the certainty of tomorrow into the safety of the Little Blue country, down home. This was Minnesota, not Missouri.

The sodden horse blankets hung from the gaunt bushes, leaking more rain than they shed. Beneath them, cold, sick, wet to the shaking bone, crouched the six survivors. Bob Younger was irrational with fever and pain. Cole hunched over him, muttering and growling like the wounded grizzly he was, fighting off the torture of his own hurts as he guarded those of his brother. Beyond them, close enough to touch in the darkness, huddled Frank James, Jim Younger, and Charlie Pitts. Beneath another bush, ten feet away, alone and invisible through the sheeting rain, Jesse glared out into the blackness.

Presently, he arose, felt his way, tree trunk by tree trunk, to the tethered horses. His clasp knife slashed quickly in the gloom, severing the reins of the first mount. Above the pelting drip of their blankets, the others heard his snarled —

"*Hee-yahh,* get!" — and the answering smack of muddy hoofs and startled neighs which crashed away through the showering foliage.

"What the god-damn hell?" rasped Cole, blundering to his feet.

"It's the horses," cried Charlie Pitts. "That crazy Jesse is cutting the horses loose. Jess! Jess! For the luvva Christ, hold on!"

"Shut your damn' mouth, Charlie." Jesse's form loomed through the downpour and shouldered in under the horse-blanket shelter. "All of you shut up. We're getting out of here."

"But the horses! God Almighty, man!" It was Jim Younger towering over him, eyes blazing. "You lost your god-damn' mind, Jess?"

Jesse's eyes burned like red coals. "It ain't my god-damn' mind I'm thinking of, mister, it's my god-damn' life!"

The flat way he said it, the sudden dropping of the high-pitched snarl into the low, tight way of talking, carried even to Cole. The big man caught Jim's shoulder, forcing him to sit back down. "Leave him get on with it," he told him softly. "Dingus has got a plan. He's always got a plan."

Cole's was a voice out of the past, sounding a faith which had endured from Old Man Pettis's melon patch to Lamine River's mailbags. Somehow the dispirited men sensed it, realized that in the darkness of his most desperate hour the wounded giant had come again to stand beside Dingus James. Feeling it, they took strength from it, and from Cole. They obeyed him, waiting silently for Jesse to speak.

When he talked, it was the old Jesse: tough, quick-worded, absolutely sure of himself and of his plan. "They figure they've got us treed," he began. "That we cain't run no more. Well, they figure right. We cain't *run* no more. But, by God, we can *walk!*" He paused, then swept on. "You remember what they used to call Old Jack's boys during the war?" The reference was to Stonewall Jackson and his famed Shenandoah Valley infantry brigade. His listeners understood it, nodded disinterestedly. "Foot cavalry!" snapped Jesse, "that's what, by Christ. He'd take them troops of his sometimes thirty miles in a night, and they would go where horse troops couldn't begin to follow them. The bluebellies never caught up to them." Again the pause, again the renewed fire. "Well, we got bluebellies after us here, too. They got

111

nothing but horsemen on their side, and they ain't looking for nothing but horsemen on ours. We'll just walk out on them, that's all. We can do it, boys, and I mean for us to do it. Once past them, afoot, we can grab new horses and be gone. We ain't no more than a night's ride from the Ioway line right now. Shank's mare will get us through, if we start right away. I mean now. Tonight."

Cole's gray eyes narrowed. "Hold off, Ding," he said. "Bob cain't walk and keep up with the rest of us."

Jesse bobbed his head, his plan having foreseen the objection. "I left three of the horses tied," he said. "I figured you Youngers to pull out on me."

"You figured wrong," replied Cole heavily. "You walk . . . we walk."

"But dammit, Cole, Bob will slow us down. We got to march thirty miles to-night. It's our only chance."

"Jim and me will see Bob don't slow you down, Dingus."

"You'd best see he don't," was all Jesse said. "Let's go."

Cole leaned down, touching his younger brother. "Boy, you hear what was said?"

"I heard."

"You game?"

"Help me up."

"Jim. Get him on the other side."

"I got him."

They heaved the youngster up, held him on his feet.

"You set, Bob?" asked Cole.

"I'm set, Cole. Give her a whirl."

Cole turned to Jesse. "All right," he said, "let's go." Then so softly that only Jesse heard it. *"And don't forget who's behind you, Dingus. . . ."*

They marched all of Friday night and hid away the daylight hours of Saturday on a tiny swamp isle. With dark, they moved again, ploughing the night away through a calf-deep mire of lowland mud and sheet-water. Sunday there was another interminable fireless camp so close to the hamlet of Marysburg they could hear the church bells tolling the sundown.

Darkness again at last. They stumbled on.

Shortly before ten o'clock they blundered on an outlying hen coop. They caught three of the chickens before the baying of the farmer's dog sent them back into the endless swamp. The fowl were torn bodily apart, devoured raw — the first food in forty-eight hours. Bob could not make it, vomiting on his second mouthful. Cole ate Bob's share on top of his own, forcing the slimy flesh down, locking his teeth to keep it there. His strength *had* to be fed.

They went on, homing more certainly now that a hole in the scudding clouds had shown them a brief glimpse of the North Star.

At 2:00 P.M., three miles north of Mankato, they reached an abandoned farm house. Human flesh could endure no more. They had been on the retreat for four days and three nights and were still less than fifty miles from Northfield. The last thirty of those miles had been covered in fifteen hours, on foot, with no food other than the sickening flesh of three summer-molted hens. Stonewall Jackson would have been proud, but safety was still a far bell, beckoning in the distance from a reef of disaster.

The torrential rains sluiced on.

That storm is still talked about in southern Minnesota. Beginning on the night of the Northfield robbery, the rain fell steadily for twelve consecutive days. By the time Jesse and his men reached the Mankato farm house, every tributary stream for a hundred miles above the Iowa line was out of its banks. The gang was cut off at last, not by any cordon of human enemies, but by a relentless posse of bursting creeks and inundated lowlands. The halt was called.

All day Monday, Monday night, and Tuesday until dusk, they stayed inside the house. Charlie Pitts and Frank James forayed out late Tuesday night, returning with five more chickens. This time a small fire was risked.

Cole tore out the living-room partition with his hands, kindling the little blaze in the center of the parlor. The molding horse blankets were hung across the paneless front windows, their owners sleeping uncovered on the bare pine floor. By now the light of a fire meant more to the inner man than did the warmth of a wet blanket to the outer.

The last of the chicken was rationed out and re-cooked at dusk, Wednesday. The bones were cracked, and the marrow sucked to the wing tips. The shanks and scaly feet were eaten to the toenails. They awaited full night, strengthened by the food, the fire, the respite of shelter from the unending rain. After an hour, Jesse said he was going out on a scout and that some action would be taken upon his return. He then talked guardedly to Frank for five minutes, and left.

The gang waited his return with varied hearts.

Frank had not said ten words since leaving Northfield. Pitts and Jim Younger had been equally glum. Bob Younger was still talking wildly with fever, and none in the dreary room but knew he had traveled his last mile, afoot or a-horseback. Cole, the indomitable, still stood head and shoulders the tallest of them all.

Since saying he would walk with Jesse, he had done so. If a man stumbled in the dark, it was Cole who helped him up, who slapped his muddy buttocks, and grinned him or cursed him on. If a path were lost in the rain and Jesse hesitated in the lead, it was big Cole who moved up beside him, pointing the way. It was: "Left, Ding, she appears to open out thataway." Or: "Take the right fork, she bears southwest, and that's our line." And, again: "Straight ahead, Dingus, that's Missouri wind a-blowing! Cain't you smell it, boy? We ain't far to go now."

Indeed, it was not his brother Bob, alone, whom the towering outlaw carried those last miles. He carried every one of the others as well, and not excepting Frank and Jesse James in the number.

But now as those others waited with

him, their thoughts were not on Cole, or what lay ahead. They were on Jesse, and what lay ahead. Even as they wondered, Jesse returned.

He said he had gone down to the farm where Frank and Charlie had got the chickens. Down there, he had stalked the farmer to the barn, meaning to get a gun on him and force him to give over some food and bandages. But as he was about to make his move, a posse had ridden into the barnyard. They were from Mankato, and what they had to say to the farmer had stood Jesse's ears out from his head.

The German Lake surround had just found the three tied horses they had left behind them. The word now was that the James gang had walked out of the trap, had a four-day start, and were undoubtedly safe on their way to Missouri. A few Pinkertons and diehard posses of local deputies were still on the lookout for them, but the bulk of the one thousand men who had been in the field as of Sunday night had quit and gone home. "Boys!" Jesse concluded, pale eyes flickering nervously, "you know what this means? It means we got a chance. We're going to make it now, you hear?"

"Damned if it don't look like we ain't,"

breathed Charlie Pitts. "Seems like, if we could get horses again, we're same as safe. You spot anything good down yonder? Frank said something about a nice pair of grays . . . ?"

Jesse shot a sidelong glance at his brother. "Frank's crazy," he shrugged, passing it off. "Them grays was wolf bait. Besides, they belonged to the posse, and they took them along. Cole, what about Bob?"

"What *about* Bob, Dingus?"

"You know we cain't make it, toting him."

Jesse said it flat and certain. It had come down to cases now. Cole knew it. They all knew it.

"We can leave him some water and all the blankets," Jesse went on, "then send some farmer back to haul him out once we're clean away. We ain't no choice, Cole."

Cole let him finish it, trying to see his side, knowing, too, that the others must be thinking the same thing, or close to it. They had to be.

"All right," he said at last. "You all go along . . . that's only fair. Jim and me will stick with Bob and bring him along the best way we can. But we ain't leaving him."

"You got to leave him," rasped Jesse. "One way or another, he stays here. He ain't tagging us no more."

Cole stood up slowly. "What you mean . . . *one way or another?*" he said.

"I mean he stays here," said Jesse. "Dead or alive . . . !"

Cole shook his big head, his voice not rising. "You cain't mean that, Dingus. You cain't mean you'd put a bullet in a boy who's backed you since we was all kids."

"Cole . . . comes to my life or his . . . you god-damn well *know* I mean it. Now make up your mind. We're moving."

Cole stepped back. The flashing glide of his right hand caught them all gaping. The heavy Colt glinted dully in the day's dying light.

"Jesse, get out."

None of them had ever heard him use that name before. They stood frozen now, not believing what they saw, not accepting what they heard.

"Get out," said Cole, *"before I kill you."*

Jesse's guns were holstered at his sides. He still had his Winchester in his hands from scouting the farm. He made no move with the Colts, did not lift the carbine.

"Turn around," said Cole, "and walk out."

Jesse looked at Frank.

"I'm coming," said Frank James, and stood up.

"Anybody else?" asked Cole, his eyes never leaving Jesse.

No one answered; no one moved.

"Once you're through that door," he said to Jesse, "don't never let me see you again."

Jesse moved for the door. Frank hesitated, stepped toward Cole. "Bud," he said, using the old childhood name, "what are you doing? Wait a minute, now . . . we can still figure this out."

"Buck," answered Cole, in a return of nicknames lost in the dust of the Pleasant Grove schoolyard, "get out. You go with him. That's your job now. I'm giving it over to you. You can read all about it in the Book of Genesis . . . four . . . nine," he finished softly.

" 'Am I my brother's keeper?' " murmured Frank.

Cole nodded, waiting.

Frank winced, but did not drop his eyes as Jesse had. "I'm mortal sorry," he said. "I reckon you know that."

"I reckon I do, Buck. Good bye."

Frank looked away from him to Jesse, waiting impatiently near the door. Just before he turned to follow his brother out, he nodded, low-voiced, to Cole: " 'All that a man hath, will he give for his life.' "

Watching them go, Cole said a cynical — "Amen." — after them. If Frank heard it, he did not look back. He never did look back. He was, indeed, his brother's keeper, and his brother had already gone before him.

It was the last Cole Younger ever saw of Jesse James.

He stood staring after him a long time. At last, he said it, very softly and to himself — and maybe to Old Hickory's ghost, standing out beyond the twilight's shade: "I ought to have killed him. I ought to have killed him a long, long time ago."

A hundred yards from the farm house, the brush closed behind Frank and Jesse James. As it did, the latter wheeled on his older brother, reddened eyes blinking furiously.

"You darned ninny, you near fixed it for sure!"

"Fixed what? What you talking about?" stammered Frank, genuinely puzzled.

"The grays, you idiot! You told them about the grays!"

"Sure I did, Jesse. What you getting at?"

He had his answer in the cold spread of Jesse's grin and gasped unbelievingly: "Jess, for the love of God, you weren't lying about those grays being picked up by the posse! Lord, God, you were. They're still there."

Jesse's eyes slitted. "Don't preach to *me*, Frank. There was just two horses. Cole only made it easy with his damned bull-head ideas about Bob."

Frank said nothing. Jesse had said it all. Jesse had a plan; he always had a plan. You could take it or leave it.

The rain, sheeting down with renewed sullenness, hid them from view almost at once. They walked fast, with no talk. Inside thirty minutes they had the horses and were riding. An hour later saw them five miles on their way, guiding the stolen grays due west. Seventy-two hours later they had crossed the South Dakota line and were free.

There is no documentation for the seven days of hell which ensued for Cole and the others. The trail picks up one week after Jesse's defection at the Mankato farm house. The point was just outside the remembered village of Madelia. Four facts, alone, have been agreed upon concerning those seven days of dead trail. The hue and cry over the Northfield fugitives, which had nearly died away, burst into full clamor again with the news of the theft of two gray horses near Mankato, and the successful dash of those two grays and their riders through a picket line post on the Crystal Lake Road shortly thereafter.

The four outlaws remaining in the abandoned Mankato farm house left that refuge sometime during the morning of Thursday, September 14th, within hours after Frank and Jesse had fled it. Early the succeeding Thursday, September 21st, they were sighted, by the farmer's seventeen-year-old son, Oscar, crossing the dairy pasture of the Suborn farm, close by Madelia. Madelia is a scant twenty-five miles southeast of Mankato.

Twenty-five miles.

Twenty-five miles in seven days and six nights. Twenty-five miles by grievously wounded men across a land as alien to them as the hinder surface of the planet Mars. Twenty-five miles through a region again swarming with the hornet's nest of lawmen posses and rural pickets stirred up by Jesse's desertion. Yet Cole and his companions were not once seen until that last morning outside Madelia!

There is no frontier record of stoic courage and superlative retreat to match it.

But, then, following Oscar Suborn's alarm, posses from Madelia and nearby St. James closed off the country north and west. Other posses moved swiftly in from east and south. Four hours after the first discovery report, two hundred men were converging on Hanska Slough, the last reported sighting of the desperate quarry.

Hanska Slough was a backed-up side channel of the Watonwan River. Below the slough the channel spread out into a breast-deep swamp pond called Hanska Lake. Below the pond, the channel proper of the Watonwan resumed.

First cry of fox was raised by the posse of Madelia's Sheriff Glispin. Prying along the west shore of Lake Hanska, the sheriff suddenly saw the fugitives struggling along the mud flats about twenty yards out from his own, the west, bank of the lake. Waving his men to take cover, he carefully studied the four outlaws.

All of them were unkempt and filthy, with heavy, rain-wet beards. Their clothes were shredded and ripped, and Glispin at once noted the absence of the famed linen dusters. The largest of the bandits, their leader, was walking in front of the others, leaning on a crutch-like stick. The two following this first man were nearly as large as he, but not as old. One of them appeared badly wounded, for the other was supporting him bodily. The fourth man, smaller than the others, did not appear to be wounded but was staggering from exhaustion.

Glispin now rose up from the reeds and shouted the order to halt. He might as well have ordered the rain to stop falling. The bandits, signaled on by the big man, ran for the shelter of a low mudbank ahead of them. They got safely behind this cover, and the silence which followed was more unnerving than any gunfire. Sheriff Glispin took the opportunity to reëvaluate his position.

His posse was small, only five men. The mud flats were naked, offering no cover for an approach to the waiting outlaws. The time for the kill, the Madelia officer decided, was not yet. His low orders to his men were as quick as they were wise: "Pull back, boys. We had better wait for some of the others to come up."

In his later explanation of the withdrawal, Glispin merely remarked: "They were all mighty desperate-looking men, though the fourth one wasn't near as big as the others."

The Madelia sheriff might as well have added that it was a chore beyond the capacities of most men to be as big as a Younger.

With this Madelia posse thus hesitating to close in, Cole led his followers in the one direction open to them — straight away from the west bank, out across the lake itself. Somehow, they made the crossing. Wading, slipping, floundering, time and again, almost going under in the deeper holes, but always, miraculously, keeping their precious revolvers arm-high and out of the water, they got to the east bank. In the crossing, Glispin noted the desperate efforts to protect the side arms from immersion, the actions calling his attention for the first time to the fact that the bandits had abandoned their carbines, apparently to lighten their flight. The fact excited him, and he again took up the chase he had so recently called off.

But the horses of his posse would not take the water, and hurriedly the sheriff ordered his followers south to the ford at the outlet of the pond. Here he led them across the Watonwan and at a hard gallop up the east shore. As they rode, he shouted them on, having deduced from the outlaws' course their east-bank objective: a number of pasturing saddle horses, loose in a lakeside field.

It was a race of fresh horsemen against exhausted men on foot, three of whom were critically wounded. Still, Glispin won it by the narrowest margin, cutting between Cole Younger and the grazing mounts, just as the latter led his band off the mud flats into the pasture.

Again the sheriff's cry to halt and surrender rang out.

The Missourians, caught on the open grass, replied in the only tongue left them. It was a ragged, thin volley, but one of Cole's shots raked the ribs of Glispin's horse. The animal reared, throwing its rider. In the confusion, the outlaws got back onto the mud flats and into the lakeside reedbeds, working through this cover down toward the outlet at the ford of the Watonwan.

They reached the ford safely and across its narrow span beheld a sight of princely wealth: the hunting camp of a group of St. Paul sportsmen — and in that camp, not a hundred yards from where they stood, were the hunters' four fine saddle mounts — picketed, under leather, full-bridled, ready to ride!

Had Frank James been at that moment

on the east bank of the Watonwan, he might have quoted Richard III with telling point. As it was, the kingdom of Cole Younger's Missouri raiders was up for unquestioning trade for a horse, Richard or no Richard.

"Four horses!" croaked the big outlaw, hollow-voiced, and plunged into the Watonwan.

Behind him came Jim and Charlie Pitts, dragging the groaning Bob between them.

"Go on, go on!" pleaded the barely conscious youngster. "For God's sake, leave me stay here, and get out yourselves. I cain't ride no more."

"Easy, boy," gasped Jim. "We'll make it now, never fear. Look yonder, there! Old Cole's almost acrost . . . !"

The wounded youth raised his head and renewed his effort to go on. Cole *was* almost across!

But the gunfire up the lake had alerted the St. Paul hunters. When they saw the bearded apparitions rise up from the reeds across the river and then plow toward them through the water, they ran for it. When Cole reached the west bank, the camp was deserted, hunters and horses gone alike. And Cole had not stood wearily upon that bank for more than thirty seconds before his haggard glance told him that, with his crossing of the Watonwan, the Clay County fox had brought his ragged pack to its last earth.

They were trapped.

The ground upon which they found themselves formed a five-acre triangle of wild grape, willow, box elder, and plum. The triangle was based on the head of Lake Hanska. Its right side was an impassable twenty-five foot, perpendicular bluff. Its left, the channel of the Watonwan River.

The end came then with merciful speed.

Within minutes after the fugitives blundered into the deadly triangle, the bluff top was crawling with posse men. Across the river, other scores of manhunters suddenly appeared. They were boxed east, west, and south. Behind them — north — lay only the open expanse of the lake.

Trail's end.

Cole came to bay in a heavy tangle of grapevine and willow near the tip of the triangle. Here there was some protection from the bluff-top fire. And they could, with their own fire, cover the river side, and the lake base, of the triangle. More hope than this, they had not.

Cole helped Jim make a bed of brush for

Bob. They then joined Charlie Pitts to crouch and hold their breaths and peer through the wooded tangle, waiting for the rest of it. The waiting proved singularly brief, a tribute to the nerve of a county sheriff whose name is remembered only in Madelia, Minnesota. Glispin could have waited for starvation to do his work for him. Instead, he selected six riflemen and closed in on foot immediately.

The lawman's skirmish line advanced across the base of the triangle in plain view of the hidden outlaws.

At two hundred feet, the posse spotted movement in the vines ahead. They held up, and Cole's gun roared. Seven rifles crashed in reply. Pitts began firing now, and Jim. A fourth Colt boomed, and the posse men knew the wounded Bob Younger had somehow forced himself up and into the fight. Glispin's riflemen moved on now, straight in, answering the scattered revolver fire with heavy, aimed volleys of their more deadly weapons. At point-blank range, later taped off as thirty feet, they blasted their last rounds into the outlaw cover.

All sound ceased within the grape thicket.

Then a vine moved.

From beneath it writhed the body of a man. He rolled to his knees, struggled to his feet, stood facing the posse. He was a mass of fresh blood, but the Colt revolver still dangled from his left hand. His right hand was strapped in a dirty sling across his chest, and the blood on that hand was old and black and fly-encrusted.

"I surrender," whispered Bob Younger. "They're all down but me."

"Drop your gun, then," commanded Glispin.

The stiff fingers loosened. The gun slid from them. It struck a rock in falling, bounced into the sodden leaf mold, lay there, motionless and dully gleaming under the rain drip of the thicket.

Bob followed it down, falling heavily as the posse eased forward. He landed in a grotesque sprawl, and did not move again.

"Keep your guns on cock, man," said Sheriff Glispin, and stepped over the body of the young outlaw. Behind him, his posse men circled gingerly around the body, keeping their eyes on the brush ahead. They followed Glispin into the thicket, fingers inside trigger guards, jaws set, rifle muzzles probing the silent vines. All sensed the shadow of fear falling ahead of that last, interminable moment of time. None

131

sensed the longer shadow standing beyond that silent thicket.

An era had died with the dropping of Bob Younger's gun. Only an epic of outlaw courage remained to be played out. What Glispin's men found in that Watonwan River covert, outside of a priceless, last glimpse of Cole Younger at his indestructible best, was supplied within a handful of wordless minutes. Within the grapevine fortress Charlie Pitts lay dead, five bullets having done the job several hundred had failed to do at Northfield. Bob Younger had a fresh, deep chest wound, in addition to the shattered wrist and right elbow sustained in the First National Bank ambush. Jim Younger, like Pitts, was carrying five rifle bullets, the last one of which had smashed his jaw and the entire lower half of his face to a pulp. Cole, the only one of the four still conscious, was bleeding from eleven wounds, six of which he had received within the past ten minutes.

In the words of Robertus Love, an emotional James-Younger historian: "Thomas Coleman Younger, who looked like a bishop and fought like a Bengal tiger, lay upon the ground soaked with the rainfall and with his own blood — and smiled as he saw approaching him Colonel Vought, proprietor of the Flander's House Hotel, in Madelia, where Cole and his brothers had stayed overnight on the way to the Northfield Raid."

What Colonel Vought heard, as he stood staring down at his recent guest, may not belong in John Bartlett's quotations. It certainly belongs in any proper memorabilia of the flinty-humored head of the Younger clan. Rearing himself on his left elbow, Cole swept off his slouch hat with his mangled right hand. And managed, somehow, to do it with a flourish that matched the white-faced grin which came with it.

"Good morning, landlord," nodded the big outlaw. "You will excuse me for not getting up, but I have taken on a bit of weight since last we met, and do not feel so well because of it." Then, still grinning, and just before he slumped, face forward, into the boot-churned mud: "How are *you*, sir?"

The morning of September 23rd found the Youngers held under guard in their hospital rooms in Madelia's Flander's House, whence Glispin had transported them by wagon from the Watonwan. Cole and Jim shared one room and a single bed. Bob, considered nearer death than the older brothers, had been granted a room to himself. The only person admitted to see them, other than the several churchwomen of Madelia who were acting as their nurses, was a city reporter from the St. Paul *Pioneer Press.*

Cole's sole response to the questions of the latter was to ask him to express publicly the brothers' thanks to the citizens of Madelia who had treated them with such kindness. He added that he was considerably surprised at this treatment, and mightily grateful for it.

Jim, his multiple-fractured jaw disfiguringly swollen and badly infected from the inside, could not utter a word. When offered pencil and paper and asked to make any statement he might wish to reach the public, he only shook his head "and turned his poor, mutilated face to the wall."

Bob, although assumed to be dying, and perhaps because he agreed with the assumption, talked with more freedom. Thanking the *Pioneer Press* man for a proffered cigar, he apologized for his shackled hands and asked politely for "the loan of a match." With the panatela lit, he inhaled deeply, made comment of its fine aroma, then stated calmly the terms under which he would like posterity to remember him and his brothers.

To begin with, he and Cole and Jim were all grown men. They knew their situation perfectly well and were ready to abide its clear consequences. Naturally, they all regretted their situation, but they had chosen their own way of life and were not complaining about it.

He would not discuss the murder of Heywood, the Northfield cashier, beyond saying that the witnesses undoubtedly knew which of the bandits had shot him. Neither would he talk about the disappearance of Frank and Jesse James, nor admit they had even been along on the robbery. In the same line, he refused to identify any of his other outlaw companions. He was reluctant to say anything of his own previous life, or of the adventures of the gang prior to Northfield. About Northfield he spoke in detail, dwelling at particular length on the stark sufferings of the escape march from the Mankato farm house. He concluded by taking the full blame upon himself for the capture of his companions. Their loyal insistence on staying with him had, in his opinion, cost them a freedom they could otherwise most easily have won.

There the interview ended. The St. Paul

135

reporter provided his own grim postscript to it: "Sheriff Glispin will proceed to Faribault by way of Mankato, leaving here at 5:45 A.M. The body of the dead robber (Pitts) goes on the same train to be embalmed. The trip will be hard on those wounded men, particularly the one shot in the jaw. He suffers much. The doctor here objected this morning to moving them, but the men are plucky and said they will go along all right."

The wages of their crime were promptly paid. Under Minnesota law, a confessed murderer could not be hanged. Cole, Jim, and Bob, in turn, pleaded guilty to the principal charge: accessory to the murder of J. L. Heywood, cashier of the First National Bank of Northfield, Minnesota. Judge Samuel Lord sentenced them all to life imprisonment in the state penitentiary at Stillwater.

Just before the trial, and afterward, all three relented and spoke freely of their past misdeeds and present regrets. Each continued to insist soberly, however, that he and his brothers were victims of a troubled time and had been largely "drove" to their lives of crime. At no time did any of them, from the moment of capture to the day of his death, admit the identities of the other five men who had been with them on the Northfield job. They had come to the end of their road. They willingly admitted it had been a bad one. Past that, there were no other apologies, no added details or explanations.

The best farewell of the Youngers was spoken outside the walls of Stillwater Prison, as they all stood before its gate, breathing deeply of the last of freedom's air and gazing, far-eyed, across the heads of the small crowd which had gathered to see them committed.

It was Cole who spoke its major theme, young Bob who delivered its quiet last word.

A Madelia lady, one of those who had nursed Cole through the hours of his worst suffering at the Flander's House, broke forward impulsively in the final moment to tell him how glad and grateful she was that the brothers had fallen into her town's Christian hands and that they had all been so well taken care of.

Cole, his handsome face thin from the weeks of courtroom testimony and the unhealed torture of his wounds, still had one smile left. "I am grateful, too, ma'am," he said. "But I cain't say we deserve it." His voice dropped low, and he spoke the words as a child might speak them, bringing them back from the long-ago with thoughtful, head-nodding finality. " *'Man that is born of woman is of few days and full of trouble.'* That's from the Book of Job, ma'am. It tells a heap of living, as I have known it."

He paused, gray eyes finding the horizon again, tired smile fading sadly.

"Circumstances, ma'am, sometimes make men what they are. If it had not been for the war, I might have been something. As it is, I am only what you see."

And, then, this typically gentle valedictory from Bob, standing at Cole's side and speaking to the Madelia lady from his heart, although his eyes and memories were as far away along the back trail as his older brother's: "Please, ma'am, don't worry about us. We are rough men and used to rough ways."

With these few softly spoken words, the gates of Stillwater Prison closed upon the last of the Youngers.

But the storied clang of steel on stone, behind them, was not their knell, alone. It rang, as well, for Jesse James, and for the legend which had been his. In folklore's final reckoning, Dr. Samuel's pale-eyed stepson must stand in the shadow of a taller man than he. A man who, but for circumstances, might have been many things better than right-hand bandit henchman to Jesse Woodson James. A man whose name, today, is all but hidden beneath the maze of lies and half-truths laid emotionally upon the grave of his traitorous leader.

It is a simple name, and easy to remember: *Thomas Coleman Younger.*

"... Fired by the Hand of Robert Ford"

Although it was delayed five mysterious, driven years, the end came as certainly for Jesse James in St. Joe, Missouri, as it had for Cole Younger and his brothers in Northfield, Minnesota. And it came with a poesy of justice not equaled in frontier history. No minstrel of olden times ever sang truer song than this:

> **The dirty little coward**
> **Who shot Mr. Howard**
> **Has laid poor Jesse in his grave.**

Yet in September, 1879, when fate commenced to gather her coils about the celebrated bandit of the Missouri borderlands, the anonymous bard who composed this most enduring of Jesse's epitaphs had not begun to "gaze in silent tears into that lonesome box of pine," and the flesh of his bearded hero was many a murderous mile

141

from Bob Ford and the "little white house on the hill" in old St. Joe.

But what of the three missing years in Jesse's history, since the gates of Stillwater Prison had closed upon Cole and Jim and Bob, the forthright, gentle-spoken Younger brothers? Nothing is written of those years, because nothing is known of those years. Not one solid tangible thing has been introduced into the record to document the gap in the trail.

The honeycombed warren of the Missouri woodlands, as it had so often before when the hounds of the law bayed too hotly upon the bloodied track of the Jameses, simply swallowed up Frank and Jesse without a trace. So say the history books.

Some very old men in Missouri know better. In the month after the great Northfield raid, Jesse and the Bible-quoting Frank passed secretly through Clay County, collecting their wives and children. The combined families departed the home state "in the dead of the night and in a single rickety covered wagon driven from Kansas City by their stepbrother, John Samuel."

Tradition has Jesse hiding in the wagon with the women and children, while Frank outrode the perilous journey on horseback.

No man from Missouri likes to question the homeland's legends. But it takes a little faith in local lore, together with a lot of innocence of Jesse's inherent wolfishness of character, to picture him cowering in a wagonload of women and children. It is the safe assumption that where Frank's horse stepped during that flight, no matter how warily or far in the lead, he was stepping in the tracks of Jesse's black.

The files of the Pinkertons today disclose the amazing geography of that three-year hegira which began that blustery, dark fall night from Kansas City. During its bewildering course, Frank and Jesse, always with their wives and children now, lived in Kentucky, Tennessee, California, Texas, and Missouri. Jesse used the name of Howard, Frank, the family surname of Woodson. So complete was Jesse's peculiarly faceless and common look of type that at one point in the Pinkertons' relentless pursuit of him he "entered and rode his famous black gelding in the Nashville races with the fairgrounds alive with Pinkerton and local detectives."

For all his crimes of murder and the worldwide notoriety they had brought him, Jesse was still a man literally without a known face to his trackers. The only picture ever made of him remained the one which "hung in the locket around his poor mother's neck." It is not entirely beside the delightful point, for one who would remember the real Jesse James, to recall that he not only entered and rode his renowned black in the Nashville Derby — he won the race! But if the point is, in its twisted Jamesian way, delightful, it is by the same token singular.

It is the last recorded bit of Jesse's steel-sharp sense of humor. Beyond this one small, pale-eyed smile, the trail turns exceeding grim.

With the passing of the third year, the considerable loot of the Lamine River robbery — harbored more carefully by the Jameses than by the Youngers — ran low. The pressure from the Pinkertons, successfully defied while the family funds were in relative abundance and could provide unrestricted bribery, mounted with sudden intensity. In September, 1879, thirty-six months precisely since the fiasco at Northfield, a telegram went from Kansas City to the Chicago headquarters of William Pinkerton, now replacing his noted father as head of the national detective agency. It was unsigned and consisted of five words:

He is back in Missouri.

A thousand-word deposition over Jesse's own signature could not have told William Pinkerton more. By now he knew his man, and he knew his methods. Thirteen years on the trail drew at once into spotlight focus. The beam fell glaringly on Clay and Jackson Counties. His operatives held it there, waiting with that enormous patience which was Pinkerton's and with that deadly faith of the trained manhunter in the credo of his calling: *the criminal will always return to the scene of the crime.*

In the late twilight of October 7th, 1879, Jesse returned. The scene was Blue Cut on the Chicago & Alton Railroad near Glendale, Jackson County, Missouri. There were six men in the gang. The old guerrilla method was employed.

The horses thundered into Glendale on the dead run. The Rebel yells echoed, the Colts roared, the window glass crashed. The employees at the dépôt were pistol-whipped, herded into and locked in the baggage room. The train was flagged down and boarded. William Grimes, the express messenger, sought in vain to hide the $35,000 in his charge. He was beaten senseless and left for dead. The escape was

145

as complete as had been the surprise of the assault. There was no attempt to "take the coaches."

Instantly, the Pinkertons pounced. Witnesses by the score were dredged out of the Clay and Jackson Counties back country. Fearful testimony was given and taken in secret. The old immunity was broken, and within twenty-four hours the Chicago officials released a bulletin naming the new gang: Jesse James, Ed Miller, Wood Hite, Bill Ryan, Dick Liddell, Tucker Basham.

Searching that miserable roster, Frank James might have muttered: "Samuel . . . one . . . twenty-seven. 'How are the mighty fallen!' "

Where, indeed, were the magic names of old? The night-riding Rebel faithful of Todd and Anderson and Quantrill? Where were Cole and Jim and Bob Younger? And Jim Cummins, Clell Miller, Big George Shepherd, and fierce-eyed brother Oll? Where, indeed, was Frank James himself? The answers echo hollowly. Only the names respond. The men are gone. But sorry crew or not, $35,000 in very live money was missing. And missing with the money, shadowy and swift as ever the old, famous gang, were Jesse and his new recruits.

For months the border was quiet. Then a sudden, smoldering flare sprang to life. Big George Shepherd, comrade of the Civil War, "Bloody Bill" Anderson days, was released from the Missouri State Penitentiary. A legend came back to life, a forgotten era reincarnate, Big George strode briefly and shadow-tall across the darkening stage.

His last statement on entering prison had been to Yankee Bligh, the famed Pinkerton operative who had trailed and jailed him, following the old gang's Russelville robbery.

"I don't know any of the men who were with me," Big George had insisted to Bligh.

The gray-walled years had changed Big George's mind. On his release, he went to the office of the Kansas City marshal. That officer, listening to his proposal, furnished him with a fake newspaper clipping purporting to relate how Shepherd, unswerving in his allegiance to his bandit pals of yore, had become the object of a widespread manhunt by the very officials with whom he now meant to work. With this sorry bait, Big George set out to seek his former outlaw comrades.

Weeks later, he returned to Kansas City,

and the headlines blared: **JESSE JAMES IS DEAD!** Shepherd's story was simple. Jesse and the boys had welcomed him heartily. At the right moment, he had gotten Jesse aside and shot him, holding the gun under a wrapped coat to muffle its sound. For William Pinkerton the tale was too simple. He demanded a body. None was forthcoming. Pinkerton denied the Shepherd story in print. The Missouri folk believed him. You did not just walk out and take old Jesse with any phony newspaper yarn. Not hardly! But then the months rolled by. There was no more sign of Jesse. No more sighting of the new gang. Public opinion wavered.

Damn, maybe Big George had got Jesse, after all. Maybe Dingus was six feet under like he said. It was certain George had been a member in good standing of the bunch which took the Russelville, Kentucky bank. And he had for sure taken his medicine for that job without squawking on Dingus or Frank or any of the boys. Good Lord, maybe Ding *was* dead! Maybe he had let George get to him.

William Pinkerton shook his stubborn head, went back to his watching and waiting.

1880 wore away. Then 1881 began. Still no Jesse.

January passed. February. The first week in March set in. And *only* set in. On its first day the gang, with Frank back at Jesse's side, struck like lightning and far afield: at a stagecoach outside Muscle Shoals, *Alabama!*

It was a feint.

On July 10th the first of the real blows fell: on the Davis & Sexton Bank in Riverton, Iowa — to a net result of $5,000 and a spot-clean getaway.

But now the Pinkertons had their man back in the glare of their waiting searchlight. All-points bulletins were dispatched into the key states of Iowa, Missouri, Kentucky, Tennessee and Texas — the hallowed James stamping grounds. These bulletins were a classic example of the famed manhunter's sixth sense as to the anatomy of the criminal mind, particularly that warped example of same which sat behind the pale-blue and sandy-lidded eyes of Jesse Woodson James.

Missouri, the home state, is no longer safe for the gang. Its backwoods hideouts are all under twenty-four-hour Agency surveillance. Its local peace officers are at last alert under an anti-James ad-

ministration. Jesse James is on a last, desperate raid to make a final, king's ransom killing and perhaps quit the outlaw trail forever. . . .

Five days after this telegraphed warning, history fulfilled William Pinkerton's singular prophecy. Jesse began the forecasted killing.

The engineer grumbled, jerking the throttle closed and throwing the sand and steam to the drive wheels. He had been late getting out of Kansas City, and the Chicago, Rock Island & Pacific's Train No. 23 was running twenty minutes behind schedule into Cameron Station, sixty-four miles out of Kansas City. Train No. 23 was running into something a little more sinister than a late schedule at Cameron Station.

Three husky, bearded men made their way into her smoker as she pulled out for Gallatin, another sixty miles up the line. They were rough-looking men, their smoker companions remembered later, wearing black broadcloth suits of a back-country cut, dirty riding boots, and wide, dusty, black hats. They spoke quickly among themselves in guarded tones, pulled their hats over their faces, slumped in their seats, and "went promptly to sleep."

It is to be assumed, from what followed, that this honest slumber was broken now and again by the half-lidded gleam of a professional eye scanning the smoking car's assortment of "plug hats" (fat prospects) from beneath those dusty, pulled-down hat brims. And that, further, on the part of at least one set of those eyes, the covert regard of the "customers" was shuttered by a chronically sore-lidded and rapid blinking.

At 10:01 P.M., No. 23 pulled into Gallatin, sat wheezing nervously for six minutes, then chuffed impatiently on toward Winston, eleven miles ahead. It was 10:29 P.M., July 15th, 1881, when she rolled into the Winston dépôt. The engineer had made up fourteen minutes and was feeling considerably better. He began to unburden himself along these lines to his fireman. While he was thus pleasantly engaged, four other events of somewhat more than comparable importance were taking place behind him, along the body proper of his train No. 23.

One of the bearded travelers in the smoker was coming half awake and was, his curious fellow passengers noted, sleepily waving a large, white handkerchief apparently to the deserted platform of the Winston dépôt. The smoker's conductor was swinging to the dépôt platform, chatting with the station agent a moment, swinging back aboard, reëntering his smoking car, and beginning, "with an affable smile," to collect his tickets and stick their tabs into the hatbands of the new passengers.

Two men were sliding out of the shadows north of the dépôt, running to the baggage car's hand rail, swarming up it to the roof of the car, and crawling stealthily along it toward the fireman's tender and engineer's cab.

The three bearded slumberers in the smoker were leaping suddenly to their feet, jerking out single-action Colt revolvers, blasting a round of warning shots over their fellow passenger's heads, and shouting the old familiar order: "All right, get them up! Get them up! Don't nobody move, or you'll get your heads blowed off!"

With the order, their leader fired three shots at the oil lamp at the far end of the car. The lamp shattered. On the signal of its crashing glass, the Great Winston Train Robbery was under way.

The conductor ran toward Jesse, who stood near the forward lamp of the smoker, crying: "Don't break that other lamp! We don't want a fire in here!" As he came up to Jesse, the full light of the remaining lamp fell on his face, and for the first time the bandit leader had a clear look at No. 23's smoking-car conductor. The former's eyes widened with sudden fury, the latter's with belated fear.

Over his shoulder, Jesse snarled to Frank and Wood Hite. "You remember this son-of-a-bitch, boys? Look at the bastard careful, Frank. Look at him mighty careful."

"Westphal! Dear Lord, it's Billy Westphal . . . !"

Frank's gasp of recognition was seconded by the explosions, at point-blank range, of both Jesse's Colts.

The shots smashed into the conductor's groin. The trainman staggered back, turned, and stumbled down the aisle toward the rear door. Jesse followed him, pumping deliberate shot after deliberate shot into his back. Somehow, the dying man reached the vestibule door.

Jesse stood back, out of his way, letting him fumble the door open and fall down the outside steps to the dépôt platform. Following only as far as the last car-step, Jesse shot him four more times as he lay writhing on the pine planking.

Once back in the smoker he simply nodded to Frank and Wood Hite. *"He'll take no more trains into Kearney."*

Seven years before, conductor William Westphal had been in charge of the special Hannibal & St. Joe train which had crossed the Missouri River to sidetrack at Kearney with a load of Pinkertons and local lawmen the night of the notorious bombing of the Samuel farm house — the night in which Jesse's mother had her right arm mutilated and his half-brother, eight-year-old Archie Samuel, lost his life in the bomb blast ever after attributed to the Pinkerton men, and as long and stoutly denied by them.

It is not made clear how Jesse remembered Billy Westphal after all those bitter years, and there is only folklore to say *that* he did, or that Frank James was in the smoker with him *when* he did. But that he killed Westphal, and did it with "nine bullets, none fired at a range greater than ten feet, and five of them from behind," is an inhuman fact, based on eyewitness affidavits of fifteen fellow passengers and upon the inquest findings still on file in the Daviess County coroner's office.

In her lean black book, fate was closing out the account of Jesse W. James. At the hour of the Winston robbery, there remained to his dark credit in that grim ledger but three mistakes yet to be made. The moment William Westphal died, those three became the less by one.

The Winston robbery was an incalculable failure. Jesse had possessed information that the combination baggage-express car was carrying upward of $25,000. His informant had neglected to state that the money was in the form (non-negotiable by wheat sack and saddle horn) of fifteen-pound ingots of mint silver. Outside of this bullion there were only $600 in the United Express Company's safe! And the affair in the smoker had been miserably bungled.

Another passenger, unnerved by Westphal's murder, had tried to run out of the car, and Jesse had shot him down in brutal turn. Frank and Wood Hite, stampeded by the double murder, had backed out of the car, abandoning the raging Jesse. At the same time, alarmed by the shooting in the smoker, the conductors in the train's only other cars — two coaches and a sleeper — had bolted their doors and put out all their aisle lights. Then, during the following assault on the express car, the engineer — his guards called off to aid in the fruitless search of the express company safe — had extinguished his cab lamps and headlight, plunging the entire train into darkness.

Cursing, the bandit crew had run for their horses, a disorganized, inept, sorry facsimile of the once terrible James gang. They had not time to steal a single watch or lift one passenger's purse. The high cost of outlaw living was not dropping a penny, but the wages for murder were going down drastically. Splitting the $600 with his four accomplices, Jesse found he had paid himself $60 each for his two homicides — a life for a life, and cheap at the price — but for that $120 Jesse had purchased his own death warrant.

Governor Thomas Crittenden, who in 1881 had just come into Missouri's executive mansion, signed the necessary legal paper. Crittenden had won the governorship on a lethally simple platform: *"The solemn determination to overthrow and to destroy the outlawry in this state whose head and front is the James gang."* Missouri law forbade the offering of more than $300 in reward money. But when the news of the Winston robbery and murder reached the state house, Crittenden forgot the law. He summoned a secret conclave of railroad company heads to Jefferson City and, on July 28th, one week after the Winston disaster, called in the press and released the terms of the warrant Jesse had drawn with his own revolvers:

A reward of $5,000 for the capture of Frank and Jesse James and $5,000 for the conviction of each is hereby posted. It is understood that the railroads will supply the funds.

For the first time in fifteen years a *real* price had been put upon Jesse's head. In simple terms, since conviction was certain, it meant that his captors would stand to pocket $10,000 in hard cash. Judas Iscariot had hired out for thirty pieces of silver.

Five years to the day after the citizens of Northfield had begun to lower it with their rifles and shotguns along Division Street, the last-act curtain rang down on the career of Jesse James. Enemies were now everywhere. Pinkertons swarmed over the state. Local peace officers, fired by avarice, were at last on the blood prowl. Private citizens, ex-guerrillas, sometime outlaw comrades of the past, all pricked hungry ears and took the golden trail. The governor's ten thousand pieces of silver stared at the hunted gang from every cabin door in western Missouri. But while the huntsmen prowled the orchestra pit, the star of the drama came out of the wings.

Curtain time was 8:00 P.M. of the evening of September 7th, 1881. The stage was twice familiar to the veteran cast — Blue Cut near Glendale, Missouri.

Act One was redundant. The pile of cross-ties athwart the rails of the Chicago & Alton roadbed. The screech of the whistle, the lock of the sanded drive wheels. The rough, bearded men leaping aboard the slowing cars. The engineer covered and escorted to the express car by the nervous, blinking, leading man of the piece.

But Act Two had been rewritten by the temperamental chief actor. And in the deviation, Jesse withdrew from fate's dwindling account book the second of his remaining mistakes. For the first time in the history of the play, and for a reason known only to the author, Jesse James introduced the members of the cast to the captive audience. With a flourish of his revolvers, the bearded hero bowed to the engineer and the express messenger.

"Allow me to introduce myself," he drawled. "I'm Jesse James." Then, without awaiting the applause: "This is my brother, Frank. The boy with the big grin and the bad front teeth is my cousin, Wood Hite. That's Clarence Hite, standing with him. Yonder there is Dick Liddell, Ed Miller, and Charlie Ford. I don't believe I caught your names, gentlemen . . . ?"

What possessed Jesse in this moment of peculiar rashness can scarcely be imagined. Nothing could have been less typical of him. What would bring a man who had made a lifetime passion of hiding his face and name, and who had for fifteen years demanded and gotten a fantastic loyalty from his followers as to their own or their fellow robbers' identities, suddenly to make a stage play of this sort is simply impossible to comprehend.

The only key was furnished years later by the self-effacing Jim Cummins, speaking to a Kansas City *Times* reporter in reply to the question. Said quiet Jim, looking back across the fading yesterdays: "After Northfield, Jesse was never the same. He got a little crazy, I think. Me and most of the others from the old bunch got a little leery of him after that. You couldn't trust him no more, and we fought shy of him." Then, after a long pause, the final soft drawl: "We always figured he never got over sneaking out from under Cole at Mankato. Cole was really the smart one, you know. Nobody

159

else could ever handle Jesse after he was took at Madelia. We all thought a heap of old Cole. He was the best of the lot."

Yet, whatever possessed Jesse in the opening moments of the second Blue Cut robbery, and whatever the key to it, he quickly recovered. With his theatrical introductions over, he returned to the standard book for Act Three. The safe was cleaned out, the passengers fleeced, the wheat sack filled and tied, the getaway made on flawless schedule. But it was a lean autumn for highway harvests. Total gleanings from the second Glendale cutting amounted to a bare $2,000 in cash and jewelry.

And the blood-money noose was tightening.

The identification of the gang's members was on the telegraph wires within twenty minutes of the robbery. By daybreak, Missouri was teeming with bounty-hunting badge toters.

By dint of immediate split-up and all night, wild riding, the gang got across the state and safely away. With nightfall of the 18th they were over the Tennessee line. They reached the pre-arranged hide-out at the home of Frank James outside Nashville the next day. Here they held together for three days. Then the disintegration began. It had been building hourly since Jesse's quixotic naming of his fellows in the Chicago & Alton express car. When Frank returned from a scout into Nashville and reported that William Pinkerton himself was in the city, the long-delayed break-up of the gang was on.

Charlie Ford, the first to go, disappeared without good-byes during the night of the 22nd. Clarence and Wood Hite followed him twenty-four hours later. Dick Liddell was next to depart. In leaving, he told Jesse that the Hites had gone to their family hide-out in Kentucky and that Ford was heading for his Ray County, Missouri farm. Ed Miller, brother of the dead Clell, stuck it out until that third night, then announced that he, too, was cutting his stick.

Jesse studied him for a time, and said: "Wait up . . . I'm coming with you."

Even in his last den, the Clay County wolf had a plan. He had let too many of the pack get away. Running loose as they were, their howling was bound to be heard sooner or later. This last one of them to leave had better be followed. It was the least a man could do.

For brother Frank, he had a parting bit

of advice: "You had best stick here, Buck. Things are going to pop up yonder. I will get in touch with you."

He and Ed Miller crossed into Missouri that same night, bound for the Samuel place in Clay County. Somewhere short of that destination, Jesse murdered Clell's brother.

The facts are few. Early on the morning of the 25th, a farmer who knew Jesse saw him riding south of Norborne, Carroll County, "with a companion on a brown horse." Later that day, the farmer heard a man's body had been found in some blackberry bushes north of Norborne. He rode over and had a look. It was the man on the brown horse.

Meantime, other murderers were afoot. The morning of his arrival in Ray County, Charlie Ford held dark council with younger brother Bob, a sometime hanger-on of the James gang. Within an hour, Bob saddled up and rode away — straight for the governor's mansion in Jefferson City. There the business was short, the chief executive's answers sweet. Yes, his excellency did still guarantee the $10,000 for the James boys. He guaranteed it — even if his proclamation was obscure on the point — for either Frank *or* Jesse. Especially

Jesse. And, yes, the guarantee did read and did still stand: *Dead or Alive*.

Bob Ford was back at his brother's farm by dusk.

A few days later, he and Charlie were in Kansas City, where Jesse, as "Mr. Howard," had joined his wife and children in a rented house. Charlie stayed with the family in the rented dwelling for several days, a welcome and trusted guest. But brother Bob rode back to the Ford farm immediately.

In Kansas City, Jesse's sojourn was brief. Before the month was out, he accompanied Charlie Ford to the latter's Ray County farm. Here they were in time to learn that Wood Hite had come in from Kentucky some days earlier. They did not get to talk to Cousin Wood, however. The previous night, Liddell and Bob Ford, fearful that Hite had gone over to the law, had murdered him in the farm house living room, Bob delivering the *coup de grâce* with "a single shot through the head."

This was not, of course, the story Cousin Jesse was given. And Liddell, seeing the narrowed blink with which the hunted leader received the substituted lie, reached a notably sound conclusion. When Jesse suggested that he "take a little ride with me and Charlie," Liddell politely refused the opportunity.

In his subsequent statement, Liddell put the refusal succinctly: "They tried to get me to go with them," he said, "but I declined to go. I mistrusted Jesse by that time and believed he wanted to kill me. When he had come up from Nashville leading Ed Miller's brown horse and told us Ed had been took sick and he didn't think he would get well very soon, we all knew what had happened. So I put off going with him and Charlie, and they left."

The year turned tensely.

Jesse flitted through the mid-Missouri backwoods like a ghost, now sleeping a night at the Samuel barn, now lurking a nervous week with his wife in Kansas City, now returning for a few days with the Fords in Ray County. Finally, he removed his family to St. Joseph, renting the ill-fated little white house on the hill.

Fate checked the ledger, nodded silently.

Mr. Howard had made his last remove.

February passed. March drew to a close. And through every hour of their inching progress the Fords, through a third brother, Elias "Cap" Ford, were in touch with Jackson County's Sheriff Timberlake, Jesse's long-sworn and mortal enemy. Timberlake, in turn, kept his posse on a twenty-four-hour standby alert and held a special train in Kansas City "under full steam and prepared to roll on ten minutes' notice."

The trap was ready, and straining at its springs. On March 29th, the last ounce of weight was placed on its sensitive pan. Dick Liddell, who had surrendered to Timberlake on a promise of clemency from Governor Crittenden, signed the fourteen-page confession "of shame," in which he named dates, places, and faces for every job the gang had pulled since the post-Northfield reorganization.

Liddell's "coming in" had been well guarded by the authorities. It was not until his confession hit the front page of the Kansas City *Times* on April 2nd that his former companions had any idea where he had gone and what he had done. Even then, the news was overnight in reaching St. Joe. Jesse's first hint of it was when he stepped out on the front stoop of the Howard home to pick up his copy of the St. Joseph *Gazette* the morning of April 3rd.

Behind him in the "little white house" at the moment were his mother, his wife, and two children, and Bob and Charlie Ford. In his statement at the inquest, Bob Ford related that Jesse walked into the living room from the porch holding the paper, unfolded.

"He stopped just inside the door," Ford said, "opened the paper and looked at it. He gave a little start and then just stood there, staring over the top of the paper and blinking like he always did when upset."

Ford's next line was unquestionably the correct translation of that last, pale-eyed blink.

"I knew then I had placed my head in the lion's mouth. How could I safely remove it?"

It was shortly after 8:00 A.M. the morning of April 3rd, when Bob Ford asked himself that fearful question. A few moments later, history answered it for him.

For the first time in sixteen outlaw years and to this day, unaccountably, Jesse took off his guns. Fate was waiting. It was the third of his remaining mistakes. The account of Jesse W. James was overdrawn. Quietly, the black book closed. Its last page bore the purple cancellation stamp of the infamous telegram dispatched to Governor Crittenden and Sheriff Timberlake at 8:27 A.M.:

I have killed Jesse James. St. Joseph.
Bob Ford.

The news struck a stunned Missouri to her editorial knees. On the front pages of every paper within the state, the voice of a shattered folklore was heard crying.

JESSE BY JEHOVAH solemnly announced the St. Joseph *Gazette*.

THE KING IS DEAD! trumpeted the Osceola *Democrat*.

JUDGMENT FOR JESSE, tolled the *Evening News*. **The Notorious Bandit At Last Meets His Fate And Dies With His Boots On!**

The Kansas City *Journal* said it best. Her banner was the heartbeat of a homeland, faithful even unto death. **GOOD BYE JESSE!**

The coroner's inquest was held at 3:00 P.M. in the old circuit courtroom of St. Joseph's Buchanan County courthouse. Present were Mrs. Zerelda Samuel (Jesse's mother), Mrs. James (his wife), and Dick Liddell and Bob and Charlie Ford, the latter "all heavily armed." The brief rest is best told in the testimonies of the two principal witnesses: Robert and Charles Ford.

The latter was first under cross-examination:

"Well, now, will you explain how it was that you came to kill him?"

167

"Well, we had come in from the barn where we had been feeding and currying the horses, and Jesse complained of being warm and pulled off his coat and threw it on the bed and opened the door and said that he guessed he would pull off his gun belt as some person might see it. Then he went to brush off some pictures, and, when he turned his back, I gave my brother the wink, and we both pulled our pistols, but he . . . my brother . . . was the quickest and fired first. I had my finger on the trigger and was just going to fire, but I saw his shot was a death shot and did not fire. He heard us cock our pistols and turned his head. The ball struck him in the back of the neck, and he fell. Then we went out and got our hats, and we went and telegraphed Sheriff Timberlake what we had done. . . ."

Robert Ford was then called and followed his older brother on the witness stand. It is remembered that he gave his evidence in a "clear, firm voice and did not once falter."

"And did the governor then tell you anything about a reward?"

"He said ten thousand dollars had been offered for Jesse or Frank dead or alive. I then entered into arrangements with

Timberlake. I afterward told Charlie of the conversation I had with the officers and told him I would like to go with him. He said, if I was willing to go, all right. We started that night, and went up to Missus Samuel's and put the horses up. Jesse's stepbrother, John Samuel, was wounded, and they were expecting him to die. There were some friends of the family there whom Jesse did not wish to see him, so we stayed in the barn all night until they left, and that was pretty near daylight, and we stayed in the house all next day, and that night we started away. That was on Thursday night. Friday night we stayed at his brother-in-law's. We left Missus Samuel and went about three miles into the woods for fear the officers would surprise us at her house. We started from the woods and came up to another of his brother-in-law's and got supper there and started from there here."

"This was last week?"

"Yes. We came at once to Saint Joseph and then talked over the matter again, and how we would kill him."

"What did you tell Jesse you were with him for?"

"I told him I was going with him."

"Had you any plans made at the time to rob

any particular bank?"

"He had spoken of several but had made no particular selection."

"Well, now, will you give us the particulars of the killing and what time it occurred?"

"After breakfast, between eight and nine o'clock on this morning, he, my brother, and myself were in the room. He pulled off his pistols and got up on a chair to dust off some picture frames, and I drew my pistol and shot him."

"How close were you to him?"

"About six feet away."

"How close was the hand which held the pistol?"

"About four feet, I should think."

"Did he say anything?"

"He started to turn his head but didn't say a word."

"Do you know anyone that can identify him?"

"Yes, sir, Sheriff Timberlake can, when he comes. He was with him during the war."

For three days the witnesses came forward, each in his somber way declaring his association with the bandit chief, and swearing to the identity of the bearded corpse. His mother, Mrs. Zerelda Samuel, was the last witness called. Her broken testimony concluded the inquest over all that

170

was mortal of Jesse Woodson James.

"I live in Clay County and am the mother of Jesse James. Oh, my poor boy. I have seen the body since my arrival and have recognized it as that of my son, Jesse. The lady by my side is my daughter-in-law, and the children are here. He was a kind husband and son. . . ."

Nothing remained but the inevitable postscript returned by the coroner's jury twenty-eight minutes after filing out: that the body of the deceased was that of Jesse W. James and that he came to his death by a wound in the back of his head, caused by a pistol shot fired by the hand of Robert Ford.

Thus, officially, closed the last act of DEATH OF A LEGEND, the parable of the Peasant Grove schoolboy turned deadly killer of the middle border. With the dimming of the house lights in the circuit courtroom of Buchanan County, the play was over.

The body was taken by train to Kearney. For twenty-four hours the coffin stood open in the lobby of the Kearney House, the town's one hotel. All day the pushing crowds of curious filed past the casket, fighting and shoving for a look at the famous outlaw. By nightfall, untold hundreds had gazed upon the fabled face of Jesse James. Perhaps in the entire gawking multitude there were a lone, hard-eyed handful of bearded, rough-clothed strangers who knew it well, and from a hundred wild night rides, and who looked up from it and nodded silently, the one to the other, before they went soundlessly away. Even in the last, still, cold hour, Jesse James was only a name. In death, as in life, he had no face.

Funeral services were held at the Kearney Baptist Church. The text was from the Book of Job, xii, 8: *"Man that is born of woman is of few days and full of trouble. . . ."*

At 4:00 P.M., the cortège wound slowly across the graying hills toward the Samuel farm house. Once more, Zerelda Mimms, Jesse's schoolgirl bride of the many, many autumns gone, stood in a farmyard beneath a tree and watched them bring her lover home. But this was not a catalpa tree, and not her father's farmyard. And this was no wounded nineteen-year-old guerrilla-hero cousin for whom she waited in adolescent wonder. Sixteen weary, dangerous years had fled. Sixteen years of outlaw hate and greed and warping fear. The day was grown late. The sun dropped low.

By its last light, the coffin was lowered into the grave at the foot of the lone coffee-bean tree fronting the Samuel place. The clods showered hollowly down, the shovels shaping the mounding of the heavy earth. The kinsmen went away, still-faced. Their women stayed to weep.

Presently, Mrs. Samuel shivered to the evening breeze. She drew her faded shawl closer, moved away toward the house and toward the beckoning warmth of its yellow lamplight. Zerelda Mimms was alone with the shadows and the crushed flowers and the faint marble memory of the man for whom she had waited a thousand lonely nights:

JESSE W. JAMES
Died April 3, 1882
Aged 34 years, 6 months, 28 days
MURDERED BY A TRAITOR
AND A COWARD WHOSE NAME IS
NOT WORTHY TO APPEAR HERE

When the moon came, she was still there, still waiting for Jesse.

Somewhere, far out in the ghost land of the crowding hardwood forest, away and across the silent Clay County hills, a lonesome hound bayed keeningly and with great sadness. *The legend was dead . . . long live the legend.*

Rainy Day in the Line Camp

When the dawn is rank and dismal
With the clammy pulse of driving rain
That hammers down our hopes, its
　　fierce
Tattoo a-lash against the line-shack pane,
It's then my courage, heart, and spirits,
All, fall heavily, running free before the
Stampede's rush, it stumbles and goes
Down, the whole race run in vain.

It's then I wonder, as a cowboy ever will,
Just what in God's good Name we find
　　here
Within this milling herd called Life
Which pays its forty-per so dear
That we are led to think the guiding
Light, on high or hell below, must be
St. Elmo's fire, so ghostly faint and blue
Its intermittent flash of cheer.

What brand burn I, which later on

Will prove of any smallest worth to me,
Or any other shiftless son, like me,
Which deeds to each of us, alone,
That gives us any joy amid the pain
And this lean gift, ah, marvelous! the
Unasked charity of squalling birth.

A gift some better man has said we did
Not seek — hell no, far less — say nay!
For later, when we tire of it, we throw
Its priceless, sweet-sad boons away
As carelessly and loose of foot, withal,
As if the Lord had granted us Eternity,
So harsh and callously do we lay waste
Its span, before we rendezvous, at last,
Within His muting grasp of clay.

Oh bring us thou Immortal Gin above,
Thou Wrangler of our hopes and hearts,
Some skookum pills to overcome the
    woes
That rainy weather in us always starts
And hunches up our loins so raunchily
That, yes or no, we will or will not be,
We must, 'twixt drip and drop and spray,
Fall victim to self-pity's darts.

Give us a warming, blue-sky sun to dally
To and hang among the rafters of our
    gloom,

A sun that, bursting grand, will scatter
And dispel the vapors of this lonely
   room
Which ever seem to trail-up close the
Deluge and the steady drum of wind and
Water crying come to breed within our
Aching breasts a hurtful spell of
   memories
That mire the past in useless spume.

God or Allah, Saint or Sin, Christian
Idol, Moslem Gin, Cheyenne Shaman,
Black-Robe Priest, Fat Confucius,
   Moloch Beast,
Loose from out your leaking vaults
Answer us cowboys, hear us pray,
For Christ's sake send us some faint
   cheer
On this damn' lousy rainy day!

Home Place

"Vengeance is mine," saith the Lord.
"Ours," corrected Ben Allison softly,
and that is the way that it all began.

I
"EMPTY CABINS, WEED CORRALS"

In Texas, after the great war, the herds of longhorn cattle gone wild infested every tangle and savannah of the Big Thicket. From Matagorda Island, on the Gulf, to away out beyond San Saba and the Concho River drainage, they ran in untold tens of thousands. Killed in inhuman wholesale by hide and tallow factory hunters, decimated by army butchering to feed a desperate, dying Confederacy, the feral Spanish cattle would not diminish. Neither would they surrender. They were bred to fight, to survive, and they did so by reverting to the

179

wildness that was in them.

The spotted cows, fawn-quick calves, and dangerous linebuck bulls took to the brush and would not be dug out of it, or driven, so long as they could hide and fight and breed their untamed kind within its covert.

The soldier sons of Texas, the ranch lads, who came home from that war, were much like the cattle. They were worn thin and mean and shy, made fearful of the world about them. They wanted only to retreat within the shinnery to nurse the wounds of mind and body, to heal themselves by living out of sight, and so regain what had been theirs before the hells of Shiloh, Chickamauga, and Second Manassas.

Such an almost beaten but unbeatable man was Ben Allison, of San Saba County. Like the wild longhorn, the gaunt San Saban's bloodstream coursed too fiercely free for surrender. Ben was one-quarter Kwahadi Comanche Indian, a heritage that would not submit to the white man's rules of defeat. The Kwahadi understood but one victor. So long as there was life, no man was the slave of another.

And so Ben came home. He and his brother Clint had ridden six weeks and eighteen hundred miles from Appomattox Courthouse. The home ranch had been their sustaining vision each mile of the way. It was all they had to come back to. All that both had so achingly yearned for of the remembered past. It was home, the home place. And now there it was before them.

The pasture was gone to salt sage. The corral was weeded over with rabbit brush. Its poles were down. The gate swung emptily on one leather hinge. The well windlass was fallen in. The double-cabin "dog run" Texas ranch house was burned to its mud sills. Its only remaining skeleton was the spine of the centerpole, with its jack oak rafters for ribs that even fire could not consume. The evening wind whirled the gray ash, tugged at the crazily tilted corral gate. A rusted fin of the sheet-metal stock tank grated and banged to its stir.

The brothers dropped their eyes.

They had no home. They had come back to nothing.

The family they had left to ride away into the glories of war, younger sister Starr and kid brother ArJay Allison, might yet be found. They would make proper inquiry. And useless. Instinct told them that. Men such as themselves, four years hardened to the guttings of fire and the stink of abandonment, could smell the difference in a set and an accidental burn. And they were smelling the difference here.

Yet Ben Allison, raising his shaggy head, only nodded to Clint and said: "We will rest the horses tonight, then go on." And when Clint nodded back and said — "Where to?" — Ben let his pale eyes look far out over the tawny grass and catclaw shinnery of the San Saba, and answered finally: "To wherever they went, that drove Starr and ArJay off the home place."

The two men climbed down stiffly from their hard-used mounts. They were too worn to talk. Words would have weighed more than the patched saddles they dragged from the wiry mustangs. Leaving bridles on but slipping the bits, they led the animals down to Hawk Shadow Creek.

They had come late in the day to the home place clearing and ought to have cast for sign with the little light remaining. But the horses came first.

In that vast and menacing openness, running from the San Saba River to the storied Pecos, a man's mount was, even before his gun, the most precious guardian of his life. Without weapons, man had many options to protect and defend his existence. There was no limit to it but his own cunning. Yet no wile and no intellect could increase the options of the man without a horse in West Texas. He had only two of them. They were called his feet.

And the Comanches had horses.

So Ben and Clint Allison saw to their saddle mounts before even *thinking* of the other options, or urgencies. Leading the little animals into the long pool below the ranch fording place, they let them drink. The horses sipped sparingly. Unlike settlement animals, they would not founder themselves. Knowing this, the men permitted them all they wished of the creek's swirling flow. At the same time, they washed the sweat and lather cake out of their coats with Stetson hats dipped full of the cool, green water. The horses grunted and whickered low answers of gratitude for the treatment. Coming out of the water, they shook themselves, showering Ben and Clint. The men slipped the headstalls of the bridles, and let them go on graze. Going again to the charred ruin of the ranch house, they did not look back at the freed animals. There was no thought that they would run off. These were Texas ponies, true as dogs.

Twilight was now down. Sight tracking would need to wait on sunrise. But, coming to the ruin, Ben knelt to examine a deep pile of the burned débris. Such wood ash and ember made a prairie clock — if you found it in the first forty-eight hours of its smoking out — that was accurate within a half day, even less. Now Ben looked at Clint and held up two fingers.

Clint nodded, understanding his brother had found heat. And heat enough to gauge a time. Two days. Whoever had been here and done this evil thing was but two days in front of them. Both men exchanged looks, Ben returning Clint's nod with one of his own. It was better than they might have hoped for. From the weed-grown look of the ranch, it could have been two years since life was laughing here, and the cabin walls unburned. They still didn't know.

They wearily sought backrests against the standing rock of the creek-stone fireplace. They made smokes, ate from their Indian-small store of parched corn and antelope jerky. There was no more talk. Only their eyes moved, watching the emptiness about them. They had the look of men who had been hounded as far as they intended to be. If they said nothing of the fact, neither threatened nor cursed any

184

enemy over it, their silence but deepened the resolve. These were dangerous men. God, or somebody, had better help those whom they would follow away from the desolated clearing of their home place. *That* was the cold truth of their stillness.

Clint slept first. He was the uncomplicated brother. Sunny-natured when sober or uncrossed, Clint Allison would kill you quicker than another man might think about it, when drunk or affronted. To such, sleep came easy.

Ben Allison was likewise a simple man. But Ben did not sleep at once, if at all. He was a thinker, not a talker like the outgoing Clint. Some believed him slow because of his few words. These learned better. Or regretted it. Ben Allison was hardly the man you weighed short. Not when the fix of his pale eyes pinned you from that face narrow and dark as any Plains Indian's. Or when his soft and gentle drawl finally did say something you could hear — maybe like: "Don't move."

Old men around San Saba, Paint Rock, and like settlements would say that Clint might kill you by mistake. Ben never would. When Ben took a man's trail, it was the end for somebody. Clint might quit along the way. A bottle or a barn dance or

185

a big-busted blonde would do the trick for brother Clinton. Ben, tall, slow-smiling, bashful Ben, would go on alone. "Having Ben Allison behind you," one old-timer remembered, "was like your shadder had a shadder. It wasn't no use to duck or to dodge. Ben would beat you there. Saving only for Tom Horn, and him only mebbe, Ben Allison was the deadliest man-tracker ever lived. Leastways, in Texas, the Injun Nations, or the Arizonny Territory."

Whatever the truth — and old men always lie both ways against the middle — Ben Allison lay watchfully awake the entire night of his homecoming to Hawk Shadow Creek. When the first pink tinge of day broke to the east, he saddled the Texas ponies and prodded Clint awake.

"I've unraveled our sign," was all he said. "Roll out."

II
"TRACK OF THE JACKASS"

The Texas brothers crouched by the pole corral, studying the maze of horse tracks. Disgruntled at the sunrise awakening, Clint dug at sleepy eyes, fumbled to roll the first cigarette. He was trying to follow the explanation of what they were supposed to be looking at but kept coming up short.

"What the hell," he scowled, "all I see is they set up their picket line here. Fence tied their bronc's, and not for long. Not enough apples piled for overnight. Christ Jesus, Ben, have you got to heathenly roust a man out of his beauty slumbers to tell him that?"

"Shut the mouth, pry open the eye, unplug the ear," Ben said. "You conscious yet?"

"I'm working on it."

"All right," Ben said, pointing again to the clutter of hoof prints at the corral. "There was only five of them rode in here. You see that? But there was six of them laid these tracks away. They tooken somebody with them on that sixth horse, Clint . . . you hear me? Somebody scant of weight, and the horse on a lead rope, not rode free. Now you tell me who it likely was on that horse."

"ArJay," Clint guessed hopefully. "They got ArJay."

"You know better," Ben said. "It was little sister."

Clint Allison did not want to think the renegades had their teen-aged sister. "God damn it, Ben," he snapped, "how the hell you know it ain't ArJay on that horse?"

187

"Look closer," he said.

Clint cursed, coughed, threw away his cigarette. "Son-of-a-bitch," he breathed savagely. "Jackass tracks overlaid . . . that's ArJay follering them on Gimpy."

"You're awake," Ben agreed. "Here's your horse."

"Hold up," the younger brother frowned, not taking his mount from Ben. "I got to have my coffee. You Comanch' cowboys may be able to set a horse without your morning's java, but not this old Confederate cavalryman."

"Oh, Christ," Ben said. "Boil it quick."

Clint made the coffee. When it had boiled over and smelled bad enough, he poured the battered tin cups full. He and Ben gulped wincingly, searing their mouths. Ben endured the pain. Clint turned the air blue. Both brothers laughed aloud, needing the relief.

"Well, iffen we was partways bright, we wouldn't have go'd to the war in the fust place." Clint grinned. "And as sure as bull chips burn clear wouldn't have come back here, oncet we did go. Leastways," he added, face shadowing, "not excepting for sister Starr and ArJay, we wouldn't have. Ben, I got the fantods. We ain't going to find them."

Ben shook his head. "We sure could use old cousin Pawsah," he conceded. "But I ain't whupt yet."

Clint had forgotten their full-blooded Tamparika Comanche cousin. His name meant "crazy," and Ben was right: they could surely use him now. For they might call him Cousin Crazy and the West Texas settlers the Tamparika Madman all they wanted. By either name their red kinsman could cold trail human game where mortal trackers would not know a mouse had paused to make water.

"Don't fret it, Ben," he said. "Ain't Pawsah taught you the trade, personal? You'll come up to them."

Ben said nothing. He was staring westerly along the trail of the vanished horsemen. *Would* he come up to the scavengers? *Would* he and Clint be in time? *Would* sister Starr be still all right? God, talk about the fantods!

The tall man broke his gaze, and his thoughts, away from such dark ideas. They would find Starr and ArJay, and they would be all right. Maybe even fine. Why, it could have been that these riders found them in want and took them along in good heart. Hell, who really knew?

Ben Allison knew. These weren't good

men. Good men didn't burn down ranch houses. Not even old Texas dog-kennel ones of the poor kind on the Allison place.

Ben handed Clint the reins of Clint's mount. He got up on his own horse, quick and easy. Clint followed in fluid kind. "Let's ramble, brother," he said, and Ben nodded and led out. *"Coo-ee,"* he said gently to the wiry small beast, and gave the mustang his head.

The big white men swung rhythmically to the peculiar traveling gait of the wild-bred horses. It was a shufflng rack, half kin to a singlefoot, hybrid to a park canter. It got over the ground unbelievably. It ate up the silent grassland miles. It took the riders skimming toward the westward curve of the prairie earth like swallows flying free above the buffalo pasture. When dark fell that night, they were but half a day behind the mounted band and had sifted the campfire ashes of two halts made by its members since leaving the gutted ranch on Hawk Shadow Creek.

"We will nail the bastards tomorrow noon," Clint Allison growled. Brother Ben shook his head, Indian-dark face turned to the panting mustangs.

"*We* won't nail them no time, Clint," he said. "The horses is rode out."

"Sure they are," Clint shrugged. "But, hell, come morning they'll be fresh as a cowflap on its way to the ground. They ain't going to get away, Ben."

"I know that," Ben said. "What I said was that *we* wouldn't be coming up to them. I will."

Clint had been loosing his double-rigged Texas saddle. He stopped. "Run that bull calf past me one more time," he said. "I didn't catch his brand."

Ben already had his saddle pulled. He dumped it to the ground. "You're staying here," he said. "With the horses. You bring them on tomorrow, soon as there's light to see by."

"You mean light for a white man to see by," Clint corrected.

"That's right. I'm going on tonight."

"You god-damn' Comanch'," Clint scowled. "Horses cain't run no more, but you're just getting started, eh?"

Ben looked out through the darkness. "One night me and Pawsah run thirty mile afoot. We had to go wide around. Some Kioways had shot our horses. We wasn't but fifteen that summer."

"Did you get away?" Clint asked.

"No," Ben answered him. "Pawsah made it clean, but they got me down with a lucky long hit. Bullet went right in here a-hint the ear." Ben pointed carefully.

"Why, shit," Clint objected. "That would have blowed your brains out."

"It did," Ben said. "Hurt like hell."

Clint made a lunge for his brother, missing badly in the dark. When he regained his feet, he had also recovered his good humor and was laughing in spite of the fact one of the mustangs had spooked and stepped on his backbone, when he went sprawling.

"Well, Christ Jesus," he said, "I'd ought to know by now that you ain't as dull as you act, but somehow I never seem to wise up." He broke off, peering hard all about him. "Ben?" he said. Then, when there was no answer: "Ben, god damn you, say suthin'."

Ben Allison did not say anything. He could not. He was no longer there, when his brother Clint called his name into the darkness.

"Injuns!" Clint said disgustedly, and turned to rub down the ponies with dried grass. This time he put hobbles on them. They were thirty miles out into Comanche country, and crazy Pawsah's cousin Ben had deserted them. It was no place to lose your horses.

III
"CALIBER FORTY-FIVE"

The heavy cloud cover which had prevented tracking the previous night had blown away. A glare of white moonlight lay over the roll and break of the grassland. Under such a Comanche moon even a quarter-breed Kwahadi could read trailing sign. He could, that was, had his Comanche teacher been Cousin Pawsah. Ben experienced scant delay in pursuing the broad path of the shod horses. Repeatedly he found the overlain small and unshod hoof marks of the mule ridden by ArJay. The last time, well along toward morning, rest-halting to get his wind and scan the way ahead, he believed he saw the little animal. *Believed*, hell. Was there any other such gaudy runt mule running loose in West Texas? It had to be Gimpy.

Well, that was *puha* news, powerful good. Ben purely admired Gimpy. The diminutive mule, hand-reared by ArJay and sister Starr, was out of an Allison mare by a wild black Spanish jack. Gimpy was a red-and-white paint like his roving dam but with black eye splotchings and a perfect black butterfly patch on his rump, from his inky

193

sire. He was one of a peculiar kind, was Gimpy. Very peculiar. Of him, brother Clint said: "He was half the size of a Mexican burro, could easily outrun a chaparral jack rabbit, had the savvy of a chickenhouse coyote with the sociability of a Texas red wolf and would bite anybody but Arjay and me, but only if I was damned careful."

Female-like, sister Starr had soft-boiled it down. "To know that mule is to love him," she said. "In somebody else's corral."

Ben had shared their salty ranch estimates, and laughed softly now to think of them again. But he wasn't short-guessing Gimpy's heft. It heartened him that the bad-tempered, pony-sized mule was with ArJay. It was like the boy having along a 450-pound cross between a fly-teased bear and a rusty buzzsaw that was his friend and loved him dearly. Whatever of other more commonly used weapons little brother might have with him, he didn't need it. Gimpy was worth his weight in a hell of a lot worse than wildcats. You would have to put him in the scale-pan with horned rattlers, scorpions, red soldier ants, and hydrophobic bats. He just wasn't nice.

Ben laughed again in the moon shadow where he had paused on sighting ArJay's mount. He looked up to the blaze of stars above him.

"Kadih," he called aloud. "Lay me a short trail and leave me to run it in long moccasins. *A'he!*"

It was, of course, a Comanche saying. If it was manhandled a bit by Ben's twangy West Texas drawl, it still lost none of its essential Indian sense. Kadih, as would seem from the upward glance accompanying his name, was the Comanche great spirit. In his many Comanche summers out of the buffalo pastures with the Indian grandfather he loved so well, Ben had learned that Kadih listened better than the Lord God Jehovah. Despite his widowed settlement mother's despairing labors to rear him up in Christian decency, tall Ben had gone to the blanket gods. For him, imprecation was not as rewardingly voiced in brother Clint's — "Jesus H. Christ!" — as it was in Ben's: "Kadih, you old bastard!" And a man couldn't be comfortable with a God he couldn't cuss out fluently.

So Ben Allison slid out from the moonshadow of the rocks where he rested, his prayers said. He ran on through the patchy light of a gathering buttermilk sky. There

195

were no more good memory grins. Now and again he glanced at the clouding night above, and was grateful. He could see from the lay of their trackline where the raiders were heading — Kwahadi Springs, over past the sandstone ridge where he had briefly seen the spotted mule. Old Kadih had heard his adopted Texas son. He was swiftly blotting out the moonlight to cover Ben's approach. It would be a windy murk up at the old Comanche water hole. What crazy Cousin Pawsah called "a killing dark." Just right.

When Ben reached the camp of the marauders who had burned the home place and borne off sister Starr, he would not need Kadih. Or any god. Or any piebald mule or break of cloud to show him the way. Ben's hand dropped to the worn walnut butt of the single-action Army revolver, swinging at his side. He would deliver his own justice to the guilty. Its name would be Colt, its caliber Forty-Five. There would be six members on the jury. Five of them would speak. And a man would die each time. With one round remaining in the judge's chamber for such of the bastards as might yet be crawling around appealing the verdict.

"*A'he*, amen."

The True Friends

Pancho López and Tacho Segura were friends. There was never any doubt of that in Tehuantepec. Everyone in the village knew it, as they knew, also, what great drinkers the two *compañeros* were. This night in question the comrades were exceedingly mellow. Good feeling flowed between them, and love, as freely as tequila and mescal. Life, as it will, came under discussion.

Pancho shook his head, regarding his less fortunate companion with a compassion none but the truly spiritual may feel for a fellow creature. Tacho had a fat wife and three unlovely children. Pancho lived to himself, the master of his destiny and, through a burst of inspiration, now, of Tacho's.

"Tacho," he said, "why don't you make yourself happy like me?"

"What do you mean?" complained the

other. "In all the world nobody is more happy than Tacho Segura."

Pancho López slid a little farther into the gutter, so that he might rest his back against the curbing. He appeared to be pondering the impasse. His friend Tacho stayed on the curbing but reached and patted him on the head. This gesture of consolation, implying that Pancho had lost the argument, was scarcely designed to bring peace in the breast of a López. A López had been with Benito Juárez in Oaxaca, and with Pancho Villa in Sonora. This was not a breed to lie in the gutter spinelessly. In the gutter, yes. But never without a spine.

"Listen, *amigo*," he challenged Tacho Segura, "do you like to go in the river fishing with López?"

Tacho palmed his hands eloquently. Where was any argument here? "But of course," he granted. "This you know as you know my name is Tacho."

"*Sí*," said the other. "And can you go to the river with López when he asks you to go? You cannot. You say to me . . . '*Dispenseme, hombre*, but my wife María has said it that I may not go in the river fishing with that bum, Pancho López.' Is that not correct?"

The other shrugged. "Well, only that she said I could not go with you. As for you being a bum, well, *amigo mío,* you know I do not share that opinion."

"And that is fine with you that a fat woman says no to you?"

"Fat, yes, but a good wife. I wouldn't trade her for a team of mules. Well, not unless it was a genuine pair of Jalisco jennies, or at least they should not be blind or galled about the withers."

López smelled defeat but circled it to sniff again and be certain. There are ways and ways to an end. "Look, *amigo,* does it make you happy *not* to go in the river fishing with López?" he asked.

"No, of course not. I love to go to the river fishing with you. I cannot think of a thing I would do before I went in the river fishing with you. Well, at least nothing the priest would permit to pass in confession. Why do you ask such a jackass thing?"

"Look, you dumb *cholo,* you," explained López, "if you are not happy about something, then you are unhappy about it. You understand that?"

"*Sí.* Clever thinking, Pancho. What a mind you do have. Go on, I am listening now, *amigo.*"

"Good. And who is it, my friend, that is

the only one in Tehuantepec who says to you no all of the times that you would love to go in the river fishing with López? Who is this fat sow of a wife which does this thing to our friendship? Think hard, now, the name will come to you."

"María!" brightened Tacho. "You mean my fat wife, that no good pig! She is the one who ruins my life. Who says no to me all the time. *¡Por Dios!* I am unhappy as hell. You are right, good friend."

"Well, then, why don't you make yourself happy like me? There is nothing to it."

"What do you say, you loafer? The true meaning now, before I give you one in the *cajones. ¡Alta!*"

"Kill the barren old cow. You've had your children by her. At least, you call them children. Just bash her in the head and be happy with me."

Tacho thought it over very seriously. He must have sat on the curbing another fifteen seconds. Ten, anyway. Then he got to his feet, after three tries, and bore off down the murky street toward his adobe *hacienda*. María Segura was asleep, and Tacho, not wanting her to miss the point, awakened her. There was just no fairness in opening up her head with her eyes closed. She might look back and think it had been an accident, which was not the idea of López, at all. When a husband arrives at the place where it is necessary, in the name of Juárez and Villa and Independence, to part his wife's pate with a sugarcane machete, why then common decency demanded she be conscious party to the agreement.

"*Hola, María,*" he muttered, holding the lamp in her blurry eyes. "Tomorrow I am going in the river, fishing with Pancho López. You see, I don't ask you, I tell you. You are a fat, selfish pig. *¡Muera Comanche!*"

SSWWwwaaackkk!

Juliano Francisco Oñate Díaz Cabeza de Vaca López was sorely troubled. After all, the matter was somewhat his responsibility in that he had to a degree suggested the solution to his good friend, Tacho. But a sugarcane machete? *¡Ay de mi!* That drunken fool. *¡Ai, chihuahua!* What a bad friend was this tequila. Poor Tacho.

Poor Tacho?

What about poor Pancho? Was not he, Pancho, sharing this same damnable cell in the Tehuantepec jail with his friend whom the newspapers down in the city were calling *el tigre de Tehuantepec?* Was not he,

201

Pancho, in almost the same manner of difficulty? Well, no, not quite. The lawyer had said it would not go as badly for López. After all, what reasonable human being could expect that *idiota* to go home and whack up his wife with the sugarcane knife just from the recommendation of a friend? Ah, but it was still close and hot in this tiny *celda de castigo,* still a worrisome thing to be a prisoner in the town *cárcel.*

Pancho López went to the single, small, barred window. Sighingly, he looked out. Beyond the town he saw the rolling sweep of the plateau running away to the blue Sierras. He longed to be out there with the coyotes and the hawks and the jack rabbits, free like they were. He wished that he and Tacho Segura were out there on that plateau pretty soon. Not just now in the daylight. Later on. When the night came down. And with two good *caballos* underneath them and a head start of like twenty miles toward Texas.

¡Pobre de mí! Why had he told Tacho to split the old bitch anyway? It had just been mescal talking. Gutter dreams. My God, to go in the river fishing was not worth spending so much time in the *cárcel* without even one small drink of anything save water. *¡Ai!*

Well, at least López was *hombre duro* enough to realize it was largely his fault. And to worry about his good friend, Tacho, being arrested for cutting up his fat wife and being called the Tiger of Tehuantepec and all of that. Moreover, he, López, would think of something to help his friend. He would think out a good plan to save his life. There must be some clever way. Of a sudden, the sun rose behind Pancho López's dark face. *¡Santísima!* He had it.

"Hey, Tiger, listen to this!" he cried, leaping toward his disconsolate cell mate. "I have the idea. You are saved. Concern yourself no more."

"Please, López, do not call me the Tiger, eh?"

Tacho Segura was the etching of last despair. He crouched on the edge of his straw pallet, swaying to and fro and counting his beads hour by hour. Thus he had mumbled and swayed the entire thirty-five days of their waiting for the *juez federal,* the government judge, to come to Tehuantepec and pass sentence upon the caged tiger of the town, and, of course, in that lesser way, upon his good friend and keeper, Francisco López.

"Listen, *tigre* . . . er . . . ah . . . Tacho, *mi amigo*. All in the world there is for you to do is compose a letter to *el gobernador*. Do you not think he is on our side, the excellency of the whole state? *Por supuesto*. The governor will hear you. Just tell him that you make apology. You are sorry to have put the machete into the fat, old wife. You are unhappy. It will not happen again. You are *muy triste*. You know it was wrong, and you admit it."

"That's all?" asked Tacho, blinking.

"Of course! What more could there be? How stupid we are. All this time we have sat here, when we might have been out going in the river to fish. Come, *amigo*, let us write the letter. *Aquí es papel . . . aquí es lápiz*. Go ahead, write!"

Confronted by such eloquence, Tacho Segura saw no choice and was grateful. What a wonderful thing to have a friend like Francisco López. He seized the lead pencil and began to print:

El señor gobernador, mi querido:

I am sorry that I killed my wife, fat María. She was a good woman. I did not see a better one in 23 years, although I tried many times. I think now it was a wrong thing to hit her so hard with the machete, espe-

cially in the head three times like that. I want very much to get out of this *cárcel* and go in the river fishing with my friend López, who told me to kill my fat wife. I promise you, dear governor, not to do it again, if you will only give me one more chance. I will sell the machete. It as good as ever, with not even the hair washed off of it, or anything. I won't hit anybody with it again. . . .

At this point, Tacho broke off, frowning. "Say, Pancho," he said, "how about those kids? Do you think I ought to tell it that I am sorry about them, also?"

Pancho frowned in turn. "Hmm. I am not sure," he said. "But I believe that I would do it, yes. Of course, they would have had much trouble with no mother to care for them, no arguing that. But still I think you had better be careful what you say. Maybe the governor is most fond of the children. He might not agree with you about how they would suffer with no mother. Yes, say you are sorry about them, too."

"You sure now, *compadre?*"

"Yes. Remember how that judge told you that for María alone it would have been twenty years of hard labor because you were drunk? *Sí.* But remember how he said you would get dangled by the neck for chopping up all those kids, too? *Sí.* I think you better write it in the letter that you are sorry about the kids."

Tacho nodded his thanks, screwed his tongue into the proper funnel, and commenced to print again:

So, dear governor, yes, I promise you I won't hit anybody more with the machete, and especially those three kids. Those little bastards . . . I liked them very much and won't do that again. I want to go home. I don't like this *cárcel* too much any more. I want to go in the river fishing with Pancho López who got just the five years for advising me how to cut up my fat wife. Please, dear *señor* governor, talk with me and let me have the pardon paper. I am sorry I killed those kids, too. So now you send me the paper, and Pancho and I can go to the river. I love the government and have had no drink in 35 days and want to go in the river fishing.

your son,
Tacho P. Segura

López took up the letter, frowning his way through it. It was not precisely what he had pictured in his fertile brain, but there was no denying that it did have about it some quality of native honesty and *sentimiento* which was certain to have its effect with the governor.

After all, did not sly López know it as a fact that his excellency was from Tehuantepec himself?

Seguro que sí. Tacho the Tiger was as good as free. In a week or ten days back would come the paper from the government and the good friends, Pancho López and Tacho Segura, would be on their way to the river and to those fish, waiting so long and patiently.

In due course the governor of the state of Santidad, so named because there is no map which shows it, although the real name of the state will be easily guessed by many a compatriot, did receive the simple plea of Tacho Segura. He read it with care and showed no prejudice. His *mayordomo* was dispatched on the very day scheduled for Tacho's execution with an order releasing the prisoner and directing he be brought to the Executive Palace in Ciudad Santidad.

Tacho was brought in to face the great

man, and he was not afraid. Who could look at that round, kind face, those smiling, soft, brown eyes, that grand dignity of white beard and high brow of justice, and know anything of doubt that here sat a man who truly loved all of his Mexican children, and not the least of these, Tacho P. Segura. Tacho's heart was full, his spirit uncluttered. He had confessed his contrition. He was as good as a free man. Else why had the governor called him. All that remained was for his excellency to announce the pardon, to say its actual words into the ears of Tacho Segura, with the *mayordomo* and the other clerks of the high office standing there to hear it, also.

Ah, that López! What a cunning rascal! Tacho's confidence did not seem misplaced, either in his good, dear friend, Pancho, or in the august governor.

His excellency was clearly sympathetic. He smiled at Tacho Segura as a mother at a naughty child. Tacho said to the governor that he loved him, that he was truly grateful for this great kindness. The governor smiled back at Tacho and assured him that Tacho, too, had his love in warm turn. He went even further and told Tacho that all his little ones in the state of Santidad had their governor's love. Why else would he have sent for Tacho Segura? It was, of course, to hear his side of the story. To hear him patiently and fairly on the matter *"en favor de un criminal,"* to consider seriously his petition for a pardon and his freedom. Would Tacho, then, be so very gracious himself as to tell *el gobernador* . . . in his own simple words, now . . . just how it had been that he had come to cut up with a sugarcane machete one perfectly faithful, good, fat wife and three normal, if somewhat homely and stupid, young ones? Ah! Tacho would be that kind? *Por favor,* then, please to begin.

Tacho told the story with much emotion. He told it surpassingly well for such a simple man. He did not neglect the importance of going in the river fishing with his best friend. He was fair to the fat wife and the ugly children. He admitted that he drank upon occasion with his dear *amigo,* Pancho López. He admitted it was wrong to use a machete as he had. He vowed he would not do it again, unless provoked, or refused permission to go in the river fishing with Francisco López.

The governor was visibly affected. He wiped an eye and sniffed audibly. For a long time, when Tacho had finished, he just sat in his high-backed, red-velvet chair, as if overcome by the pathos and poignancy of Tacho's plea. Finally, however, he stood up. Smiling benignly, he gestured for Tacho to join him.

"Come with me, Tachito, little one," he murmured. "Come and look out this large window with me. As we gaze on God's great earth, recall that you are a man sentenced by law to be executed on this very day, yet here you stand with your governor, drawing the good, sweet breath and looking calmly out upon your gallows tree, a most remarkable thing.

"Eh, little one, tell me how it all looks out there to a man who was supposed to die today? Wonderful? Beautiful? But of course. Yet it will all disappear on this very day, if I do not grant you the pardon you seek."

Here the great man paused to smile reassuringly.

"But, come, do not grow so pale. You are not dead yet, Tachito. I merely wish for you to study all the lovely things you gamble upon losing when you drink the mescal and the tequila and go home to gain your freedom with a sugarcane machete. Eh, little one?"

The governor placed his arm about Tacho's thin shoulders and pointed dramatically beyond the gallows tree out over the rolling plateau of Santidad state. He spoke in a low voice, with very great gentleness and absolutely certain sympathy.

"See out there, Tachito. Is it not beautiful? Do you know what time of year it is, *niño?* Yes, it is the summertime. Is not the summer a wonderful time, Tachito, child? In the summer we are all so happy. Is not the summer the time of the ripening grain? Does not the corn grow tall and tassel splendidly? Does it not do this, little one, so that the tortillas, the enchiladas, the tacos, the burritos all shall be rich and tasty? Is not everything dressed in the ripe green of the full sunshine? Look at the trees. Look at the grass. Look at the flowers. Look at the river, cool and clear. Look at the mountains, blue and snow-capped. Ah, Tacho Segura, is not it a remarkable thing to be alive in *el verano* . . . in the summertime?

"*Sí,* and then what comes after the summer, Tachito? Of course, it is *el otoño,* the autumn. In the autumn we make the harvest. All the corn for the tortillas, all the *fríjoles* for the chili, all the red peppers for the *salsa,* all the good food is gathered now. We are ready for the *fiestas.* The dancing, the music, the marimbas, the *señoritas,* ah!

211

Tacho Segura, surely the autumn is the grand time to be alive!

"Now, little one, child of my heart, we must think of what comes after *el otoño. Sí,* of course, one can see that you know how good these times are, how much it means to be alive in them, especially in *el invierno,* eh, *niño?* Oh, but is not the winter a glorious time? The clean, fine snow, the sparkle of the frost, the crystals frozen on the windowpanes, the little children laughing and playing as the snow falls to make a fairyland all about. The gay feasting at the Christ birth, *la Natividad.* The time of warm fires, good comrades, fine wine. The taste of the mellow beer, the *cerveza* made of the fat grains, ah! The winter is also a marvelous time to be alive. *¿No es verdad, Tachito?"*

The governor paused to draw a long breath at the thought of so much splendor of living. All went happily here for Tacho. Had he not seen a small tear in *el gobernador's* fine brown eye but the moment gone? Of course, he had. What a prince of a man, this white-haired *hidalgo!*

"And then, Tachito, my little squirrel," his excellency resumed expansively, "what comes next? Is it not *la primavera,* the beautiful springtime? *Sí,* we know that it is, eh, little chicken? The very most wonderful time of the year comes then. The little animals, the new grasses, the fresh young flowers, all of God's world and the creatures in it, returning to bring the promise of eternal life once more to us, His children. All of the good people, singing and dancing, glad with the joy of being alive in the spring. Feeling the warm sun on their backs and in their faces. The planting of the crops, the smell of the freshly turned earth, the lowing of the cattle, the calling of the new calves, the whickering of the mule as he leans heavily in the trace, bearing the shining plow through the brown waves of the earth! What a time this is, Tachito, my small rabbit. For a man to put his strength with that of the beasts of the field so that the ground may bear its fruit and bring the joy of life again to all. There is no better time for a man to be alive, eh, child? We know that. *¡Ai!*"

Here the governor hesitated for many seconds. Tacho Segura grew restive to be away and to tell to Pancho the good news. At last, however, the great man spoke again, and Tacho could see that now he was genuinely moved. Tacho had to force himself to remain calm. It would not be proper to let the governor see that he understood, beforehand, the nature of his charity. Instead, Tacho thought of that lazy bend in the river where he and his dear best friend, Pancho López, would run to the moment that the governor let Tacho go back to Tehuantepec. In his reverie, the words of his benefactor now entered once more. Tacho smiled softly, barely listening.

"And then, finally, Tachito, my duckling, after having come and gone the summer, the autumn, the winter, and the sweet spring, do you know what then comes again, little one?"

"But of course, *gobernador!*" responded Tacho, his face brightening as a child's. "Comes then one more time *el verano,* the summer. *¿No es verdad, gobernador?*"

"*Sí,* Tachito, my true child. That is right. And then do you know what will obtain . . . what will be . . . after that? After the summer, like now, has come again? Do you know what you will have been by that time?"

The governor waved his slender hand and spoke finally with a great, soft gentleness. Yet, at the same time, his luminous smile vanished, and now the words, although soft, crackled like *chispas,* like sparks, into the expectant ear of Tacho

Segura, the almost-free man.

"By that time, Tacho, my son," murmured the governor of Santidad, *"you will have been dead just precisely one year."*

Blizzard at Bald Rock

The Bald Rock Gun Club was in regular bad-weather session. The blizzard which had struck the Bald Rock Basin that morning was still hammering the bunkhouse. Trapped, the elite winter crew of the Tumbleweed Land & Cattle Company had exhausted its small stock of indoor cowboy games — stud poker, penny pitching, tossing cards in the hat — and had come to its ordinary apogee of self-reliance in a pinch: big game guns and the men behind them.

Hunting was the passion of these rough Westerners, and not for jack rabbits. In Wyoming's Bald Rock country they had it all — bear, moose, elk, the big deer, antelope, sheep, goats — everything which the land offered except the buffalo which roamed no more on any range. And, as with all true hunters, the essence of the passion was the weapon. Big game and big guns, that was the question. What rifle for what game and in which caliber?

Every known and several unknown makes and models of shoulder arms had been suggested, dissected, sworn by and at, by the five irrefutable authorities in the Tumbleweed bunkhouse — men whose fame and reputation in the field were unchallenged from the swamps of Saigon to the tundra of Siberia. On the adjacent Rafter-T and Rockhouse Ranches, or in the Bald Rock post office or Bullpine Saloon, some question might have been called, it is true. But from Saigon to Siberia the Tumbleweed nimrods reigned supreme.

Smooth-Mouth Madigan, who owned the only set of store teeth in the county and never wore them, held stubbornly for his ancient '76 Winchester lever-action in caliber .40-60. Curly Bill Brokaw — whose daddy had been a traveling Semite corset salesman and whose mother was a friendly Indian customer, giving Curly Bill some separate regional note as the only Jewish Arapaho in Wyoming — Bill held as stoutly for his more modern "Big '86" Winchester in caliber .50-110, an extremely rare and potent piece. John Wesley Hardin Schultz, namesake of a gunman of some minor rank in another field, declared loudly for the "Old Reliable" or "Bull

Thrower" Sharps he had inherited from his grandpaw. Baldie Simms, who wore his wild mustang's mane sheared off at the collarline and had to shave three times a day just to see out, stood fast for his Model '95 Winchester in the .40-90 boring; while Teton Smith, the foreman, just returned from his tour with T. R. and the Rough Riders "down in Cuba," naturally took up for the brand-new U.S. Krag carbine in the issue caliber.

An hour having gone and the discussion degenerated into some name-calling not concerned with firearms makers, Teton appealed to the sixth, or silent, member of the Bald Rock Club. This was Swampie, whose duties about the Tumbleweed included "mucking out" the bunkhouse every so often or when the patina of corral stompings, cigar butts, cigarette shucks, and the amber of Brown's Mule became higher than the tops of Teton's boots, which were admittedly but ten inches. Swampie, being somewhere between Moses and Methuselah for age, was regarded as not the swiftest of chore boys but certainly among the most sagacious. His previous opinions had been sought on everything from the best way to make pemmican (don't) to how to shoe a kicking mule (shoot him) and the surest cure for hiccups (strychnine). Now it would seem that somewhere in his endless past Swampie ought to have found the answer to the best caliber for big-game hunting. The confidence went not unrewarded.

"Well," said the ancient one, "let me get a smoke built, and I will tell you what you want to know."

He edged his gaunt bulk around the better to face his listeners. He had learned long ago not to turn his back on the bunkhouse crew of the Tumbleweed, when adjudicating any matter involving the morals of manhood. His blue eyes, still keen and clear beneath the snowy brows, played watchfully about, as he finished with his cornshuck cigarette, struck a big wooden match to it, leaned back, and let memories return with the curl of the fragrant blue smoke.

"Now, boys," he began, "as far as your arguments went, they was fair enough. Problem was they didn't go far enough. If you're going to pick out the really top caliber, you got to do it on the basis of its knockdown power . . . its putaway pill . . . on the very biggest stuff. That's following the proposition that what will pulverize the biggest, will likewise dissolve anything up to that. You see that?"

Smooth-Mouth nodded. "Sure, that figures, go ahead on."

"Yeah," agreed Curly Bill. "Keep them moving. Don't bog down in the dust."

Baldie and Wes Schultz were equally friendly to the postulation, but Teton Smith, an educated man, required some defining of terms.

"In my four years at the Rock Springs School," he said, "I seen many books on all sorts of critters, and it's my learning that we ain't got no elephants in these parts, and them's the very biggest game there is. What you talking about?"

"Who said anything about *these* parts?" Swampie was not the least flustered. "Why, you didn't even let me get to what parts I was going to. But it ain't necessary to answer your rude interruption. The biggest game ain't far off in any land."

"All right, name it." Teton assumed he had the old man busted flat and three legs tied, but he wasn't tired at all. Swampie rode right with him, smooth as China silk.

"Well," he drawled, "it's common as cow chips. Nowhere near extinct. Found in each and every hemisphere that I know of. And while its actual size ain't alarming, it's the attitude of the individual animal hisself

221

that makes these critters the very biggest game there is."

"Bosh," snorted Curly Bill disgustedly. "You're talking about two-legged critters. That ain't fair!"

"Fair or fribulous, you name me something more dangerous to go after with a gun."

The others frowned diligently but to no end. Smooth-Mouth shook his head. "Cain't be did. But it still ain't a square shake. Why, you can kill a man with a squirrel rifle."

"Yeah," agreed Swampie, "and you can miss a mouse with an elephant gun. You want to hear the rest?"

They did. Outside, the blizzard wasn't letting up one rip. It looked like a long night. "Go ahead on," ordered Teton Smith. "Ain't no doubt an *hombre* can make mean tracks, happen he's a mind to."

"That's right," said Baldie, bobbing his unshorn mane. "Ain't no animal can be as bad as a badman. Lay to it, Swampie. I'll cold-cock the first one interrupts again."

Since Baldie stood six feet, five inches with his boots put away under the bunk, and weighed thirteen pounds less than a long yearling elk, with the temperament of a Brahma bull holding his belly against a bucking strap, the guarantee was a good one. Swampie receipted for it with a grateful nod.

"Thank you, Mister Simms. As we have a scholar in the crowd in the person of our esteemed foreman, it is only fair that we admit a gentleman, as well. Now that I've been garnished my diplomatic impunity. . . ."

"It's 'garunteed,' not 'garnisheed,' you dumb-ox dolt!" Teton Smith sometimes believed he never would get these waifs and strays up to recognizing their own names written down. But a man had to keep trying. "Go ahead on like I told you," he concluded. "Just steer around the six-bit spots. Keep it simple. You ain't no Ruddjerd Kipling, you know."

"Roger who?"

"Never mind, god dammit . . . get on ahead with the story!"

"That's what I aim to do, soon as you give me room. I ain't going to fight you for the floor, though, dad blame it."

"I sure wouldn't do that," agreed Teton acidly. "You might win. Then, where'd you be? Buried alive in cigar butts and cigarette shucks, that's what. Mister, I never did see such a filthy bear-pit as this here bunkhouse!"

"Mister Teton." Baldie towered over the

223

slim foreman. "I reckon I don't want to get set adrift in this here snowstorm, but you got to quieten down. Swampie's been give impunity, but you keep breaking in on him."

Teton Smith retired to the edge of his bunk, not precisely defeated but at least given pause. Swampie, after building a fresh smoke, lit up and set sail, at last.

"This here was in the Massai country."

"That's down there in Arizony, ain't it?" asked Smooth-Mouth. "Like around Prescott or Bumblebee or Horse Thief Basin? Seems like I remember that name. Apaches, ain't they? Same as the Cherrycows and Mimbreños and the like?"

Swampie studied him carefully. The sky-blue eyes were calm beneath the craggy-beetled brows. They rested in the shadow of the hawk-like great nose. They regarded Smooth-Mouth from behind the ambush of the cascading handlebar mustache, yellowed with age and amber.

"Baldie," he directed, "th'ow him out."

The giant cowboy started to obey the order, but Teton Smith understood when authority had been made enough mock of. He threatened to call out the boss from up at the big house, providing the story did not proceed in a better-greased way and without any more axle squeaks. Swampie, as he had begun to warm to his subject, accepted the conditions.

"These here Massai was black savages in Africker," he said. "You know them painted devils with the slit noses and the earrings and the bones through their lips and all of that? This here hunter I got the story about, he was setting off into this Massai country because he had a score to settle with the big chief, a real Cochise or Mangas Coloradas of a black man what was the head cheese of the whole tribe."

Wes Schultz, a boy who wouldn't weigh one hundred and thirty-nine pounds carrying a wet saddle, and who was never noted for his urges to charge the enemy, drunk or sober, here braved the silence which greeted Swampie's opening statement.

"Now just a sky-blue minute," he demanded, stretching to his full five feet, four inches. "When the heck was you ever in Africker?"

Because Wes was anemic and had also taken a bad bump on the head from a kinky broncho some time back, he was allowed to live. Swampie even took the time to be kind to him.

"Wesley, did I say that I was ever in Africker?"

"No, blast it, but you sure as heck implified it!"

"Not at all, boy. Only thing I said was that this here hunter fellow I knowed and got the yarn from . . . he was there."

"How'd you come to know him? I've lived here in Wyoming twenty-nine years, and I ain't ever knowed any Africkian hunters, nor no Apache colored men, neither."

"You forget, my boy, that I wasn't even warmed up twenty-nine years ago. Why, I was already past forty before I ever heard of Wyoming."

Wes Schultz was not swift, but he was not all that slow. He waved apologetically. "Sorry, Swampie. I forgot. It's just that you don't look a day over ninety-eight."

"You're cute," nodded the old man. "Where was I? Oh, yes. This here hunter, Gus Bell, owed this here Massai chief, Ten Lions, a bad debt from long ago. Never neither one of them said what it was, but it was strong enough to bring Gus Bell back after nearly fifteen years. Now, this here American kid . . . he didn't know a cussed thing about any of. . . ."

Baldie Simms held up a hand the size of a mutton leg. "Wait along, there. Where'd the blasted kid come from?"

"What? Didn't I tell about him? Oh, well, he's the one I really got the yarn from."

"Hold on, I thought you said you got it from the hunter?"

"The heck I did!"

"The heck you didn't!"

"Go ahead on," Teton Smith ordered from his bunk. "It don't matter which it was. It's a double-back lie anyhow."

"I'll pass that," said Swampie. "Now I'm started, nobody heads me. So this here young American kid . . . he was sort of picked up along the sea coast in one of them terrible slum-dump towns where slaves and frankincense and all of that was peddled wholesale by the A-rabs and other villains. Gus Bell . . . he took ahold of this young bu . . . well, he was not a bad kid, just a wanderer . . . and he give the kid a chance. That is, he said for him to come along, and he would make a big-game hunter out of him. You know kids. Even kids wild enough to be beached in some crazy-tail Africkian coast village. This boy . . . he followed off after Gus Bell like as if Gus was the second coming of Allah, or at least of Mohammed.

"They got on famous. The kid had sand, and Gus paid off more on nerve than on

227

notions or high ideas. He allowed that a cape buff', or a nursing lioness, or a sore-tusk bull elephant didn't savvy no moral persuasion nor none of that sort of nonsense. But he reckoned good hard nerves was mighty useful in the bush where they was going.

"Deeper and deeper they got into the inner country. They had them a A-rab guide, a slave trader from Izambique, the town they set out from. Fellow's name was Kabar, Ali Kabar. He was black almost as a colored man and with the ideals of a hyena or jackal crossed with a warthog. But for some reason he was loyal to Gus Bell and so the kid trusted him, too.

"Ali . . . his job was to keep track of the coast-bearers they had lugging along all their truck, camp stuff, tents, food, ammunition, spare gun, all of that. And it was the gun part of it that really got the kid's imagination to going.

"Gus had this double-barreled English rifle. It was short, thick, heavy as solid steel. It was bored six hundred caliber and used a Five-Fifty-grain bullet, or ball really, as it was a patch-bullet loader. You know, you put the powder cartridge in at the breech, drop the ball, and seat it from the muzzle on top of the powder. It was like some of them early Civil War muzzle-loaders that was arsenal-converted to semi-breechers.

"Well, this kid was no dummy. He was crazy for guns, and he'd never seen the likes of this English cannon that Gus Bell was toting and would never let one of the bearers touch, even though it must have weighed fifteen pounds, and the temperature in the bush was upwards of a hundred and twenty degrees and steamy.

"The kid had hunted some near the coast, enough to know that Gus Bell was famed throughout Africker for shooting the biggest stuff with the smallest calibers . . . he would tackle cape buff' or rhino or bull elephant with a Seven-by-Fifty-Seven M M Holland and Holland Mannlicher that most men wouldn't use for anything more argumentacious than a dik-stick, which same is a antelope about the size of a poor-wintered house cat. But here was this same Gus Bell harboring and hugging a double rifle that had holes in it big enough to chamber a worm pill sideways. Nor that wasn't all of it, neither. When the kid tried to pry out of him how come the heavy artillery, old Gus . . . he was getting a mort of age on him by then . . . just clammed up and sort of smiled it off.

"But the kid wouldn't take smiles for answers. They were getting 'way into the interior now, real near the Massai country. Their natives were getting edgy as hell and so was Ali Kabar. The kid was worried some. He kept pushing old Gus. Finally Gus told him a little.

" 'Well, kid,' he said, the smile far-off and strange-like, 'this game we've been shooting along the way is not too much. The cape bull or kopje lion hasn't been born that would sweat your Uncle Gus too free, providing I had so much as a deer rifle between me and them, and the wind lay just right. But there's bigger stuff a-coming, boy. There's wilder game than any buff' or lion in this Massai bush. Real big game, kid. The biggest. An when, as and for certain, we meet up with it, that's where this baby comes in.' He would always pause just there and give the big double a pat. Then end quietly . . . 'Yes, sir, I've waited a long span and trekked a far trail to make this one last shot.' "

"Always the kid would pester him for more details. What was this big game? When would they get to it? How really big was it? Was the Massai country the only place it growed, and like that.

"Each time, old Gus would only grin

some more, gray eyes squinting far away, as if he was seeing something the kid's young eyes couldn't make out. Then he'd mutter . . . 'You'll see, boy, you'll see. I want you to learn how to pick the right caliber for the job. You're young. You can learn. You got time to do something with your shots.' Then he'd stop and take the kid by the arm and squeeze him something fierce and say . . . 'Now, remember what I tell you. I want you to have the gun after it does its job. You keep it and always remember what old Gus told you about it. That way, I'll know you're doing all right and was able to learn from my mistakes. Any time you get in a jam, you can always think back to me and this old outside-hammer rifle, and you can be reminded to take your best shot first, instead of last like old Gus Bell. You'll *know* the right caliber like I never did.'

"That was the end of it. He would never talk past that point, and he never did tell the kid, or even hint to him, what it was that he had come to settle with this Massai chief, or what the Massai country had to do with the mystery animal that made the cape buff' and kopje lion look like dung beetles underneath a bull waffle."

Swampie peeled the cold shuck of his

cigarette from his lower lip. He began building a third smoke. Smooth-Mouth, Curly Bill, and the others noticed that his own fine old blue eyes were looking pretty far away in their own right. But they didn't say anything. Swampie was a peculiar old horse. You had to let him take his own gait. Of course, Africa was a pretty big bite, even for him. But, then, he didn't charge anything but a man's time for his stories, and the blizzard *was* still blowing outside.

"Now, then," the old bunkhouse-keeper resumed, "they was sleeping their thirty-fourth night out, when the kid overheered Ali Kabar telling Gus Bell that the porters was saying they were there, that next day would put them 'into the lion-killers' land.' The kid couldn't hear what Gus Bell answered, but he didn't have to wait long to find out.

"You see, them porters, gun-bearers and the like, were all coast natives. If there was anything they liked to keep plenty of room between them and it, it was one of them inland Massai. That Massai country was a good bit like our range. It wasn't jungle and swamp and snake-hole country, like what our bearers come from, but open and high and dry, with grand grass and rocks and thickets of mimosa thorn . . . ah, that was cattle country good as any you ever seen!"

"My eye!" broke in Smooth-Mouth Madigan incredulously. "Is this here going to wind up a cowboy story? What the heck? We can tell our own lies about cows and cow country!"

"Yeah," agreed Curly Bill. "How come that grand cattle country slid in there like that?"

Swampie eyed them with the imperious look of the minstrel who has traveled far and seen things his listeners cannot know even in their scrawny imaginations. There was utter disdain in the look, but also a degree of compassion and real sympathy for the stunted in mind and the mean in spirit.

"The reason them Massai was so different," he explained patiently, "was that it *was* cow country they lived in. They herded cattle good as any spread in the Bald Rock, but they didn't run their brands for making market steers. They never touched the meat. All's they did was to open up the jugglurr's veins in them poor critters th'oats and stick in a drain pipe and run themselves out a bucket of blood. Then they'd go to the other end of the cow and draw a gallon of milk. That was their chuck wagon. They never et

233

nothing but blood and milk, and the rascals growed to seven feet high and weighed about twict what a white man would, yet was all muscle and meanness the same as a snake. Least that's what Gus Bell told the kid next morning. He said . . . 'Boy, we're going into Massai country today, and I want you to look sharp that none of our niggers take off into the bush. Ali is a-going to take the lead. You march in the middle of the line, and I'll bring up the drag. These here coast bearers don't cotton to these big, rangy Massai lion-killers, and Ali says they been muttering about evaporating at the first blind turn in the trail.' Then Gus . . . he told the kid some little more about the Massai, and it was all of it pretty spooky . . . how they actually hunted and killed lions with nothing but a wooden lance and a bullhide shield . . . how they was really descendants of Cleopatra's Eejipshun Nile outfit, fine-cut features and slant eyes and handsome as any white men you ever dreamed to see, but blacker than the bottom of a coal pit and wickeder than a fly-bit bull and 'way bigger than anything A-laddinn ever rubbed out of that damned lamp. You can believe the kid was listening and a-watching out almighty sharp with both eyes to see him a Massai by this time.

"Well, Ali Kabar had heard right. In two days over one half our coast natives was gone. That thirty-seventh night coming on was a goose-pimpler. All during it we could hear lions grunting and coughing out in the mimosa thicket, only they wasn't *real* lions according to Ali Kabar. By gray-streak daylight, we didn't have one bearer left. They all winked out on us with the stars. I mean to say that the young American kid was not just medium scared, he was stiff-backed as any green-broke bronc'. He was walling his eyes and bunched up in the middle, set to jump four ways at once. Gus Bell just give him a pat on the back and said . . . 'Don't fret so, boy. We don't need them porters any longer. We're here, now. This is the Massai country. The big stuff is just ahead. It could be anywhere around us in the bush from this camp on. You and me and Ali will just hunt on, the three of us, and we'll do a sight better than we would have with fifty stampeded coast bearers to spook up our game a-clumping through the bush along with us. Just keep up tight and don't fall back, or stray aside. This here big stuff we're after works sneakier than a wounded cape buff'. So you just hang close to old Gus, and he'll learn you what gun to use, and when.' "

Swampie stopped talking. He was nodding to himself, blue eyes shining as though he were seeing it all again. The big handlebar mustache quivered with what could have been the scent of kopje lion, or the cold fear-sweat of terrified coast natives, running for their lives. His companions looked at one another, puzzled, and Baldie Simms reached out a gentle hand and put it on Swampie's shoulder.

"Old-timer," he said, "you're going just fine, but we don't want you to fall down with the blind staggers. You ain't no need to let on like it's all so genuine it'll bust your heart vessels thinking back on it. Heck, it's a good enough yarn so far. Ain't no call to liven it up by dropping dead on us. We ain't asked you for no swore statements. Just see that the kid, old Gus, and that there Alley K-Barb feller keep a-going like they was, a-plowing on into that there grand cattle country where them king savages was a-killing all them lions and guzzling all that there jugglarr's vein blood . . . pshaw, that's all we ask."

Swampie, well recovered, accepted a cigarette eagerly, rolled for him by Wes Schultz, and given a courtesy lick and twist in the passing along by Curly Bill Brokaw.

"All right, let's see, that was the thirty-eighth day from the sea coast, wasn't it?" he resumed. "It was late that same afternoon that Ali Kabar stopped in a brush clump among some rocks and said to wait a bit . . . he was going to sneak up ahead a ways and spy out the lay of the land. Gus Bell let him go, telling the kid that no white man alive could smell out the big stuff like Ali Kabar. But Gus forgot to tell the kid that the big stuff was even better at smelling out . . . well, never mind! . . . Gus and the kid was still crouching in them rocks, waiting for Ali to come back, when they heard this here fearsomely scream . . . *AAAAaarrrRRrGGGrraahhHH!*"

The old man cupped his hands and delivered the ear-splitting screech into the attentive silence of his listeners before any of them might imagine his purpose. Wes Schultz, never too steady since the broncho stomped him, went right straight up into the air like a cat that's been shot at. Curly Bill and Smooth-Mouth, jerking back in unison, banged skulls with a ringing solidness that left both seeing black and yellow spots. Even Teton Smith, the veteran of San Juan Hill and Guásimas, galvinated far enough to fall off the edge of his bunk and get his elbow jammed in the company spittoon. Only big Baldie Simms remained unmoved, a nodding blink and gulp of admiration the sole accompaniment to his sober testimonial: "Say, now, that there *was* a fearsome caterwaul."

"It were," agreed Swampie. "And rightly so. When they had hung quiet as pocket mice for about ten seconds after the screech, old Gus give the kid's arm a squeeze. 'That was it,' he said, voice held down low but not shook any great amount. 'The big stuff. Come along on. I don't think we'll wait for Ali.' "

"Well, if they wouldn't wait for Ali, he would sure as sin wait for them. And forever. They found him nailed to a bushbean tree, the Massai spear going clean through his th'oat and six inches out the far side of the trunk. He looked rough. Old Gus just took another tuck in that grim jaw of his, but the kid got green as breadfruit. Gus seen him go off-color and grabbed his arm again. He squoze the arm hard and whispered in his ear . . . 'Don't move a muscle. Our game is all around us. This is the real thing, kid. Hold like a rock, when it closes in!'

"The rest of it come too quiet and fast for the kid. He saw them giant Massai unfolding themselves up out of the thicket, ringing him and old Gus in so tight that a long-armed reach would have smudged black hide in any direction. They seemed to know old Gus. The leader barked out some greeting, and old Gus barked it right back. To the kid, he added with a steadying look . . . 'We're under arrest, and going to see the chief. Don't sweat it none now. I've been marching forty days and nights to get us right precisely here.'

"The kid was rooted solid with the shakes, but somehow managed to make it to the village without disgracing himself or Gus Bell. It was getting dusk now. At the village, the supper fires was jumping and gleaming, their red glows lighting up the forms and faces of the Massai like it was painting them with blood . . . and not out of them cattle's jugglarr veins, neither. The war party flang old Gus and the kid into the middle of these here fires, where there was a sort of council ground, then sent for the chief to come and look at what his big black cats had drug in.

"While waiting for the chief, the kid took his first good look at the warriors surrounding them. He had never seen such black men. They were all of them 'way over six foot tall and muscled-up like marble statues. Their sooty faces were splashed with bars of white and yellow paint, zebra-style. From every wide shoulder hung a chunk of lion pelt, with mane and claws and tail hung onto it sort of like a cape. Each black hand held a wood-hafted spear, short in the handle like a Cheyenne buffalo lance, but with a hammered steel blade about three feet long and honed to shave with.

"Back of the warriors at a careful distance, again just like any Sioux or Cheyenne village in the old days, the women and young ones crowded in to watch the harangue. The kid was still scairt stiff-jointed. But old Gus just stood there bold as brass. He even had the gall to start in on them seven-foot lion-killers, giving them Hades for not bringing up the chief at a swifter gait. The kid was getting the drift of the palaver now because Bell had shifted into Swahili, which he knew the kid could make out fairly good, it being the sort of out-loud sign language of them Africkian folks, seeing's how all the different tribes jabbered some of it. So the kid had just begun to steady down when here comes the chief.

"This fellow left the kid strick' stupid. He was *over* seven foot tall, maybe by two, three inches, and would have weighed three hundred pounds skinned-out and hung up to drain. And ugly? Why, the out-sized rascal was that scarred-up and tore-up of feature, he would make a Gila monster dipped in black mule bile look fetching by comparison. He looked like he had been in a fight with a pride of eight lions in a mighty tight gully. And that was about right, except that the kid was off two lions. Old Gus corrected that arithmetic with his quiet nod and low voice, as the chief came a-striding up.

" 'Ten Lions,' he told the kid. 'That's the name of your biggest game, boy. Now you watch the caliber I use on him.' "

"Scairt? Why, the kid hadn't commenced to know how it felt to take the chill off death yet. But there was something in the look of those glittering-eyed warriors and that mean-looking chief that didn't go with old Gus Bell's quiet voice and confident instructions, and that made the kid's knees begin to turn watery. It had all of a big sudden got too creepy-still in that Massai village. You could have heard a white man's pocket watch ticking, when that huge chief come to a halt in front of Gus Bell. And that with five, six hundred growed and half-growed lion-killers, hun-kered around in the dark and shadow of them leaping red flames, behint him!"

Swampie broke off abruptly. He cupped a gnarled hand to his ear, and said: "Say, speaking of getting quiet, ain't that wind a-letting up some outside? Blizzard's about blowed out, I reckon."

"The heck with the blizzard," breathed Curly Bill. "Get on with them Africkian Comanches."

"Yeah," Smooth-Mouth Madigan's gums clacked with impatience. "What happened when old Ten Lions . . . he begun a-pawing up the dirt in front of Gus Bell?"

"I believe it *is* letting up a bit outside," said Teton Smith, cocking an ear to the waning buffet of the storm. "I figure we'll be able to get out and hay down that bunch of heifers in the south pasture, after all."

Big Baldie Simms shook his tangled mane. "Blast them heifers," he scowled. "You go hay them down. I ain't a-setting foot out that there door, till Swampie gets that pore orphan kid away from them eight-foot savages."

"Well," said Teton, retreating once more, "if he don't get the kid shut of them right soon, it'll be spring-thawed outside, and we can feed them heifers green grass. Maybe the wind's let up out yonder, but it's sure as heck still blowing up a blue norther in here!"

"Mister Smith," drawled Baldie, "if you don't hobble your jaw, I'm a-going to nose-wrap you with that there spittoon. I done said I don't relish looking for work in the winter, but I'll hear how that pore little American kid made out with them lion-killers, if I have to stuff you under your bunk and wad you in with your own saddle turned horn to. Now I mean it."

Swampie waved a hand quickly. Direct confrontation of ranch authority was not his dish of chokeberry tea. Besides, Baldie was his bodyguard. He did not aim to lose him with another three months of winter still to be survived in the Tumbleweed bunkhouse. He cleared his throat with enough noise to rattle Smooth-Mouth's teeth in the tin cup by the shaving mirror, and set sail again, full bore.

"Well, sir, before that chief could get his mouth pried open, Gus Bell took into him. He insulted him in every word of the Swahili tongue and a few outside of it. He called him an old lady, a loud talker, a thief, a murderer, a liar, and a cheat. He said he'd known him long years ago, before he was chief, and that he wasn't really fit to be chief of nothing saving maybe a hut full of gum-boiled old grandmaws.

"The chief . . . he knowed but one way to

settle a charge like that . . . out where the lions was waiting in the mimosa brush. He come back at Bell with a challenge to go lion hunting next morning without shields and using skinning knives for spears. Old Gus just laughed at him and said he wouldn't think of going hunting with any man who couldn't even fire one shot from a white man's rifle, let alone be slicing at any live lions with a butcher knife. 'How about a little contest of strength right here in the village tonight?' old Gus said to the big Massai chief. 'Or are you afraid of the white man's gun?'

"Well, naturally, no chief can turn down a outright challenge of strength or skill . . . that's the law in the Africkian bush, same as it was here on the buffalo plains with the Sioux, Arapahoes, and Cheyennes in the old days.

"So off the whole blamed tribe marches to where the medicine man sets up a batch of rules . . . the main one of which was that, if Gus Bell won, he and the kid would go scot-free, while, if the chief won, the two white guests would end up in them supper fires, instead of at them.

"A bullhide shield was hung up on a thorn bush about fifteen paces off. This was the target. Bell said the chief was such an old woman he wouldn't even hit it, while he, Bell, would demolish it as if by thunder and lightning. Well, Bell shot first and naturally that gave him some advantage. Such as cramming in a paper-hulled shotgun full of Number Two buckshot, instead of the regular lead ball. When he fired, that bullhide shield disappeared as if it had been sieved through a sausage grinder.

"Now that was just the right barrel, mind you. The Massai didn't have no idea what two-barreled guns was, of course, so when Gus reloaded that right barrel and snapped the big double shut, they figured the chief was getting the same dose of medicine that Gus had just took. Another shield was hung up, and Ten Lions he got a-hold of that six hundred rifle like it was a quail gun. His fingers was so big he couldn't get them between the double triggers, and old Gus told him not to worry about that, just to pull both of them and make sure he got the full medicine that way. 'All the same as I did,' he said out loud and boastful, and banging hisself on the chest.

"Up went that old sidehammer blunderbuss and, naturally, you know what happened. Old Gus had that left barrel crammed halfways to the muzzle with paperjacks of powder and three of them Five-Fifty-grain bullets for elephant and the like. When the chief touched off that load, you'd have thought that Mount Vesoovius had disrupted again. Fire belched out of the old double in a solid sheet of flame four feet long. The steel-covered butt drove back into that Massai's face and shoulder with the force of a free-arm swing with a fifty-pound sledge. The chief folded up like a struck tent. He tottered back out of the smoke cloud, took about three lunkering steps, and pitched down onto his face, pickled as a piece of salt pork.

"He never even moved, except to mumble . . . 'You win.' . . . in Swahili.'

"Old Gus, he reached down and retrieved what was left of the big rifle, making sure the chief wasn't dead, but only very bad shook. Then, he made a sign to the medicine man and said something in the Massai language. The kid didn't understand it, but the medicine man and the rest of them Massai, big and little, did. They all stood back, silent as stones, and let Gus Bell and the American kid walk out of that village free into the pitchy-dark Africkian night as wild birds or beasts of the bush. Once shut of the village, Gus and the kid struck out

246

at a trot and never let up till daybreak found them far from the borders of the Massai country, and, far as I know, neither one of them has went back to this day.

"As for the gun, it was ruined and hanging together only by its sidelocks. Old Gus knocked off the butt and the barrels and traded them to a coast chief for enough ivory to put the kid on the boat for home. The action, with them two outside hammers and all smoked up from the charge that brung down Ten Lions, he give to the kid, saying . . . 'Here, ever you get to wondering what caliber to use on what game, remember what you learnt from Gus Bell . . . *you use the biggest, blinking caliber you got.*'"

Swampie shook his head sadly, or maybe it was wearily.

"That was surely a powerful long time gone," he said, and the story was ended.

His listeners eased back. If not disappointed, they were feeling somewhat shortchanged. Swampie's yarns were generally cut from a lot stronger cloth, if not as farshored.

Baldie Simms summed up the company feeling with proper charity when he looked away from the old man and said gently: "Wind *has* let up outside, Mister Smith. I reckon we can go and hay down them heifers now." The others nodded tacit agreement, and Teton Smith led the exodus. Swampie followed his friends to the door of the bunkhouse and watched them make out over the frozen ground to the corral which held the saddle stock. When they were quickly saddled and gone, he turned back to the empty room. Before he built up the fire in the stove and put on some more coffee for the boys, when they got back, he went to his bunk and pulled out his old warbag, which was more a sea chest than the ordinary cowboy trunk.

Opening it, he dug into the mildewed trivia of half a century of life. Presently, he brought out a bulky object wrapped in strange, heavy animal hide. Opening the piece of hide, he stared down at the verdigrised action of a rifle with sidehammers not made on this side of the sea, or for many decades on either side of it.

"Yes, sir," he said softly, "that truly was a powerful spell back. Too bad the kid forgot his lessons. . . ."

Jefferson's Captains

It was 1803, a dark, gusting night and very late. In the White House, Thomas Jefferson consulted his conscience and his courage. Satisfied at last, he sent for his personal secretary. The latter, a scholarly captain of regular infantry, knew what the summons concerned.

For many weeks negotiations to buy the vast empire of the Louisiana Territory had been dragging on with France. The gambler's stakes involved were enormous. The land mass in question encompassed an uncharted area extending from the Mississippi Valley to the Pacific Coast and from Canada to Mexico. Jefferson's cartographers had guessed the total to be twice the size of the existing United States. The Spanish and French map-makers — Spain having held precious title — were not even that certain of what this real estate comprised. Nor had they any reasonable idea where its north and south boundaries might lie. Most especially was the northern line in doubt. Up there, Her Majesty's Britannic government still schemed to possess the "Columbia and the Ouregan Countries." Her Canadian agents probed constantly to determine this matter in favor of the Crown.

Certain American visionaries — precious few, as is ever the case — understood the nature of the British adventuring along the northern reaches of the Louisiana wilderness. Jefferson was the light that led this hardy, small band of American patriots. He realized that what actually was in progress was a silent, even deadly, struggle to set the northern boundaries of the United States. Or, from the British view, to expand the southern boundaries of the Empire's Canadian star.

The first of the two nations, the lonely President believed, that could get there — there being the mouth of the mighty Columbia River in the Pacific Northwest — would be the eventual and immediate winner. And, of course, it went without qualification that the getting there must be done overland, since the U.S. had already reached the south of the Columbia by sea and had been rudely informed by the British that, in effect, such visits by ship did not count, a most peculiar logic for the greatest sea power on earth to apply in any power contest.

The victory, the prize, for which this soundless and, indeed *sub rosa,* battle was being planned and carried on, was simply incalculable. God alone might know how many millions of acres, how many tens of thousands of square miles, how many rivers, lakes, deserts, mountain ranges, buffalo pastures, mines of precious metals, forests of primal timber, and farms of rich deep loam would, or could, be counted in the final summings of the victor's spoils.

But there was another prize within the prize. A winning which would make all the other winnings seem the merest of tinsels. It was the legend of the Northwest Passage — a navigable way by water from the United States to the Pacific, an ocean seaway *overland.* Somewhere out there in that vast brooding wilderness was "the Louisiana," a connecting course of waterways that lay waiting for its discoverer. Beginning at St. Louis, it followed upward the great Missouri River to that stream's headwaters, joining with the Columbia, then down the latter's fabled tides to the Pacific and to the trade of the Orient and the world of the Far East! This was the legend, and Jefferson believed the legend.

Aside from the excitement of the finding of the inland passage which had haunted the imaginations of Western man for four centuries, the President was realistically aware of the remaining, concrete values of his projected purchase. He comprehended precisely the immediate nature of the need to establish regency. His secretary was no less aware of the undeclared war to pioneer the way to the Columbia and the Pacific, and of its implications of empire.

Thus for the President to pay for this vast "blind bundle," which was the Louisiana Territory, was one thing, of course, while to take possession of it was altogether another. Jefferson also understood this as, again, did his secretary. Coming now to the door of the executive study, the latter paused.

Any man might well do so. The answers, waiting beyond the walnut panels, could alter the course of the young nation's destiny, could, indeed, change the history of a hemisphere. Had the President decided to go ahead with the Louisiana gamble? Had he determined to confide this news, and perhaps much more, to his faithful friend and secretary? The slender captain beyond the study door shook his head and squared his shoulders. Entering the fire-lit room, he bowed slightly.

"Mister President. . . ."

Jefferson turned from the rain-lashed western window. He did not reply other than with a least toss of his leonine head. Then followed a searching examination of the secretary's tense face. Seeming reassured by what he saw, the President's own grave countenance softened. He returned the small, formal bow.

"Mister Secretary . . . ," he replied, then let the silence resume a moment. Suddenly he straightened, eyes alight. "Old friend," he said, "how would you like to beat the British in a boat race to the Columbia?"

It was as simply said as that, and the secretary trembled. How would any old soldier like such a challenge to his country's future? How would any professional captain respond to the question of contesting the world's mightiest nation for the prize of an empire at the cost of a planted flag? But the secretary was a man of iron. He merely made his little bow once more.

"I would like that just fine, sir," he said.

"And do you think you could win the race?" Jefferson watched him very closely now.

"It can be done, sir."

"Can be?"

"No sir . . . will be."

"Hah! That's the answer. All right, no more on that. Now you will need a second-in-command. I want two captains along. If one should fall, or fail, the other must be as fully equal in his ability to succeed. You will be the senior, of course. Now do you know your other man?"

"Yes, sir."

"Who is he?"

The secretary gave the name, and Jefferson nodded.

"If he satisfies you, I'll not say no to him. Get him."

"There must be a condition, Mister President."

"What? A condition, sir? At a time like this?"

"Yes, sir. My companion must have equal command in every sense. There can be no senior or junior between us. Not with this man. Otherwise, sir, I cannot accept the commission. He might. I could never."

Jefferson's frown sharpened with his words. "You're a generous fellow, Mister Secretary. Few would be so charitable, or, indeed, so reckless, with this opportunity."

"I understand the risk, sir. The condition remains."

"You're blackmailing me, Mister Secretary."

"Yes, sir. You will see to the equal commissions then, sir? That is, you will make certain yourself that they are drawn alike in every way?"

The secretary was justly concerned. He knew well the evanescence of agreements given in the heat of important Presidential discussions. Yet now Jefferson was scowling in angry earnest. The secretary was aware he must tread here with consummate skill, if not outright luck.

"You see, sir, my man is older than I and also outranked me in my first service. He commanded the rifle company to which I was attached as an ensign. Moreover, he is the best soldier for this service of yours in the entire nation. You know him. You know his brother. In or out of the regular forces there is no man to call his peer, or theirs, in point of this type of undertaking. To share equal command is the very least I might offer this true patriot and soldier."

Jefferson's scowl only added another browline. "I would remind you, Mister Secretary, that you would not be offering the command, or any share of it. It would be I."

"Yes, sir. You will see to the matter, then, sir? You will guarantee an equal commission for him?"

Jefferson, if not out of patience entirely, was at the point of stiff reprimand. He stomped over to the western window. In a moment, he swung back around.

"You would appear to me, sir," he rasped, "to be in a strange position to be bargaining with me. I am not at all certain that I care for your attitude, or will accept it. You are not the *only* captain I've considered."

"You don't know the man as I do, Mister President. And if you will be staking the future of our nation upon this strike for the Columbia, I will be staking my life."

Jefferson, confronted with such courage and conviction, such readiness to sacrifice a career for no more than an old comrade's honor — a comrade who would never know if the secretary had, or had not, stood fast for him — could not persist in his inclination toward dismissal. His smile was no less rare and bright for its certain rueful tinge.

"No," he said, "I do not know your friend as you do. But I've a sneaking suspicion that I am going to do so before too long. Go and fetch him. He has his equal commission and you my word for it."

"Thank you, Mister President."

With another, final, small bow the secretary departed the study. When he had gone, Jefferson turned again to the dark panes of the inland window. He stood, staring out into the gusting windiness and wet of the storm, the sense of time and decision heavy upon him.

Westward nine hundred miles rolled the wide and muddy tide of the great Missouri. Beyond that mother of American rivers lay the sunset and the Pacific Ocean. Between, stretching two thousand and more unknown miles through no man knew what terrors and perils, the legendary Northwest Passage waited for his two captains. The incubus of the hour, the enormity of the odds, the sheer recklessness of the expedition's conception were well-nigh past calculation.

Was he in time? Would his captains be in time? No mortal could say. He could only prepare, and pray.

Jefferson came away from the window, head down and frowning, hands laced behind his coattails.

"I don't know," he mused softly aloud. "Lewis and Clark . . . somehow the names don't seem to ring just right. . . ."

Comanche Passport

The officer's eyes, watery and red-hawed from ten hours of High Plains sun, squinted through the smoke of the night fire at the silent man across from him, his words coming slow and careful the way a wise man's will when he's talking to a hard case like Bass Cooper.

"You and I aren't exactly new to one another, Cooper, and I feel I can speak frankly to you."

His companion's answer was a flat stare, unvarnished by any other acknowledgment, and the cavalryman, flushing to its direct challenge, finished lamely.

"I may as well tell you, right out, that the men didn't buy your story about that captive Comanche you brought in from Pawnee Fork this afternoon."

The silent one, a medium-tall man, looking taller from the slack way his greasy buckskins gaunt-draped his frame, returned the officer's gaze, level-eyed.

"And me, Captain Hughes, I don't give a hoot what your troopers are buying. As long as I'm scouting for this supply train, they'll buy what I bring in to sell."

Captain Henry Hilton Hughes, Troop B, Fourth United States Cavalry, wasn't just the man you put the spurs into like that, without you got some back-hunching out of it. His words stiffened with the jut-out of his broad jaw.

"Let me remind you, Cooper, that your record in this man's Army smells like a sick dog. And as far as the men in this immediate command are concerned, per- haps you'd better remember that the *other* supply train was a Fourth Cavalry outfit. Maybe that'll let you see how this whole thing looks to these men."

Bass Cooper could see the way it looked without any trouble whatever. All the while the captain had been getting his worries into hard words, the lean scout's mind had been running that two-year-old back trail to the Comanche ambush that had kept him off the service payroll until this pres- ent outfit's regular scout had come out second in a knife seminar in Kansas City and young Captain Henry Hughes had re- luctantly accepted Bass's plea for the chance to get back to Army scouting.

That ambush, two years ago, had been no more Bass's fault than it had been God's, but the facts that he had lived with the Comanches, spoke their tongue better than he did his own, and knew half their head chiefs by their teepee names, had made up the Army's mind against him. The clincher had been the particular chief who had done the job — old Oudlt' eidl, the notorious Big Head.

Bass had known Big Head as well as he knew himself, had received him as a friend in that Army camp the night before the Pawnee Fork Massacre. The post commanders at both ends of the Santa Fé Trail had looked at one another and nodded. And suddenly had no more service for the best civilian scout in the business.

For two long years now, Bass Cooper had haunted the Trail, lone hand, hoping to get at Big Head some way. But Oudlt'eidl's outsize cranium was stuffed with good red brains. He had pulled his lodges after the ambush, headed south for old Mexico and an easy career at horse-raiding the big Spanish ranches in Sonora, and been seen no more along the South Trace.

Bass, looking at Captain Hughes across

the fire now, knew he couldn't blame the youthful officer. Nor was there anything he could say to him. The look-alike of the two cases was too cozy. That other train had been a post-supply outfit, too, even toting along the same kind of Comanche bait as this one, a creamy horse herd of high-class cavalry-replacement mounts. His answer, when it finally came, echoed the resigned bitterness of the condemned guiltless.

"There ain't nothing I kin say, Captain. Either you trust me and follow my scouting, or you don't. I ain't going over my side of that Pawnee Fork Massacre again, for any man. You know my claims about it."

"I know them," replied the other man awkwardly, "and, as far as I personally am concerned, Cooper, I believe them. Had I not, I would never have signed you on for this hitch. But, good Lord, man, two of the tallest men in Texas couldn't see to spit over that story you brought in tonight. Let alone that shoulder-shot Comanche buck you brought along with it."

"Nevertheless, you'd best believe it, Captain. You and your men, both. I *did* catch this buck trailing me up by Pawnee Fork and I *did* wing him, just like I told you. And" — the swart scout paused meaningfully — "you *have* got a clean hundred war-trailing Comanche braves squatting acrost your path somewheres past Pawnee Fork. And you *are* toting along a horse herd that would suck in any Comanche wolf pack ever whelped."

"I'm sorry, Cooper. What you've told me so far doesn't add up. Comanches along the trail are hardly news to a regular cavalry outfit."

"Well, maybe here's something that is," nodded the scout. "I *know* that buck I brought in this afternoon."

"You what?"

"I know him," repeated the scout easily. "Name's Peidei-t'ou-dei. You can shorten that to Stiff Leg. He's subchief and general handyman to an old Comanche friend of mine. A big one. And mortal bad. Name of Oudlt' eidl."

"And how does that come out in English?" Captain Hughes's short question came edged with the irritation that was growing under the scout's laconic disclosures.

Bass Cooper looked off across the fire, staring south into the prairie-black gut of the spring night. His answer was so soft the officer barely caught it. But what he caught of it jumped the short hairs along the back of his neck straight on end.

"Big Head," said Bass Cooper, and that was all he said.

The following morning, Captain Hughes called his troopers and supply-wagon 'skinners up in the gray cold of pre-dawn and gave them Bass's amended story without benefit of his own opinions, the men saying nothing, but taking it with many a hard-eyed glance at the somber scout. After that, they set out, the officer riding the head of the wagon line with Bass, the ten members of Troop B clanking along behind in the dust of the heavily loaded supply vehicles. Ahead lay the fifteen-mile rising pull to Pawnee Fork, soldiers and 'skinners, cavalry mounts, and wagon mules settling to it with a grimness that could be felt.

Hour after hour the wagons rolled, jaw-set 'skinners keeping the ten-mule hitches as far up in their collars as the bite of a blacksnake bullwhip could drive them. Nerves were popping loud enough to outdo the whips, yet the livelong day they saw nothing — not a pony track or a pile of horse dung fresher than that of the last freight outfit in front of theirs.

Riding at the head of the sullen line, Bass Cooper could read the hard questions swept repeatedly at him by Captain Hughes's accusing glances — *Where are your Comanches, Cooper? Where is even any sign of your Comanches, mister?* — and knew, even as he rode, that his last chance of convincing the Army man lay in the cold ashes of that big ring of hostile cook fires he had spotted the day before at Pawnee Fork. If the Comanches had played it cute, had scattered and blanked-out those ashes, he was as done as a pit-roasted rack of hump ribs.

Big Head's band had played it just about as opposite of cute as a pack of High Plains hostiles ever did. Captain Hughes, his dust-caked troop of cavalry and his hard-bitten crew of Missouri and Texas muleskinners, took one long, quiet look at that stark ring of ash spots and backed off to do a batch of reconsidering about civilian scouts in general, and dark-faced Bass Cooper in particular.

By the time coffee had been boiled, and night had shut, tight-down, around the little prairie camp, there wasn't a man in the outfit but who was hunkered close to the fire, waiting, nerve-set and awkward, for Bass Cooper to expound his professional views on how a quarter of a troop of green cavalry and ten rawhide-tough Santa

Fé Trail 'skinners went about outguessing upward of a hundred hostile Comanches, under the roughest cob in the whole cornfield of South Texas trail raiders.

"All right," Captain Hughes's brittle admission came to the taciturn scout, "you can count on all of us, now, Cooper. What do you propose doing?"

Bass Cooper wasted no time in telling them. "First off, we can reckon Big Head will go on through with whatever plans he's made for attacking us. Providing he has any plans. Me, personal, I think he has."

"Yeah," — this from Cloyce Travis, a wolf-jawed Texan who was Hughes's boss 'skinner — "but the hell of it is we ain't got no way of knowing what them plans might be. And no way of finding out."

"That's where you're wrong." The scout's mouth twisted to a fleeting grin. "We got a plumb quick way of finding out, first-hand."

"What are you getting at, Cooper?"

"When you want Injun plans, get them from an Injun, that's all."

"Meaning that wing-shot buck we got tied up in the lead wagon?"

"You ain't just whistling . . . I mean *him*. That's why I brung him back yesterday, instead of blowing his bowels apart. He'll know about any plans them red sons may have hatched."

"Hell," Travis shrugged, "that buck ain't going to tell us nothing. You-all know that. He ain't said a word since we trussed him up and threw him in the wagon."

"He'll talk," said Bass. "You boys just go fetch him. Meanwhile, I'll get me my talking stick."

"What's that?" demanded Captain Hughes uneasily.

"Little Comanche invention for freeing up froze' tongues."

"Hold on," countered the young cavalryman. "I don't believe we can allow any Indian torture, Cooper. We're all Christian people here. I grant you, the red man may know something, but. . . ."

"But . . . nothing," Cloyce Travis's soft Texas drawl undercut the officer's objection. "I ain't got nothing against Christians, but that heathen red scut wouldn't know Jesus from Jed Smith. Let's leave the Lord out'n it. Bass Cooper's running this outfit until we hit Arkansas Crossing and get shut of these here Comanches. Mebbeso you-all still want your hair with you in Santy Fee, you'll bear that in mind."

Shortly the cavalry officer nodded, turned to the waiting scout. "Go ahead, Cooper. Get your stick. I'll have the Indian brought up for you."

When Hughes's troopers returned with the glowering Comanche, Bass straightened up, fetching a foot-long piece of whittled hardwood to view.

"This here's a talking stick. The Comanches call it *dei-n t'ou-e,* the tongue-stick. You give it a twist and talk comes out."

"How's she work?" Cloyce Travis eyed the small stick skeptically.

"On a very artistic principle," replied Bass soberly. "Now pay attention, because I ain't going over this twice."

Having warned the white audience, he turned to the scowling Comanche, addressing him in a short-barked string of his mother tongue. "Ho, you, Stiff Leg. You are familiar with this stick? It comes from the southern tribes, down in Sonora. Now, you listen. And while you are listening, look, too. Look at me. Hard. You remember K'ou sein-p'a-ga? You remember Black Beard?"

"You K'ou! You Black Beard. Him you!" The startled recognition burst from the sullen brave, his quick-following plea coming with a guileless, wide-mouthed grin.

"Listen, Black Beard. I've been south. I know the stick. We were friends, you and I, *kou-m,* real friends. You remember Stiff Leg? You won't use the tongue-stick on your old friend. *Kou-m, kou-m,* there is no need for the stick. Big Head means your wagons no harm. He doesn't want the horses of these pony soldiers. Hear me. I swear it."

Bass, stepping back into the full firelight, held the little stick up so the watching men could see it clearly. "You'll all observe there's a slot cut in the middle of this stick. All we do is take a good-honed skinning knife and open us a little flap of skin on Stiff Leg's belly. Just under the button. Then we flay this little strip of skin away from the meat and fat, and stick it through this slot in the stick, pulling her on through, tight."

The scout paused, watching the brave for any sign of folding, saw none, and continued.

"Now, we start rotating the stick, half a turn at a twist. What starts peeling off and wrapping itself around the stick is the three-inch strip of Stiff Leg's belly hide."

Bass hesitated again, looking Stiff Leg up and down.

"Depending on how hard this buck

don't want to talk, we keep turning the stick. Looking at him, I'd judge him to be about a three-turn man. Mebbeso, he's tougher than I think. Depending on that, we'll peel him clean down to the end of his pizzle."

"Hiii-eee!" The Comanche's snarl came with his wild lunge at Bass. The scout side-stepped as Cloyce Travis and the mule-skinners snowed the crazed Indian under.

"Spread-eagle him on that wagon wheel!" snapped Bass. "And stuff his yap with something. We don't want him wailing loud enough for Big Head to hear him."

With Stiff Leg bound and gagged on the wagon wheel, Bass stepped in, close. His skinning knife whipped up, slashing the front of the Comanches's war shirt. The captive twisted, driving his teeth furiously into the leather gag. The watching men bit just as hard, gag or no gag.

Bass made three thin cuts, his knife moving like a light streak. When he had made them, he brushed the blood off Stiff Leg's belly with the greasy foresleeve of his buckskin shirt, stepped back, grunted a short Comanche phrase at the hostile. The brave's answer, in Comanche or any other tongue, came out a snarl, and Bass shrugged, moving in with the knife again.

Stiff Leg stood up to the flap-flaying, the pulling of the flayed flap through the stick-slot, and a turn and a half of the stick itself. Then he caved in. At that, he took it better than three or four of Captain Hughes's young troopers, each of whom felt compelled to stumble off in the dark to bark up his sowbelly and beans back of the handiest wagon wheel.

Bass sloshed a dipper of creek water across Stiff Leg's belly, cut him down, laid him out on his back by the fire, daubed his wound with tallow, pasted the flap back in place, and bound it there with a strip of trade muslin. Then he propped him against the wagon wheel and threw another dipper of branch water in his face.

Stiff Leg came out of it, shaking his head and whining like a cornered bear. When his head was clear, he talked and, from the sound of it, talked reasonably straight. His story came out in a mixture of Comanche, broken English, and dramatic hand-sign language that made the confession clear enough for the greenest trooper to follow with eye-popping understanding.

"Big Head . . . him want the horses. Need ponies. Very long trip up from Sonora. Hard on the horses. Him see you.

Him see your ponies. Him remember other time, make big laugh. Him. . . ."

"*Hau, hau,*" waved Bass. "We savvy horses. How about the attack, now? Where will Big Head attack?"

The Comanche hesitated, watching the scout. Bass smiled, encouragingly, twirling the tongue-stick the least bit.

"Sandstone Slot!" Stiff Leg had gotten the point, his answer bursting out hurriedly.

The name sent Bass's mind loping up the Trail to the spot, setting it at two miles past Big Coon Creek, in the very gut of the desolate country ahead. It was a narrow, quarter-mile-long defile, hand-carved by Man Above for the ambush to be used by His savage red sons.

"Go on," he grunted, flashing the tongue-stick, "keep talking."

"Wagons go in Sandstone Slot. Horses not in yet. When wagons all in, Indians ride in . . . fast. Get between horses and slot. You trapped inside. Can't get out to fight. Indians run off horses. *Sat-kan,* it's as easy as that."

Afterward, there was a little silence, then Bass talked. And the way he talked made a man know he was thinking the thing out.

"I hate to horn in on a man's pondered plans, 'specially when he's made them with such loving consideration of his white brother. What Stiff Leg ain't told us, and which any of you mossyback 'skinners ought to know, is just this. Once them Comanches get us in that bottleneck wash, with our horse herd run off and all, they'll put a bunch of braves on either end of the slot and thirst us out. They ain't got nothing better to do, I promise you. Seeing's how I don't hanker to set in that slot till my gizzard shrivels, we'll just go ahead and do as I say. And that's to run it out Big Head's pet way . . . up to a point, leastways."

The night Bass peeled Stiff Leg's belly, the train was thirty-three miles from Big Coon Creek, the last camp before Sandstone Slot. That made it a two-day drive facing the caravan, during which, according to Stiff Leg, they could expect no bother from the hostiles. Bass was satisfied he had gotten the gospel out of the wounded Comanche, but he and Captain Hughes outrode the lead wagon wide and wakeful, all the same. They pulled the Coon Creek Crossing without a sign that Indians had ever come near the Santa Fé

Trail. So far, so good. Up to Coon Creek, leastways, it looked like the Comanche tongue-stick was big medicine.

After supper in the Coon Creek camp, Bass called the men up for the final pow-wow. "I ain't going to give you my plot before you sleep. It might keep you awake," he grinned. "But I allow you'll agree it's a good one, when you hear it. I'll give it to you, when I bust you out'n your blankets along after moon-dark. Meantime, I got to know for final and sure . . . am I giving the orders, or ain't I?"

After a moment's uncomfortable silence, Cloyce Travis spoke for the 'skinners. "You-all are giving them, Cooper," he grunted. "Leastways, so far as my boys are concerned."

"You've been right so far, Cooper. Go ahead." Captain Hughes's agreement, for all its grudging dignity, was just as definite as Travis's.

Bass nodded, facing around to take in the full group. "All right. Everybody turn in. Get all the sleep you can. When I roll you out, I want you should roll out quiet. No lights and no noise. Every one of you clear on that?"

Apparently everyone was, for his only answer was a wave of sober nods, washing

274

around the listening circle. Bass chucked his head, satisfied.

"Good enough. Truss that buck up again and throw him back in the wagon. Go on, spread out. I want this here camp dark in ten minutes."

In some minutes less than that, the camp was as out-black as a snuffed candle. Bass, hunched between the lead wagon's front wheels, smoked his short, stone pipe and turned his ears to the night-bird and small-animal talking going on in the low hills to the west.

"Keep your nighthawks whistling, Big Head," he muttered grimly. "And hold them fox barks steady. Happen things go just so, tomorrow, I'll hand you back something you hung on me two years ago."

At three o'clock the moon went down, and Bass sent Captain Hughes and Cloyce Travis to roll out the troopers and wagon 'skinners. With all hands assembled, the scout nodded shortly.

"All right, boys." The low voice carried maybe a wagon length, no more. "What I got in mind works tricky. All the same, it's the best I been able to figure."

He gave them the layout, then, and, going along, he could sense their agreeing nods, hear their low grunts of approval.

When he had finished, nobody had a word to ask. He waited a few seconds, concluded abruptly.

"We'll roll a mite early, while it's still near dark. All the light we'll need is to see the slot, when we get there. Trail's clean and smooth from here to the opening."

"And she's smooth clean on through," added Cloyce Travis thoughtfully.

"That's right." Bass's voice dropped even lower. "Now spread out and catch up your mules. And for God's sake rustle them long-ears in here, quiet-like."

Out-trail, west of the night-moving wagon camp, two kit foxes began yapping back and forth. A third and fourth joined the conversation, aided by the faster, more excited ongoing of a dog coyote.

"Listen to them damn' 'skins talking it up," Bass whispered to Captain Hughes, where the cavalryman squatted by his side in the morning dark. "Ever hear a better kit or coyote?"

"Nonsense!" rejoined the young officer uneasily. "Those are the real thing. I've been down this trail enough times to tell a Comanche talking when I hear one, Cooper!"

Bass said nothing. Let the youngster bolster himself. No point in unsettling him more than he and his green boys were already unsettled. No use for a man to josh himself, though. Even if the cocksure captain had been down the trail more times than a buffalo herd had tick birds, those were red tongues clacking out there toward Sandstone Slot.

Cloyce Travis drifted noiselessly up through the black. "All set, Bass. We got them all spanned in and the wagons gang-hitched Injun file, like you-all said."

"Good. Now," — the scout's voice picked up speed and urgency — "have four of them troopers to haze the horse herd along, easy and normal, back of the last wagon. When the last wagons are going in the slot, them boys are to leave the horses and hit into the slot, too. Get that into their heads. They got to get clean away from that herd before Big Head comes down on them. Hump your tail, man!"

"She's humped!" the 'skinner's answer drifted back, his hurrying figure fading with it. Minutes later, he was back, reporting the horse herd bunched and ready to move to Bass's order.

"It's nigh four. . . ." Bass was thinking out loud. "We can go ahead and slop the hogwash to them."

Cloyce Travis drifted out again, Bass giving him a minute before singing out —

277

"Catch up! Catch up!" — at the top of his well-trained lungs. Seconds later, the darkness was rent with the hairiest-chested imitation of a wagon- train catch-up that had ever been staged on the Santa Fé. The 'skinners had forty-five minutes of unnatural silence to make up for in their addresses to their hammerhead hitches, and they didn't miss a four-letter word. They read the 'skinner's bible backward and forward and threw in a few psalms even Bass had never heard.

"Stretch out! Stretch out!" The scout's final order boomed up the darkened Santa Fé loud enough for every red fox in the next sixteen sections to hear. The five spans on the lead wagon hit into their collars as Cloyce Travis poured the blacksnake to them. Down the invisible wagon line, other snakes were snapping and other hitches digging in. The big Murphy freighters squealed and groaned into motion, the obedient, trail-broke horse herd tagging along behind the last wagon.

Following the momentary let-up in blasphemy that always set in after the wagons got under way, a renewed chorus of fox barks and nighthawk cries sprang up around the gully-washed country flanking Sandstone Slot.

Turning to Captain Hughes, Bass laughed. "You still reckon them are the real Johnny Foxes and Willy Nighthawks out there, Captain?"

The nervous officer didn't hesitate with his fervent reply this time. "If they are, by God, they're a damned sight more interested in Army supply trains than they should be!"

Forty minutes down the trail and the sky-belly back of them was lighting to a fish-bloat gray. The pale light bounced off the scrub-beetled brows of Sandstone Slot, staining the face of the escarpment sick-blotchy. The gaping mouth of the slot itself loomed blurred and empty as a burned hole in a dirty blanket. Redbird, Bass's bright chestnut gelding, padding along, cougar-quiet, fifty feet in front of the lead wagon, kept crouching and side-skittering with nerves.

The morning wind, blowing straight at them out of the slot, was a pure blessing. Being dead on, it caught up the pony stink from the twin gullies flanking the narrow defile, carrying it parallel to the train and scattering it away on the desert behind the trailing cavalry horses. Not a horse or a mule in Bass's outfit caught one whiff of the hostile horse sweat and held into the slot steady and smooth-stepping.

Bass swung wide of the entrance, checking the hip-shifting Redbird, letting the wagons go in, past him, counting them with breath-held vehemence as they went.

The first of the tied-together groups of Army vehicles went in and on down the slot, smooth as Shanghai silk, the second group following in perfect order. But a sharp eye, given a little closer look than that afforded from the distant gullies, with maybe just a shade better light, would have seen something off-color about that entrance. As the wagon groups had rumbled past the thin scout at the slot's mouth, the number two, three, four, and five wagon of each group had discharged a strange, silent cargo. A cargo that went scuttling up the insides of the brush-choked lips of the slot, clawing for handholds in the steep-going, slipping, scrambling, and dragging the long Sharps rifles by their barrels.

Bass hadn't more than time to count the 'skinners off their Army freighters before he had other worries. Damn, where the tarnal hell were those troopers — oh, yonder they came, bulking up through the quick-growing light. Riders bent low, horses cat-jumping toward the slot under the anxious heels digging their ribs. The last four men were the troopers assigned to pilot the horse herd, moving three and one, with stolid Captain Henry Hughes riding off the flank of the last one.

A moment later, all four had disappeared into the slot, waving silently at Bass as they passed him.

The scout had a handful of seconds, then, to bat a glance up at the lips of the gully above. He didn't mind what he saw, either. Eight of the ten 'skinners on one side, the ten cavalry troopers on the other, perfect-hid by the rank sage and mesquite. Belly-flopping and squinting along the three-foot swing of their rifle barrels, his eighteen marksmen waited for Big Head and his Comanches.

Three seconds more for an eye-flick down the silent line of halted freighters in the slot behind him, showing him the other two 'skinners straining to hold the long lines of roped-together wagon mules quiet. Two added seconds for another eye-flick out beyond the slot, checking the empty throats of the twin gullies, and the even, plodding approach of the unguarded cavalry horse herd.

One second, then, and hell gave itself a double rupture, breaking loose.

The startled horse herd went dashing toward the slot, neighing and snorting their sudden terror — and Big Head was howling the howl of the Texas Comanche, and both gullies were puking a vomit of feathers, lance tassels, war bows, and grease paint. And Bass Cooper and Captain Henry Hughes were banging their faces into the dirt under the rear wheels of the last wagon, where it stood parked in the slot opening.

Watching the Comanches come, Bass allowed that, when Big Head jumped, he jumped with both splayed moccasins. The hostiles came down on that cavalry horse herd like buffalo wolves on a thrown-out batch of hot calf guts.

Sweet? Man, oh, man, it was pure sugar. The running horse herd was scarcely a hundred yards from the slot. The Comanches, cutting in between it and the slot, to block the crazed animals off, weren't fifty yards from the hidden white riflemen. And hell, a barefaced boy couldn't miss at twice that range with a smoothbore!

Bass let the converging Indian charges, one sweeping from the north gully, one from the south, get good and clotted up in front of the milling horse herd before bellowing: "Fire!" The eighteen-gun volley crashed into the packed mass of men and animals with a thud audible above the compounded war whoops and pony neighs. Indians, Indian ponies, cavalry horses, guns, hoofs, battle screams, and wild neighs went sprawling in a shattered tangle.

Ramming his patch and galena pill home, Bass prayed the reserves the Comanche chief had undoubtedly left in each of the twin gullies would hold up their relief charge until he and the boys could get reloaded, feeling, from what he knew of the red sons, that they would.

He knew them, all right, and they did.

Indians just didn't fight like white men. Swat them hard on the first rush, and nine times out of ten a man had them whipped. Big Head's reserves milled in their gullies, awaiting the return of their chief with his repulsed first waves. The second of these waves, bearing the raging Big Head in its tail-tucked van, dumped the chief, black-faced and raving, in the safety of the north gully.

Immediately, the Comanche leader began yelping his barking war cry and haranguing his braves to move in on the still unguarded and wandering cavalry horses. By the time he had sold them the idea,

Bass had his 'skinners, and Captain Hughes his troopers, primed and waiting.

"Pick your targets, boys!" the scout's call ran cheerily up the slot banks, "but leave the old he-coon to me. Anybody puts a galena pill in that outsize skull, and I'll drill him for his trouble. Big Head's my meat, and I'm namin' him so!"

"Mind what Cooper says!" Captain Hughes barked the sudden confirmation of Bass's request at his own white-faced troopers. "Leave the chief for him!"

Before Bass could answer the quick smile Hughes flung at him with the unexpected order, business was picking up again out beyond the slot.

The hidden white riflemen began squeezing off the return gallop of the redmen the minute they bombarded back out of their gullies. Results — the charge never got rolling, and Bass failed to get his sights near Big Head.

But the Comanche chief had had his share. Back in the north gully for the second time in three minutes, he waved Black Dog and four other gun-owning braves forward. "Fire the five shots!" he growled hoarsely. "Go on, fire them!" The braves nodded, skying their rifles and firing in even rotation. After a moment, the shots were answered by five more from the south gully.

Hearing the signal shots, Bass crawled out from under the Army wagon, his grin nearly unhinging his long jaw.

"Get your head out'n the ground, Captain!" he called to the crouching officer. "Them dog-eaters is hauling their freight."

"How in hell do you figure, Cooper?" The cavalryman's dirt-smeared face poked out querulously.

"Five's their bad medicine number," Bass replied soberly. "Five's poison to a Comanche or any other Plains Injun. They're through for today. Their hearts ain't good no more." Bass turned, boosting his voice to the watching men above. "Hold your fire, boys. Them five shots was their medicine signal. We won't be hearing no more red-fox barks betwixt here and Santa Fé."

"By damn, you-all are right, Bass!" Cloyce Travis, highest man on the slot ridge, called down. "I can see them filing out'n the far ends of both gullies. That bunch easing out'n the near gully is fair close enough to count their coup feathers!"

"Which one's the near gully?" The easy tones dropped out of Bass's voice, his question snapping with sudden interest. "North or south?"

"North. . . ."

"How near?"

"Three, four hundred yards. They got to hump up over a little cross ridge to get out'n it. We can see them plain. Why you-all ask?"

"I aim to holler me a good bye to one of them Comanche pals of mine!" Bass was already halfway up to the slot ridge, his answer scarcely beating him to the Texan's side. "Happen the wind and the light and the luck are just right, he'll hear me, too."

With the scout's words, all eyes swung to the bobbing exits of the Comanches departing the northern jaw of their ill-fated ambush trap. The nervous seconds sped, each one boosting another hard-spurred pony up and across the momentary bareness of the cross ridge.

Captain Hughes, having inched part way up the slot ridge to join his men in watching the hostile exodus, was counting the Comanches out, his lips moving unconsciously with those of his tight-mouthed troopers, his nerves stretching as the number grew from thirty to forty to near fifty. Still Bass held his fire.

There was a nasty moment, then, when

no more Indians came out of the north gully. *Damn! What was in that scout's mind, letting the red sons out that way? Sure it was long shooting and not much chance of a clean hit, but why hold down Cloyce Travis and those other center shots among the 'skinners? It would almost seem as though the moody trail guide was covering to let the red devils make it clean away!*

The officer's darkening thoughts scattered and broke for sudden cover — over there at the gully end a last Comanche was kicking his pony up the near side of the cross ridge! And up above, on the slot ridge, Bass Cooper was standing hard against the climbing red of the morning sun, his guttural voice booming a Comanche greeting across the morning stillness.

"Ho, Oudlt' eidl! It is I, K'ou sein-p'a-ga! You remember? Your old friend, Black Beard?"

The startled Comanche, caught off guard by the fierce yell, wheeled his painted pony, stood, for one long breath, silhouetted atop the open ground of the cross ridge.

"Wagh!" the warrior's return snarl burst as a single-worded shout of recognition, his rifle swinging up to follow it.

"TH-gyh hou'bH!" shouted Bass Cooper,

his Sharps slapping to his hunching shoulder with the words. The gun seemed to explode on contact with the lean cheek, its half-ounce galena pill blending its departing whine with the dull-boomed report of the black powder. Across the silence, a man found it hard to think he didn't hear the soapy swat of the ball going home.

The stricken Indian horseman straightened, hung poised for a second in the saddle of his hunching pony. Even at the distance, what with the clean morning light and the way he sat, so sudden-straight and still, there was no missing the bright flash of that five-foot eagle-crest bonnet, or of the grotesquely large head, its fanning feathers vignetted. The fading roll of Bass's shot was still echoing in the north gully as Big Head's pony leaped sideways and away from the nerveless thing on its back.

The charcoal-and-vermilion-smeared body hit the graveled slope of the cross ridge, rolled, bouncing and flopping, to the bottom of the north gully. There it lay, sky-staring and silent. Oudlt' eidl, war chief of the Comanches, was dead, even before the rattling gravel that was his only funeral procession had ceased following him into his last resting place.

Back on the slot ridge, Bass lowered his battered Sharps, eyes still on Big Head's distant, sprawled figure.

"Hey, Bass!" Cloyce Travis's friendly call brought the scout's gaze back to the 'skinners and troopers, crowding around him on the brushy slope. "What was that last Comanche yell you-all flung at the chief? The one you-all squeezed off with?"

"*TH-gyh hou'bH*," said Bass slowly. "Happy Traveling. Pleasant Journey. It's a thing they say when someone is about to die. About to start up the Shadow Trail. About to put in for his Comanche passport. . . ."

"Man alive," there was growing admiration in Cloyce Travis's drawl, "I allow you-all are some pumpkins with that holy iron of yourn, but that buck was some over three hundred yards! You-all don't aim to say you actually expected to drill him center?"

"You can't very well miss a shot," replied Bass evenly, "that you've been practicing in your head for the long part of two years."

"Well, what do you-all say now that you've made it?" smiled the Texas 'skinner.

"Yes, Bass," — it was the first time Captain Hughes had called him by that name, and Bass didn't miss the frank respect in the young officer's use of it — "what *do* you say, now? I'm waiting for my scout's report."

The scout looked at the straight-faced captain, and beyond him to the waiting circle of muleskinners and cavalry troopers, his narrow black eyes relaxing as the ring of friendly grins spread around to hem him in.

"Boys," — his low words, coming haltingly from the crooked, half-shy smile of his twisted mouth, left them all with their hearts full and their mouths empty — "I say, let's get them Army wagons rolling west. I want to know how it feels to be riding the head of a U.S. cavalry supply line again. With the wagons and the pony soldiers glad to have you out there where you belong . . . and the sun hitting you from *behind* for a change, as well as in front."

The Tallest Indian
in Toltepec

Where the wagon road from the small town
of Toltepec, in the state of Chihuahua, came
up to the Río Grande, the fording place was
known as the old Apache Crossing. This
was because the Indians used it in their
shadowy traffic in and out of Texas from old
Mexico. It was not a place of good name,
and only those traveled it who, for reasons
of their own, did not care to go over the
river at the new Upper Crossing.

This fact of border life was well understood by Colonel Fulgencio Ortega. He
had not forgotten the Indian back door to
El Paso on the American side. That is why
he had taken personal charge of the guard
post of his troops at this point.

A very crafty man, Colonel Ortega. And
efficient. It was not for nothing that the
descamisados, the starving, shirtless poor,
called him the Executioner of Camargo.
Chihuahua had no more distinguished son,

or another son half so well known in the ranks of the irregular *rurales,* which was to say the stinking buzzards of the border.

Now, with his men, a score of brutes so removed from decency and discipline that only their upright postures stamped them as human beings, he lounged about the ashes of the supper fire. Some of the bestial soldiers bickered over the cleaning of the mess kits. Others sat hunched about a serape spread on the ground, belching and complaining of the foulness of their luck with the cards and with the kernels of shelled corn which passed for money among them. The heat of the evening was stifling. Even with the sun now down at last beyond the Río, it was still difficult to breathe with comfort. The horse flies from the nearby picket line still buzzed and bit like rabid foxes. It was a most unpromising situation. In all of the long daylight they had wasted at the ford, no fish had come to their net, no traveler from Toltepec had sought to pass the crude barricade flung across the wagon road.

"*¡Válgame!*" announced Ortega. "God's name, but this is slow work, eh, Chivo?"

The name meant "goat" in Spanish, and the bearded lieutenant who responded to it seemed well described.

"True, *jefe*." He nodded. "But one learns patience in your service. Also hunger. Hiding. Sand fleas. Body lice. How to use corn for money. How to live on water with no tequila in it. Many things, *excelencia*."

Ortega smiled and struck him across the face with the butt of his riding quirt. The blow opened the man's face and brought the bright blood spurting.

"Also manners," said the colonel quietly.

Chivo spat into the dirt. "*Sí*," he said, "also manners."

Presently, the man on duty at the barricade called to his leader that someone was coming on the road.

"By what manner?" asked Ortega, not moving to rise.

"A burro cart."

"How many do you see?"

"Two. A man and a boy. Hauling firewood, I think."

"*Pah!* Let them go by."

"We do not search the cart, *jefe?*"

"For what? Firewood?"

"No, *jefe*, for *him* . . . these are Indians who come."

Instantly, Ortega was on his feet. He was at the barricade next moment, Chivo and the others crowding behind. All watched in silence the approach of the small burro cart. Had they begun to pant or growl it would have seemed natural, so like a half circle of wolves they appeared.

On the driver's seat of the cart, Díaz grew pale and spoke guardedly to his small son. "Chamaco," he said, "these are evil men who await us. Something bad may happen. Slip away in the brush if there is any opportunity. These are the enemies of our leader."

"You know them, Papa, these enemies of our *presidente?*"

"I know the one with the whip. It is Ortega."

"The Executioner?" The boy whispered the dread name, and Juliano Díaz, slowing the plodding team of burros, answered without moving his head or taking his eyes from the soldiers at the barricade.

"Yes, my son. It is he, the Executioner of Camargo. As you value your life, do not speak the name of *el indio* except to curse it. These men seek his life."

El indio was the name of love which the shirtless ones had given the revolutionary president whom they had brought to power with their blood, but who now fought desperately for the life of his new government and for the freedoms which he sought to bring to the *descamisados* of all

294

Mexico, be they Indians, such as himself and Juliano and Chamaco Díaz, or of the Spanish blood, or of any blood whatever. To the small boy, Chamaco, *el indio* was like Christ, only more real. He had never seen either one, but he knew he would die for his *presidente* and was not so sure about the Savior.

He nodded, now, in response to his father's warning, brave as any ten-year-old boy might be in facing the Executioner of Camargo.

As for Ortega, perhaps the sinister appellation was only a product of ignorance and rebelliousness on the part of the incredibly poor Indians of the motherland. He understood this for himself, it was certain. But being a soldier was hard work, and the people never comprehended the necessity for the precautions of military control. This did not mean that one of the Spanish blood could not be gracious and kind within the limitations of his stern duty. The colonel waved his whip pleasantly enough toward the burro cart.

"Good evening, citizen," he greeted Díaz. "You are surprised to see us here, no doubt. But the delay will be slight. Please to get down from the cart."

"*¿Qué pasa, excelencia?* What is the mat-

295

ter?" In his fear, Díaz did not obey the request to step down but sat numbly on the seat.

"Ah, you know me!" Ortega was pleased. "Well, it has been my work to get acquainted among the people of *el indio*. Did you hear my order?"

"What?" said Díaz. "I forget. What did you say, Colonel?"

Ortega moved as a coiled snake might move. He struck out with his whip, its thong wrapping the thin neck of Juliano Díaz. With a violent heave, the guerrilla leader threw the small man from the cart onto the ground, the noose of the whip nearly cracking his vertebrae.

"I said to get down, *indio*," he smiled. "You do not listen too well. What is the matter? Do you not trust your Mexican brothers?"

Díaz was small in body only. In heart he was a mountain.

"You are no brothers of mine!" he cried. "I am an Indian!"

"Precisely," answered Ortega, helping him up from the dirt of the roadway. "And so is he whom we seek."

Díaz stood proudly, stepping back and away from the kind hands of Colonel Fulgencio Ortega. He made no reply, now,

296

but the boy on the seat of the burro cart leaped down and answered for him.

"What!" he exclaimed, unable to accept the fact anyone would truly seek to do ill to the beloved *presidente*. "Is it true, then, that you would harm our dear . . . ?" Too late, he remembered his father's warning and cut off his words. Ortega liked boys, however, and made allowances for their innocence.

"Calm yourself, little rooster," he said kindly. "I said nothing of harming *el indio*. Indeed, I said nothing of your great *presidente* in any way. Now, how is it you would have the idea that it is he we look for, eh?"

All of Mexico knew the answer to the question. For weeks the outlands had thrilled to the whisper that *el indio* would make a journey to the United States to find gold and the hand of friendship from the other great *presidente*, Abraham Lincoln. It was understood such a journey would be in secret to avoid the forces of the enemy *en route*. But from Oaxaca to the Texas border the *descamisados* were alerted to be on the watch for "the little Indian" and to stand at all times ready to help forward the fortunes of his journey.

Chamaco Díaz hesitated, not knowing what to say.

His father, brave Juliano, broke into the growing stillness to advise him in this direction. "Say nothing, my son," he said quietly, and stood a little taller as he said it.

Chamaco nodded. He, too, straightened and stood tall beside his father.

They would talk no more, and Ortega understood this.

"My children," he said, "you have failed to comprehend. We do not seek to harm the *presidente*, only to detain him."

If standing tall, Chamaco was still but a small boy. He had not learned the art of dishonesty.

"Why do you stop us, then, Colonel?" he demanded. "We are only poor wood gatherers from Toltepec, going to El Paso."

"Just exactly my problem," explained Ortega, with a flourish of the whip. "You see, *pobrecito*, it is my order that every Indian going across the border must be measured against that line which you will see drawn on the dead oak tree." He pointed to the sun-blasted spar with the whip. "Do you see the line on the tree?"

"Yes, Colonel."

"Well, it is drawn five feet from the ground, *chico*. That is just about the tallness of your great *presidente*, not being too precise. Now the problem is that I myself am not familiar with this great man. I would not know him, if I saw him. But we have his height reported to us, and I have devised this method of . . . shall we say? . . . ruling out the chance that *el indio* shall get over the river into the United States and complete his journey."

"Colonel," broke in Juliano Díaz, going pale despite his great courage, "what is it you are saying?"

Ortega shrugged good-naturedly. "Only that, if you are an Indian not known to me, or to my men, and if your height is the same as that of *el indio,* and if I detain you, then I have prevented a possible escape of your great *presidente,* eh?"

"You mean that you think I, Juliano Díaz of Toltepec, am . . . ?" He could not finish the thought, so absurd was it to his simple mind. Could this Rebel colonel truly believe such a thing? That he, Díaz, was the leader, the great *el indio?* Díaz gave his first hint of a relieved look. It may even have been the trace of a smile. There was, after all, and even with the sore neck from the whip, something ironic about the idea. "Please, *excelencia,*" Díaz concluded, forcing the small smile to widen for the sake of Chamaco's courage, "take me to the tree and put me against the mark, that my son and I may go on to El Paso. I have not been well, and we need the *pesos* from this wood to buy medicine in Texas."

"Chivo," snapped Ortega, no longer smiling, "measure this Indian!"

Chivo seized Díaz and dragged him to the tree. Pushing him against its scarred trunk, he peered at the line.

"He comes exactly to it, *jefe*. Just the right size."

"Very well. Detain him."

The matter was finished for Colonel Ortega. He turned back to the fire. He did not look around at the pistol shot which blew out the brains of Juliano Díaz. To a scrofulous sergeant, even with the startled, sobbing cry of Chamaco Díaz rising behind him, he merely nodded irritably. "Coffee, Portales. *Santa María,* but it is hot! Curse this river country."

What would have been the fate of Chamaco, the son, no man may say. Chivo was hauling him to the fire by the nape of his neck, pistol poised to finish him as well, with the colonel's permission. Also, no man may say if Ortega would have granted the favor. For in the instant of death's hovering, a thunder of hoofs arose on the American side of the river and a rider, tall sombrero proclaiming his Mexican identity, dashed his lathered mount across the ford and to a sliding stop by the fire of the Executioner of Camargo.

"Colonel!" he cried. "I come from El Paso! Great news is there. *El indio* is in the town. He has already been to see the American *presidente* and is on his way back to Mexico!"

Ortega stepped back as though cut in the face with his own whip. The wolf pack of his men drew in upon him. Chivo, in his astonishment that *el indio* had gotten out of Mexico and was ready to come back into it, dropped his rough hands from Chamaco Díaz. It was all the signal from above that the quick-witted Indian youth needed. In one scuttling dive he had reached the crowding growth of river brush and disappeared, faithful, belatedly, to his dead father's instruction.

Chivo, pistol still smoking, led the yelping rush of the guerrilla band after the boy. Ortega cursed at his men, raging about himself with the lashing whip.

"Kill him, you fools!" he screamed. "He must not get over the river. Shoot! Shoot! Stomp him out and shoot him. He must not warn the Americans that we know they have *el indio!* After him . . . after him . . . you idiots!"

Deep in the brush, Chamaco wriggled and squirmed and raced for his life. The rifle bullets of the renegades cut the limbs about him. The cruel thorns of the mesquite and catclaw and black chaparral ripped his flesh. He could hear the soldiers panting and cursing within a stone's toss of his heels. He cried for his dead father as he ran, but he ran! If God would help him, he would reach the other side of the river and *el indio.*

As the desperate vow formed in his mind, he saw ahead a clearing in the tangled growth. Beyond it, the waters of the Río Grande flowed silver-red in the sunset dusk.

Riding through the twilight toward El Paso, the thoughts of Charlie Shonto were scarcely designed to change the sunburned leather mold of his features — not, at least, for the happier. A job was a job, he supposed, but it seemed to him that all the while the work got harder and the pay less.

Who the hell was he, Charlie Shonto? And what the devil was the Texas Express Company? And why should the two names cause him pain, now, as he clucked to his weary buckskin and said softly aloud: "Slope along, little horse, there's good grass and water awaiting."

Well, there was an affinity betwixt the likes of Charlie Shonto and the Texas Express Company, even if it hurt. The latter outfit was a jerkwater stageline that had gotten itself about as rump-sprung as a general freight and passenger operation might manage to do and still harness four sound horses, and Shonto was a "special agent" for the stage company. But Charlie Shonto did not let the fancy title fool him. There was a shorter term, and a deal more accurate, for the kind of work he did for Texas Express. If a man said it with the proper curl of lip, it came out something awfully close to "hired gun."

Shonto didn't care for the label. He didn't especially relish, either, the risks involved in wearing it. But a riding gun, be he on the driver's box with an L. C. Smith or Parker on his lap, or in the saddle with a Winchester booted under his knee, made good money for the better jobs. The better jobs, of course, were those in which the survival odds were backed down to something like, or less than, even money. So it was no surprise to Shonto to be sent for by Texas Express for a special assignment. The surprise might lie in the assignment itself, but the sun-tanned rider doubted it. It could be assumed that when Texas Express sent for Charlie Shonto, the "opportunity for advancement" was one already turned down by the Texas Rangers and the U.S. Army, not to mention Wells Fargo, Overland Mail, or any of the big staging outfits.

Shonto clucked again to the *bayo coyote,* the line-backed buckskin dun, that he rode. "Just around the bend, Butterball." He grinned dustily. "Billets for you and bullets for me."

Butterball, a gaunt panther of a horse which appeared wicked and rank enough to eat rocks without spitting out the seeds, rolled an evil eye back at his master and flagged the ragged pennant of his left ear. If he had intended further comment than this one look of tough disgust, the urge was short-circuited.

Scarcely had the comment about "bullets" left Shonto's lips than a respectable, if well-spent, hail of them began to fall around him in the thicket. Next instant, the sounds of the rifle shots were following the leaden advance guard in scattered volleys. Instinctively, he ticked Butterball with the spurs, and the bony gelding sprinted like a quarter-mile racer for the near bend ahead. When he brought Shonto around that bend, the latter hauled him up sharply. Across the Río Grande a tattered company of Mexican irregulars were target-practicing at a dark, bobbing object in midstream. Shonto's immediate reaction was one of relief that the riflemen had not been firing at him. The next thought was a natural curiosity as to what they had been firing at. It was then the third message reached his tired mind, and his mouth went hard. That was a little kid out there, swimming for the American side.

The night was well down. In the Texas Express office in El Paso, three men waited. The drawn shade, trimmed lamp, the tense glances at the wall clock ticking beyond the way-bill desk, all spoke louder than the silence.

"I wish Shonto would get here," complained the express agent, Deems. "It ain't like him to be late. Maybe Ortega crossed over the river under dark and blind-sided him."

The second man, heavy-set, dressed in Eastern clothing, calm and a little cold, shook his head. "Shonto isn't the type to be blind-sided, Deems. You forget he's worked for me before. I didn't exactly pull his name out of a hat."

Deems stiffened. "That don't mean Ortega didn't pull it out of a sombrero!"

Sheriff Nocero Casey, last of the trio, nodded. "Deems is right, Mister Halloran. I don't care for Charlie being late, either. It ain't like him. If Ortega did hear we had sent for Charlie Shonto. . . ." He broke off, scowling.

Halloran took him up quickly. "It's not Shonto being late that is really bothering you, is it? I counted on you, Sheriff. I didn't dare import a bunch of U.S. marshals. I hope you're not getting cold feet."

"No, sir. It's common sense I'm suffering from. This job is way out of my bailiwick. The government ought to send troops or something to see it through. It's too big."

Again Halloran shook his head. "The U.S. government can't set one toe across that river, Sheriff. You know that. It's the law. That's why we've brought in your special agent. Mister Shonto is a man who understands the law. He appreciates its niceties, its challenges."

"Yeah, I've often wondered about that," said the sheriff. "But I won't argue it."

"Ah, good. You see, there is no law which says Texas Express cannot ship a consignment such as our invaluable Item

Thirteen into Toltepec. It will be done every day now that the new Mexican Central line has reached that city."

Agent Deems interrupted this optimism with a groan. "Good Lord, Mister Halloran, what's the use of talking about what we can ship when that cussed Mexican Central Railroad starts running regular between Toltepec and Mexico City? They ain't even run one work engine over that new line that I know of. Them blamed ties that are laid into Toltepec are still oozing green-wood sap!"

Halloran's heavy jaw took a defiant set. "Are your feet feeling the chill, also, Deems? I thought we had the plan agreed to. Where's the hitch?"

Agent Deems stared at his questioner as if the latter had taken leave of whatever few senses government secret service operatives were granted in the beginning. "Where's the hitch, you say? Oh, hardly anywhere at all, Mister Halloran. You're only asking us to deliver this precious Item Thirteen of yours to railhead in Toltepec, Mexico, fifty miles across the river, tonight, with no one wise, whatever, right square through Colonel Fulgencio Ortega's northern half of the loyalist guerrilla army, guaranteeing to get our shipment on the train at Toltepec safe and sound in wind and limb and then to come back a-grinning and a-shrugging and a-saying . . . 'Why, shucks, it wasn't nothing. It's done every day.' Mister, you ain't just plain crazy, you're extra fancy nuts."

"As bad as all that, eh?"

"Fair near," put in Sheriff Casey. "We don't know if that Mexican train will be in Toltepec. We don't even know if those wild-eyed coffee beans even got a train. All we know is that you government men tell us they got the train, and that it'll be in Toltepec if we get this Item Thirteen there. Now that's a heck of an 'if.' "

Halloran was careful. He knew that only these local people — Texans familiar with every coyote track and kit-fox trail leading into Chihuahua — could bring off the delivery of Item Thirteen. Nothing must go wrong now.

"If we took Item Thirteen five thousand miles, Sheriff, surely Texas Express ought to be able to forward shipment the remaining fifty miles to Toltepec."

"Huh!" said Deems Harter. "You got one whack of a lot more faith in Texas Express than we have. In fact, about forty-nine miles more. As agent, I'll guarantee to get your precious shipment exactly one mile. That's from here to the Río Grande. Past that, I wouldn't give you a nickel for your chances of making that train in Toltepec. *If* there's a train in Toltepec."

Halloran shook his head, unmoved. "I'm not exactly thinking of my faith in terms of Texas Express, Harter. It's Charlie Shonto we're all gambling on."

"Yeah," said Harter acridly. "And right now Charlie Shonto looks like a mighty poor gamble."

"Well, anyways," broke in Sheriff Nocero Casey, who had drifted to the front window for another look up the street, "a mighty wet one. Yonder comes our special delivery man, and it looks to me as though he's already been across the river. He's still dripping."

Halloran and Harter joined him in peering from behind the drawn shade.

It was the express agent who recovered first. "Good Lord!" he gasped. "What's that he's toting behind him?"

Sheriff Nocero Casey squinted carefully. "Well," he said, "the bright lights of El Paso ain't precisely the best to make bets by, but if I had to take a scatter-gun guess at this distance and in the dark, I'd say it was a sopping-wet and some-undersized Chihuahua Indian boy."

★ ★ ★

In the shaded office of the Texas Express Company, the silence had returned again. First greetings were over. Shonto and Halloran had briefly touched upon their past experiences during the War between the States, and the time had very quickly run down to that place where everyone pauses, knowing that the next words are the ones that the money is being paid for. Sheriff Casey, Agent Harter, Shonto, even little Chamaco Díaz, all were watching P. J. Halloran.

"Now, Charlie," said the latter, at last, "we haven't sent for you to review the squeaks you've been in before." He let the small grimace which may or may not have been a smile pass over his rough features. "But I did feel that some slight mention of our past associations might prepare you for the present proposal."

"What you're saying, Mister Halloran, is that you figure your Irish blarney is going to soften up my good sense." Shonto's own grin was a bit difficult to classify. It was hard as flint and yet warmed, too, somehow, by a good nature, or at least a wry appreciation of life as it actually worked out in the living. "But you're wasting your talents," he concluded. "I've had a couple of birthdays since I was crossing the Confederate lines for you, and now I don't sign up just for a pat on the back from my fellow countrymen. I've learned since the war that a man can't buy a bag of Bull Durham with a government citation. Not that I regret my time in the silent service, mind you. But a fellow just doesn't like to be a hog about the hero business. Especially when he did his great deeds for the North, then went back to earning his keep in the South. If you spend your time in Texas, Mister Halloran, you don't strain yourself reminding the local folks that you took your war pay in Union greenbacks."

Halloran nodded quickly. "Don't be a fool, Charlie," he said. "Harter, here, and Sheriff Casey were carefully sounded out before we ever mentioned your name. They are not still afire with the Lost Cause. We can forget your war work."

"I'm glad you told me, Mister Halloran. Somehow, I still remember it every so often. Matter of fact, I still occasionally wake up in a cold sweat. Now I can put all that behind me. Isn't it wonderful?"

"Shonto" — Halloran's hard face had turned cold again — "come over here to the window. I want to show you something." He took a pair of binoculars from

311

Harter's desk, and Shonto followed him to the drawn shade. There, Halloran gave the glasses to him, drew back the shade, and said quietly: "Look yonder on the balcony of the Franklin House. Tell me what you see. Describe it exactly."

From the other's tone, Shonto knew the talk had gotten to the money point. He took the glasses and focused them on the hotel's second-story *galería,* the railed porch so common to the Southwestern architecture of the times. As the view came into sharp detail, he frowned uneasily.

"All right," he began, low-voiced. "I see a man. He's short, maybe not much over five feet. He stands straight as a yardstick. Stocky build. Big in the chest. Dark as hell in the skin, near as I can say in the lamplight from the room windows behind him. He's dressed in a black Eastern suit that don't fit him, and same goes for a white iron collar and necktie. Black hat, no creases, wore square like a sombrero. Long black hair, bobbed off like it was done with horse shears." He paused, squinting more narrowly through the binoculars. "Why," he added softly, "that's a blasted Indian dressed up in white man's clothes!"

"That," said P. J. Halloran, just as softly, "is exactly what it is." They turned from the window. "Up there on that balcony," Halloran continued, "is the most important man, next to Lincoln, in North America. I can't reveal his identity, and you will have to know him as Item Thirteen, until you have him safely on that waiting train at Toltepec."

"What train at Toltepec?" Shonto frowned. "Since when have they built the Mexican Central on into that two-burro burg?"

"Since today, we hope," said Halloran. "The idea was that, precisely as you, no one knew the railroad had been laid on into Toltepec. Those last few thousand yards of track were to be spiked down today. The gamble is that not even Ortega and the *rurales* would hear about it in time. Or, hearing of it, not realize a train was waiting to be run over it."

"That's what I'd call house odds, Mister Halloran. This Item Thirteen must be one heck of a table-stakes man."

"He's one heck of a man," answered the government operative. "Anyway, Charlie, the train is supposed to be waiting at midnight in Toltepec. If we can get Item Thirteen there, the train can get on down past Camargo by daybreak and out of Ortega's reach . . . if the train's waiting in Toltepec."

"Longest two-letter word in the world," said Shonto. "Go ahead, drop the other boot."

"Well, we know that powerful enemies lie between El Paso and Toltepec. There's no point explaining to you the type of enemy I mean. I believe you're familiar enough with Colonel Ortega and his loyal militia."

"Yes, just about familiar enough. In case you're still wondering how Chamaco and I got ourselves doused in the Río, it was meeting Ortega's loyal army, or as big a part of it as I came prepared to handle. I'd say there was twenty of them. They were pot-shooting at the kid, swimming the river. He got away from them while they were murdering his father. Butterball got excited at the rifle fire and ran away with me . . . bolted right into the river. Next thing I knew, I was in as bad shape as the kid, and, long as I figured two could ride as cheap as one, I scooped him up, and we made it back to the American side by way of hanging onto Butterball's tail and holding long breaths under water on the way. I have got to get me another horse. In my business, you can't be fooling around with jumpy crowbaits like that."

"When you decide what you want for

Butterball," put in Sheriff Nocero Casey, "let me know. I've been looking for just such a *loco* horse."

"Charlie," broke in Halloran, "are you interested or not? We've got to move soon."

Shonto nodded speculatively, a man not to be rushed.

"Depends. You haven't dropped that other boot yet."

"All right." Halloran spoke quickly now. "The small man in the black suit carries a letter of credit . . . a U.S. letter of credit . . . for an enormous amount of money. Some say as high as fifty million dollars. That's fifty million U.S., not Mexican. It's to bail out his revolution down there." Halloran gestured toward the Río Grande and Mexico. "I don't need to tell you, Charlie, what men like Ortega will do to prevent that letter from getting to Mexico City. The money means the rebels are through . . . loyalists, they call themselves . . . and that the revolution will succeed and will stay in power. As you have already learned when your horse ran away with you, Colonel Ortega has been assigned the job of sealing off the border in Chihuahua State. Now, it becomes your job to unseal that border."

Charlie Shonto's grin was dry as dust.

"Shucks, nothing to that . . . nothing that I couldn't do with ten or twelve companies of rangers and a regiment of regular cavalry."

"Don't joke, Charlie." Halloran pulled out an official document and handed it to Shonto. "Here are my orders. You don't need to read them. But check that final postscript at the bottom of the page against the signature beneath the Great Seal of this country you and I fought for, when he asked us to."

Shonto glanced down the page, reading aloud slowly. " 'Any man who may aid the bearer of these orders in the business to hand will know that the gratitude of his government and my own personal indebtedness shall be his and shall not be forgotten. [Signed] A. Lincoln.' Well now," he said, handing back the document as gingerly as though it were the original of the Declaration of Independence. "Why didn't you say so, Mister Halloran?"

"Like you" — Halloran smiled, and this time there was no doubt it was a smile — "I always save my best shot for the last target. What do you say, Charlie?"

"I say, let's go. For *him* I'd wrestle a bear, blindfolded. Who all's in it?"

"Just you, Charlie. I've brought our man

this far. Sheriff Casey and Agent Harter have handled him here in town. But from here to Toltepec, he's your cargo . . . *if* you'll accept him."

Shonto winced perceptibly.

"There's that word again. You got anything extra to go with it this time?"

Halloran picked up a rolled map from Harter's desk. "Only this chart of the area between here and Toltepec supplied by the Mexican government. You know this ground as well as any man on this side of the Río Grande. Take a look at this layout of it and tell us if you spot any way at all of getting past Ortega's patrols, into Toltepec."

He spread the map on the desk. Harter turned up the wick, and the four men bent over the wrinkled parchment. Behind them, the little Indian, Chamaco Díaz, had been forgotten. He stood silently in the shadows, wondering at the talk of these Americans. Chamaco had been to school some small time in El Paso and knew enough English to follow the conversation in the rough. Lonely and sorrowful as he was, he knew who that other little Indian in the black suit was, and his heart swelled with love and pride for these American men, that they would talk of risking their lives that *el indio* might live and might reach Mexico City with the United States money which would save the *presidente*'s brave government of the *descamisados* and *pobrecitos* such as his father, Juliano Díaz, who had given their lives to establish it. Now, Chamaco watched the four big Americans bent over the map of Toltepec — his part of the beloved motherland — and he waited with held breath what the verdict of the one tall man with the dried leather face would be.

For his part, the latter was having considerable last doubts. The map wasn't showing him anything he didn't already know. Presently, he glanced up at Halloran.

"There's no help here," he said. "I was hoping to see an old Apache route I've heard stories of. But this map shows nothing that wouldn't get me and the little man in the black suit stood up against the same tree that Chamaco's daddy was stood up against. Ortega knows all these trails."

"There's nothing, then? No way at all?"

"Yes, there's that Apache brush track. It was never found by the rangers, but they know it exists. They've run the Chihuahua Apaches right to the river, time and again, then seen them vanish like smoke into midnight air. If we knew where that trail went over the Río, we might have a coyote's chance of sneaking past Ortega's assassins." Shonto shook his head. "But there isn't a white man alive who knows that Apache track. . . ."

His words trailed off helplessly, and the four men straightened with that weary stiffness which foretells defeat. But into their glum silence a small voice, and forgotten, penetrated thinly.

"*Señores,* I am not a white man."

Shonto and his companions wheeled about. Chamaco moved out of the shadows into the lamplight.

"I am an Indian," he said, "and I know where the old trail runs."

The four men exchanged startled looks, and, in their momentary inability to speak, Chamaco thought that he detected reproof for his temerity in coming forward in the company of such powerful friends of Mexico. He bowed with apologetic humility and stepped back into the shadows.

"But of course," he said, small-voiced, "you would not trust to follow an Indian. Excuse me, *señores.*"

Shonto moved to his side. He put his hand to the thin shoulder. Telling the boy to follow him, he led the way to the office window. He held back the drawn shade while Chamaco, obeying him, peered down the street at the Franklin House.

"Boy," he said, "do you know who that small man is standing up there on the hotel balcony?"

Chamaco's eyes glowed with the fire of his pride. "Yes, *patrón!*" he cried excitedly. "It is *he!* Who else could stand and look so sad and grand across the river?"

Shonto nodded. "You think *he* would trust an Indian boy?"

Chamaco drew himself up to his full four feet and perhaps five inches. In his reply was all the dignity of the poor. "*Patrón,*" he said, "he once *was* an Indian boy!"

Charlie Shonto nodded again. He tightened the arm about the boy's shoulders and turned to face the others. "Don't know about you," he said to them, "but I've just hired me an Indian guide to Toltepec."

The men at the desk said nothing, and again Chamaco misinterpreted their hesitation.

"*Patrón,*" he said to Charlie Shonto, "do *you* know who it is up there standing on the *galería* looking so sad toward Mexico?"

"I could take an uneducated guess," answered Shonto, "but I won't. You see,

Chamaco, I'm not supposed to know. He's just a job to me. It doesn't matter who he is."

The Indian boy was astounded. It passed his limited comprehension.

"And you would risk your life for a stranger to you?" he asked, unbelievingly. "For an Indian in a rumpled white man's suit? A small funny-looking man with a foreign hat and long hair and a dark skin the same as mine? You would do this, *patrón,* and for nothing?"

Shonto grinned and patted him on the head.

"Well, hardly for nothing, boy."

"For what, then, *patrón?*"

"Money, boy. *Pesos. Muchos pesos.*"

"And only for that, *patrón?*"

At the persistence, Shonto's cynical grin faded. He made a small, deprecatory gesture. It was for Chamaco alone; he had forgotten the others.

"Let's just say that I was watching your face when you looked up at that hotel balcony a minute ago. All right, *amigo?*"

The dark eyes of Chamaco Díaz lit up like altar candles.

"*Patrón,*" he said, "you should have been an Indian, you have eyes in your heart!"

Shonto grinned ruefully. "Something

tells me, boy, that before we get our cargo past Ortega tonight we'll be wishing I had those eyes in the back of my head."

Chamaco reached up and took the gunman's big hand. He patted it reassuringly. "*Patrón*" — he smiled back — "do not be afraid. If we die, we die in a good and just cause. We lose only our two small lives. Him, up there on the *galería*, he has in his hands the lives of all of the poor people of Mexico. Is that not a very fair exchange, our lives for all of those others, and for his?"

Shonto glanced at the other men. "Well, Chamaco," he said, "that's one way of looking at it. Excuse us, gentlemen . . . we've got a train to catch in Toltepec."

He took the boy's hand in his, and they went out into the street. Halloran moved to follow them. At the door he halted a moment, shaking his head as he looked back at the express agent and the sheriff.

"Do you know what we've just done?" he said. "We've just bet fifty million dollars and the future of Mexico on a Chihuahua Indian kid not one of us ever laid eyes on prior to twenty minutes ago. I need a drink!"

The coach bounced and swayed through

the night. Its sidelamps, almost never lit, were now sputtering and smoking. They seemed to declare that this particular old Concord wanted to be certain her passage toward the lower ford would be noted from the far side — and followed.

The idea was valid.

The lower crossing, the old Apache route, was the way in which a mind of no great deception might seek to elude examination by the *rurales* at the upper, or main, crossing. The driver of the old Texas Express vehicle, a canvas-topped Celerity model made for desert speed, held the unalterable belief that the Mexican mind was so devious as to be very nearly simple. It twisted around so many times in its tracks, trying to be clever, that in the end it usually wound up coming right back where it started.

The driver was banking on this trait. He was depending on Colonel Fulgencio Ortega to think that, when the planted rumor from El Paso reached him by avenue of his kinsmen in that city, he would say: "Aha! This stupid American stageline company thinks that, if they announce they will try to cross with *el indio* at the old lower ford, I shall at once conclude they really mean to cross at the new upper ford, and that I shall then be waiting for them at the new upper ford, and they can cross in safety at the lower place. What fools! I shall quite naturally watch both crossings, and this they realize full well. What they are trying to do is see that I, personally, am not at the lower ford. They think that if they can contest the crossing with my men . . . without me . . . it will be a far easier matter. Well, now! *¡Ai, Chihuahua!* Let them come. Let them find out who will be waiting for their disreputable stagecoach and its mysterious passenger at the old lower ford! Hah! Why will they attempt to match wits with the Executioner of Camargo?"

Of course, if Colonel Ortega did not reason thus, the driver of the coach would have made a grievous error, for the entire plan depended on meeting the Executioner. The driver, a weather-beaten, leathery fellow, wrapped the lines of the four-horse hitch a bit tighter. He spoke to his leaders and his wheelers, tickling the ears of the former and the haunches of the latter with the tip of his fifteen-foot coaching whip.

"*Coo-ee,* boys!" he called to the horses. "Just so, just so." Leaning over the box, he spoke to the muffled, dark-faced passenger

— the only passenger — in the rocking stage. "*Señor,* it is all well with you in there?" He used the Spanish tongue, but no reply came in kind from the interior. Indeed, no reply came in any tongue.

A very brave fellow, thought the driver. His kind were not many in the land below the Río — or any land.

"You are a very small boy," said the somber-looking little man. "How is it that you are so brave?"

"Please, *presidente.* I beg of you not to say more, just now. We are very near to the place, and there is great danger." Chamaco spoke with awed diffidence.

"I am not afraid, boy." *El indio* patted him on the shoulder. "Do I not have a good Indian guide?"

"*Presidente,* please, say no more. You don't know Colonel Ortega."

"I have dealt with his kind. I know him, all right. They are all alike. Cowards. Jackals. Don't be afraid, boy. What did you say your name was?"

Chamaco told him, and the small man nodded.

"A good Indian name. It means what it says. How much farther now, boy, before we cross the river?"

They were moving on foot through a tunneled avenue in the river's brushy scrub of willow and rushes. It was the sort of thoroughfare frequented by the creatures of the night. None but very small men — or boys — might have used it at all, and then only very small Indian men or boys. If the rangers had wanted to know one reason, just one, why the Apaches raiding up from Chihuahua had been able to disappear before their eyes on the American side of the Río, it would have been that they were seeking some hole in the brush which would accommodate an ordinary mortal, not a Chihuahua Indian. But Chamaco Díaz was not alone a small Indian boy, he was a patriot.

"*Presidente*," he now pleaded, "will you not be quiet? *¡Por favor, excelencia!* We are coming to it this moment."

The small man in the black suit smiled. "You dare to address me in this abrupt manner!" he said. "You, an Indian boy? A shirtless waif of the border? A brush rat of the river bottom? *¡Ai!*"

"*Presidente*," said the boy, "I will ask it one more time. I know that you do not fear the Executioner. I know that I am only a *pobrecito*, a *reducido*, a nothing. But in my heart you live with the Lord Jesus. I will die for you, *presidente,* as I would for Him, even sooner. But I have sworn to guide you across the river and to the rendezvous. I have sworn to get you to Toltepec by midnight this night. Therefore, why should we die, when you must live for the people of our suffering land? I am taking you to Toltepec, *presidente.* And if you continue to speak along the way, I will die for nothing, and Mexico will never get the money you bear, and she will not be saved. But mostly, *presidente,* you will be dead. I cannot bear that. You are the life of all of us."

They had stopped moving. *El indio,* in a streak of moonlight penetrating the arched limbs above them, could see the tears coursing down the dark cheeks of Chamaco Díaz. He reached quickly with his fingers and brushed away the tears.

"An Indian does not weep," he told the boy sternly. "Go ahead, now. I shall be still."

Chamaco swallowed hard. He dashed his own hand quickly at the offending eyes. His voice was vibrant with pride. "It was the brush, *presidente,* the small limbs snapping back and stinging me across the face. You know how it is."

El indio nodded once more. "Of course, boy. I have been in the brush many times.

Go ahead, show the way. I have been an old woman, talking too much. We are both Indians, eh? Lead on."

Straight as a rifle barrel, Chamaco Díaz stood before him a moment. Then, ducking down again, he scuttled on ahead. *El indio* watched him go. Just before he bent to follow, he glanced up at the patch of moonlight. The beams struck his own dark face. They glistened on something which seemed to be moist and moving upon his own coffee-colored features. But then, of course, in moonlight the illusions are many, and the lunar eye is not to be trusted. Had he not just said himself that Indians did not weep?

The coach of the Texas Express Company splashed over the old Apache Crossing and came to a halt before the flaring bonfire and wooden barricade across the Toltepec road.

"*¿Qué pasa?*" the tall driver called down to the leering brigand who commanded the guard. "What is the matter? Why do you stop me?"

"*De nada.* It is nothing." Lieutenant Chivo smiled. "A small matter which will take but a moment. I hope you have a moment. *Yes? Very well. Colonel,*" he called to the squat officer drinking coffee by the fireside, "the stage for Toltepec has arrived on time."

The colonel put down his tin cup and picked up a long quirt. Uncoiling the whip, he arose and came over to the barricade. He stood looking up at the coachman. After a moment, he nodded pleasantly enough and spoke in a friendly manner.

"Please to get down," he said.

"Sorry, I can't do it," replied the driver. "Company rules, Colonel. You understand."

"Of course," said the guerrilla chief easily. "Without rules nothing is accomplished. I'm a great believer in discipline. Did I introduce myself? Colonel Fulgencio Ortega, of Camargo. Now do you care to get down?"

"*The* Colonel Ortega?" said the American driver, impressed. "*Jefe*, this a great honor. And these are your famed *rurales*?" He pointed with unqualified admiration to the surly pack stalking up, now, to stand behind the colonel and his lieutenant. "My, but they are a fine-looking troop. Real fighters, one can see that. But then, why not? On the side of justice all men fight well, eh, Colonel?"

Ortega ignored the compliments. "Did

you hear what I said?" he asked. "I wish you to get down. I do not believe I have met your passenger, and I think you should introduce me to him. My men will hold your horses."

His men were already holding the horses, as the driver was keenly aware. Also, he did not miss the fact the soldiers were holding something else for him — their rifles, pointed squarely at him. But he was the steady sort, or perhaps merely stupid.

"Passenger?" he said. "I carry no passenger, Colonel. Just some freight for Toltepec."

Ortega stepped back. He looked again into the coach.

"Freight, eh?" he mused. "Strange wrappings you have put around your cargo, *cochero*. A black suit. Black hat with round Indian crown worn squarely on the head. And see how your freight sits on the seat of the coach, just as if it were alive and had two arms and two legs and might speak if spoken to. That is, if fear has not sealed its cowardly Indian tongue!" His voice was suddenly wicked with hatred, all the smile and the pretense of easiness gone out of it — and out of him. "Chivo!" he snapped. "Please to open the door of this coach and help *el presidente* to dismount!"

The stage driver straightened on the box.

"*¿El presidente?*" he said to Ortega. "Whatever in the world are you talking about, *jefe?*"

"We shall see in a moment." Ortega nodded, in control of himself once more. "Hurry, Chivo. This *cochero* does not understand the importance of his passenger. Nor is it apparent to him that jokes about 'freight' which walks and talks like an Indian are not laughed at in Chihuahua just now. *¡Adelante!* Get that coach door opened, you fool!"

Chivo, grinning as only a dog wolf about to soil the signpost of his rival may grin, threw open the door of the Concord and seized the lone passenger by the arm. With a foul-mouthed oath, he pulled the small figure from the coach and hurled it viciously to the ground.

His surprise was understandable. It is not the usual thing for a victim's arm to come off at the shoulder and remain in the offending hand of its assaulter while the remainder of the torso goes flying off through the night. Neither was it the usual thing for the poor devil's head to snap off and go rolling away like a melon when the

331

body thudded to earth.

"*¡Santísima!*" cried one of the brute soldiers of the guard. "You have ruined him, you dumb animal!"

But Lieutenant Chivo did not hear the remark, and Colonel Ortega, if he heard it, did not agree with the sentiment, except perhaps as to Chivo's intelligence. For what the guerrilla lieutenant had pulled from the Texas Express Company's Toltepec stage was quite clearly a dressmaker's dummy, clothed to resemble a very short and large-chested Mexican Indian man who always sat straight on his seat and wore his black hat squarely on his head.

Moreover, Colonel Fulgencio Ortega was given no real time in which to comment upon his soldier's awed remark or his lieutenant's amazed reaction to the arm in his hand and the head rolling free upon the fire-lit bank of the Río Grande. For in the small moment of stricken dumbness which had invaded all of them when *el presidente*'s body had come apart in mid-air, the American driver of the Toltepec stage had wrapped the lines of his four-horse hitch, stepped to the ground in one giant stride from the precarious box of the old Concord, and all in the same motion slid out a long-barreled Colt revolver and buried its iron snout in the

332

belly of the Executioner of Camargo.

"*Jefe*," he announced quietly. "if you make one false movement, your bowels will be blown out all over this riverbank."

This statement Colonel Fulgencio Ortega had no difficulty whatever in comprehending. "Chivo!" he cried out. "In the name of *Madre María,* hold the men. Let no one touch a trigger!"

"Yes, Chivo." The leather-faced American *cochero* nodded, spinning Ortega around so that the muzzle of the Colt was in his spine. "And so that you do not in greed seek to replace your beloved *jefe* in command of the *rurales* of Camargo . . . that is to say, that you do not in this moment of seeming opportunity make some move deliberately to get me to shoot him . . . permit me to introduce myself."

"Ah?" queried Chivo, who truly had not yet thought of this obvious course of treachery to his leader. "And to what point would this be, *cochero?* Do you think that I am in fear of stagecoach drivers?"

The tall driver shrugged. "Well, I think you ought to have the same break I give any other man I'm paid to get past."

There was something in the way that he spoke the one word *paid* that penetrated Chivo's wily mind. He hesitated, but two of the soldiers did not. Thinking that they stood well enough behind their companions to be safe, they moved a little aside from the pack to get a line of fire at the big American. The instant they were clear of their friends, however, flame burst from behind the back of Colonel Ortega — one lancing flash, then another — and the two soldiers were down and dying in the same blending roar of pistol shots.

"Shonto," said the stage driver to Chivo, the smoking muzzle of the Colt again in Ortega's spine. "Over there across the river, they call me Shonto."

"*Madre María*," breathed Chivo, dropping his rifle, unbidden, into the dirt of the wagon road. "Carlos Shonto? *Por Dios, pistolero,* why didn't you say so?"

"I just did." Charlie Shonto nodded. "Now you better say something. Quick."

Chivo shrugged in that all-meaning way of his kind. "What remains to die for?" he inquired. "You do not have *el indio* in the stage. You have fooled us with the dummy on the ground over there. Somewhere, *el presidente* is no doubt riding through the night. But it is not upon the stage for Toltepec. Another of our guards will get him. For us, the work of the day is over. Command me."

Shonto then ordered all the soldiers to drop their rifles and cartridge bandoleers. All knives, pistols, axes went into the common pile. This arsenal was then loaded into the stage along with Colonel Fulgencio Ortega, bound hand and foot by his faithful followers. The work went forward under Chivo's expert direction, the spirit of the *rurales* now totally flagged. With their chances of snaring *el indio* had gone their interest in being heroes. Like soldiers everywhere, they were of no great menace in themselves. Deprived of leadership, they were just so many surly dogs, quarreling among themselves. Shonto had gambled on this, and gambled exceedingly well.

Yet, as in every risk, there lurks the element of the unknown, the thing that cannot be depended upon except in the name of luck. Shonto's luck ran out with the command he now issued to the scarfaced Chivo.

"All right, Lieutenant," he said. "Up you go. You'll be the *cochero* now. I'll ride shotgun. You savvy *la escopeta?*" With the question, he reached for the double-barreled Parker laid across the driver's box, and Chivo nodded hastily. He savvied shotguns very well. One did not argue with them at close range, not ever. But Shonto had made his basic mistake some time ago, when he had put the thought of succeeding to Ortega's place of power in Camargo in the mind of the brutal lieutenant. Such towering aspirations had never flooded his dark brain. True, he would have seen Ortega killed in a moment, should that suit his purpose. This much was exactly what Shonto had guessed. What the wary gunman had not foreseen, however, was that, until he, Shonto, had mentioned the matter, Chivo had never really thought about the possibility of promoting himself over his colonel.

Now the prospect inflamed his jackal's mind.

"Whatever you say, *jefe,*" he told Shonto, fanging a smirk which the latter hardly supposed was a grin of good nature. "You see, I climb to the seat gladly. I take the lines and am ready to drive for you. Come on. Let's go."

Shonto started to swing up after him. For one moment both hands were occupied. It was in that moment that the boot of Lieutenant Chivo drove into his face. Shonto fell backward, landing hard. The shotgun was still in his grasp but was useless from that angle. Above him, Chivo was shouting the horses into motion. The coach lurched forward. Shonto made it to his feet in time to leap for the trunk straps in the rear. He caught one of them, held on, and dragged behind the moving stage for fifty feet. He still had the shotgun in his right hand.

The soldiers, sensing his helplessness, ran toward him. They seized clubs and picked up rocks on the run. Chivo, in response to their yells, slowed the stage, thinking to allow them to beat and stone the dragging American.

Shonto held onto the trunk strap. When the snarling soldiers were near, he raised the shotgun and fired it with one hand into their faces. The first barrel and the second blasted as one. The soldiers fell away, three to stagger and fall mortally wounded, two others clutching at their shredded faces, screaming in the agony of the immediate torture and the knowledge, even in their terrible pain, that they would never use their eyes again.

Chivo, on the driver's box, turned in time to see Shonto haul himself up over the rear of the Concord. He had no weapon, now, but neither did the *rurale* lieutenant.

Chivo knew the one way open to him and took it. Over the side he went, rolling to the ground and free of the speeding wheels, the excited teams running wild the moment he flung away the lines. Shonto, weaving precariously, made it to the driver's box and threw himself down between the straining horses to recover the lines.

His luck now returned. He was able to gather up the lines and return to the box, the coach under control and still upright on the wagon road to Toltepec. But now he knew the wolf pack behind him had a leader again. He could guess how long it would take Chivo to mount the survivors and take up the pursuit.

"*Coo-ee, coo-ee,*" he called to the snorting team. "Steady down, you beauties. You've not begun your night's work yet. Save that pep and vim for the last lap."

Where he had said he would be waiting beside the wagon road to Toltepec with *el presidente,* there Chamaco Díaz waited when, half an hour's loping run from the Río, Shonto pulled up his panting horses and hailed the underbrush. The Indian boy had guided his charge without fail and on foot through the night and between the prowling soldiers of Colonel Ortega four miles south of the river. The ancient and secret Apache escape route from Texas, which the two had traveled to reach their rendezvous with Charlie Shonto and the stage for Toltepec, lay still unknown behind them. Shonto did not ask Chamaco where it ran, and the boy did not tell him. He was an Indian, even now, and Charlie Shonto was a white man.

Swiftly, then, the last part of the plan was put into operation. The four horses were unhooked from the coach. Four saddles and bridles were brought from the coach trunk, and the mounts were readied. Colonel Ortega was removed from the stage and hung over the saddle of one mount in the manner of a sack of grain. Shonto tied his hands to his feet under the horse's belly, halfway hoping the ropes would not hold. Where the rutted track of the road bent to go past the rendezvous, an eighty-foot bluff rose above the Chihuahua plain. Over this drop, Shonto and his two Indian friends now tossed the Concord's load of firearms. There was no time for more effective disposal. Mounting up, the party set out, away from the road, Chamaco leading, Shonto bringing up the rear with the pack horse of the Executioner of Camargo. The goat path along which the small Indian boy took them disappeared into the desert brush within a pistol shot from the wagon road. Shonto had no more idea where the trail led than did Ortega or *el presidente*. No options remained in any event. Behind them, along the road from the river, they heard now the shouts of men of Mexican tongue and the hammer of horses' hoofs in considerable number. In a pause to listen, they all recognized the high yelping tones of Lieutenant Chivo, discovering the abandoned stage and guessing, amid a goat's beard of rotten curses, the manner of flight of his enemies. And more: from Chivo's murderous bleats, they made out that he had with him another patrol of Ortega's *rurales*, evidently encountered along the way. These new soldiers, whatever their number, would be armed and were clearly being commanded by the colonel's good lieutenant. All might still have been well — yes, surely would have been so — considering the depth of the brush land and the blindness of its cover. But in the press of time and because he had not thought ahead to the complication of Chivo's picking up more arms *en route*, Shonto had not taken the precaution he ordinarily would have of gagging the captive colonel.

He thought of it, now, as Ortega's galling

shout echoed down the slope they were climbing.

"*¡Aquí, aquí, muchachos!* I am here! I am here!"

His head was hanging on that side of the horse nearest Shonto. The shout for help was cut off by the toe of the gunman's boot knocking out four front teeth and knocking out, too, the owner of the teeth. But the price of poker had just gone up, regardless.

"Chamaco," he said, "we have one chance . . . to split up."

"Never, *patrón.*"

"Listen, kid" — Shonto's voice went hard as quartz — "you do what I tell you. I'm running this show."

"No, my American friend, you are not." The denial did not come from the boy but from the small man in the black suit. "It is I who must say what will be. And I say we stay together. You are not with Spaniards, my friend. You are not with traitors who call themselves Mexicans. You are with Indians. Lead on, boy."

Shonto knew he was helpless. He knew, as well, that they were helpless, that it would be but a matter of minutes before the *rurales* would come up to them, blind brush or not. They were so close behind that they could follow by ear the sounds of

341

the stagecoach horses, breaking through the brush. The rifle firing would commence any moment, and a bullet, unaimed except by the noise of their ponies crashing ahead, would soon enough find all and each of them. There was no other end within reason.

Yet Chamaco Díaz was no victim of such knowledge. He had been supported by his *presidente,* had heard him with his own ears say: "You are with Indians." What was not possible in the service of such a man?

"Patrón!" he now called to Shonto, voice high and sharp with excitement. "There is a way. Follow me, and don't worry about making noise. The rangers from your Texas side of the river did not always obey the law!"

Their horses were plowing on up the slope now, and true to Shonto's fear the guerrillas were beginning to fire blindly at the sound of their progress. The bullets hissed and sung about them. But the boy's shout had intrigued Charlie Shonto.

"What's that?" he yelled back.

"The rangers of Texas," answered the boy, laughing for the first time in Shonto's memory of him. "Many times they would run the Apaches right on across the river, *patrón.* Then the Apaches had to have a

342

way on this side to lose them. I know the way, *patrón*. Ride hard and jump your horse when I demand it."

Shonto wanted to know more about that "jump" business, but the guerrillas were too close now. All he could do was bend low in the saddle and hope the bullet with his name on it went astray. It did. They came to Chamaco's jumping place without a wound. The place itself was a declivity in the trail — dug by hand in centuries gone — where no rider, not knowing that it waited beyond the steeply descending hairpin turn which hid it from above, could ever lift his mount over it in time. The animal's momentum, coming down the roof-steep pitch of the decline, would have to carry it and its rider into the "ranger trap." And this is the way that it worked with the eager *rurales* of Chivo. All of the horses of Chamaco's party, even the pack horse with Colonel Ortega's unconscious form, cleared the break in the trail, leaping it like deer because spurred to the effort by their desperate riders. But the mounts of the guerrillas, scrambling around the hairpin, snorting furiously under the urging of their savage masters — the scent of the kill hot in the nostrils now, so close were they — had no chance to see or to lift themselves and their riders over the yawning pit. Into the waiting blackness of the man-made chasm the first dozen horses and soldiers went screaming and kicking. Another dozen soldiers and their mounts piled up in the trail above and did not plunge into the abyss with the others. But neither did they seem to retain their previous eagerness for the blood of *el presidente* and the elevation of Lieutenant Chivo to the rank of Executioner of Camargo.

As for Chivo himself, Shonto never knew if he was among the first group of riders, or the second. All that he did know was that, following the first spate of screamings from the fallen, he did not hear again the harsh, yelping voice of the bearded lieutenant.

"*¡Madre!* Chamaco," he said to the Indian boy, in the first moment of stillness following the piteous cries from above, "what is in that Apache trench up there?"

"Tiger's teeth," said the youth, "their points burned to hardness of iron, their butts set in the cracks of the mother rock. I don't wonder at the screams, *patrón.* I've looked down in that hole."

"*¡Santísima!*" breathed Shonto. "A staked pit!"

"For a pack of animals, the death of a pack of animals." The Oaxacan accents of *el presidente* seemed sad. "Let us go on and catch that train in Toltepec. There is so much work to do in Mexico. The people cry out to me, and there is little time, so little time, for me to answer them."

Shonto did not answer, feeling the moment belonged to another. Chamaco understood the courtesy.

"Yes, *presidente*," he said softly. "Please to follow your humble servant."

At once the small man in the black suit spurred his horse up beside that of the Chihuahua Indian boy.

"You are no one's humble servant," he said sternly. "Remember that always. You are a citizen of Mexico, a free man, humble to no one. If you believe in a god, you can thank him for that. If you believe in a man, you can thank a man."

"Yes, *presidente*, I thank you *and* God."

"In that order, eh, boy?" A trace of warm amusement crossed the dark Indian features. "But you are wrong about the man, *muchacho*. It is another *presidente* whom I charge you to remember. See that you don't forget his name, citizen. You owe it your life. Burn it in your mind, if you are a true Mexican . . . Abraham Lincoln."

It was all downhill from there. Some

minutes short of midnight, Shonto rode into Toltepec with his charges. By a quarter past the hour, Item Thirteen was aboard the waiting train. Steam being up and the dawn all too near, the parting was abrupt. Camargo must be run past in the dark. Also, for the benefit of good health, those who must remain behind when the train pulled out would do well to be drawing in American air come sunrise of that risky day. *El presidente,* surrounded by his faithful guard aboard the train, was virtually taken away from Shonto and Chamaco. So, as well, was the one-time Executioner of Camargo. In a last-second view, *el presidente* seemed to spy the tall American and the tiny Indian boy, sitting their horses in the lamplight spilling from his car's window. Shonto and Chamaco thought they saw him wave to them, and they returned the wave, each with his own thoughts. If the Texas gunman saw the bright tears streaming down the dark cheeks of Chamaco Díaz, he said nothing of the matter, then or later. Each man was permitted his own manner of farewell. But when the train had pulled away from Toltepec — before, even, its smoke had trailed into the Chihuahua night behind it — Charlie Shonto knew all he ever cared to know of the ending of the story. His big hand reached through the dark to touch the knee of his companion.

"Come along, Chamaco," he said. "We had better make long tracks. It's forty-nine miles to the river."

The boy nodded obediently, saying nothing. They turned their horses and sent them into a weary lope.

As they rode, Shonto's rawhide features softened. He was watching the proud set of the thin figure riding by his side. He was aware, surely, that the small Indian man in the ill-fitting black suit had been Benito Juárez, the liberator of Mexico, his people's Abraham Lincoln. But that part of it did not impress the big gunman unduly. For Charlie Shonto, the biggest Indian he saw that night was always a little Chihuahua boy who barely reached to his gun belt. History would not record, Shonto suspected, the secret fact that Juárez had been spirited to Washington, D. C. History would never record, he knew certainly, the added fact of the strange manner in which the legendary *el indio* had been returned safely to his native land. But Charlie Shonto and Texas Express would know the way that it was done, and so would the tallest Indian in all of Toltepec.

When he thought of that, somehow even Charlie Shonto felt better. As the shadows of the Toltepec hills closed behind them, he was sitting as straight in the saddle as Chamaco Díaz.

But, of course, not as tall.

The Streets of Laredo

Call him McComas. Drifter, cowboy, card-sharp, killer. A man already on the road back from nowhere. Texas of the time was full of him and his kind. And sick with the fullness.

McComas had never been in Laredo. But his shadows, many of them, had been there before him. He knew what to expect from the townsfolk, when they saw him coming on, black and weedy and beard-grown, against the late afternoon sun. They would not want him in their town, and McComas could not blame them. Yet he was tired, very tired, and had come a long, tense way that day.

He steeled himself to take their looks and to turn them away as best he might. What he wanted was a clean bed, a tub bath, a hotel meal, and a short night's sleep. No women, no cards, no whiskey. Just six hours with the shades drawn and no one knocking at the door. Then, God willing, he would be up in the blackness before the dawn. Up and long gone and safe over the border in Nuevo León, old Mexico, when that Encinal sheriff showed up to begin asking questions of the law in Laredo. The very last thing he wanted in Texas was trouble. But that was the very last thing he had ever wanted in any place, and the very first he had always gotten. In Laredo it started as it always started, everywhere, with a woman.

Still, this time it was different. This time it was like no trouble which had ever come to him before. Somehow, he knew it. He sensed it before his trim gelding, Coaly, set hoof in the streets of Laredo.

Those border towns were all laid out alike. Flat as a dropped flapjack. One wide street down the middle, running from sagebrush on one end to the river on the other. Some frame shacks and adobes flung around in the mesquite and catclaw, out where the decent people did not have to look at them. Then, the false fronts lining the main street. And, feeding off that, half a dozen dirt alleys, lying in two lines on either side like pigs suckling a sow asleep in the sun. After these, there were only the church, school, and cemetery. It was the last place, clinging on the dry-hill flanks of town, where the land was even too poor for the Mexican shacks, that McComas and Coaly were presently coming to.

It lay to their left, and there was a burying party moving out from town, as they moved in. McComas had to pull Coaly off the road to let the procession pass. For some reason he felt strange, and hung there to watch the little party. It was then he saw the girl.

She was young and slim, with a black Spanish *rebozo* covering her head. As the buggy in which she was riding with the frock-coated parson drew abreast of McComas, she turned and stared directly at him. But the late sun was in his eyes, and he could not see her features. Then, they were gone on, leaving McComas with a peculiar, unpleasant feeling. He shook as to a chill. Then, steadied himself. It was no mystery that the sight had unsettled him. It was a funeral, and he had never liked funerals.

They always made him wonder, though. Who was it in the coffin? Was it a man or woman? Had they died peaceful or violent? What had they done wrong, or right? Would he, or she, be missed by friends, mourned by family, made over in the local newspaper, maybe even mentioned in the San Antonio and Austin City papers?

No, he decided. Not this one. There were no family and friends here. That girl, riding in the preacher's rig, wasn't anybody's sister. She just didn't have the look. And the two roughly dressed Mexican laborers, sitting on the coffin in the wagon ahead of the buggy, were certainly not kith or kin of the deceased. Neither was the seedy driver. As for the square-built man on the sorrel mare, heading up the procession, he did not need the pewter star pinned on his vest to tag him for McComas. The latter could tell a deputy sheriff as far as he could see one, late sun in the eyes, or not.

The deputy could tell McComas, too. And he gave him a hard looking-over as he rode by. They exchanged the usual nods, careful and correct, and the deputy rode on, as any wise deputy would. Directly, he led the buggy and the wagon into the weed-grown gate of the cemetery, and creaking up the rise to a plot on the crown of the hill. There, the drivers halted their horses, let down their cargoes. Still, McComas watched from below.

The two Mexicans strained with the coffin. It was a long coffin, and heavy. A man,

McComas thought. A young man, and standing tall. One who had been taken quick, with no warning, and not long ago. No, this was no honored citizen they were putting under. Honored citizens do not come to boothill in the late afternoon with the town deputy, riding shotgun over the ceremony. Or with only a lantern-jawed, poor-bones preacher and a leggy young girl in a black Mexican shawl for mourners. Not by considerable.

McComas might even know the man in that coffin. If he did not, he could describe him perilously close. All he had to do was find the nearest mirror and look into it.

Again, he shivered. And again controlled himself.

He was only tired and worn down. It was only the way he felt about funerals. He always felt dark in his mind, when he saw a body going by. And who didn't, if they would be honest enough to admit it? Nobody likes to look at a coffin, even empty. When there is somebody in it and being hauled dead-march slow with the wagon, sounding creaky, and the people not talking, and the cemetery gates, waiting rusty and half-sagged just down the road, a man does not need to be on the dodge and nearly drunk from want of sleep to take a chill and to turn away and ride on, feeling sad and afraid inside.

In town, McComas followed his usual line. He took a room at the best hotel, knowing that the first place the local law will look for a man is in the second- and third-rate fleatraps where the average fugitive will hole up. Laredo was a chancy place. A funnel through which poured the scum of bad ones down into old Mexico. If a man did not care to be skimmed off with the others of that outlaw dross, he had to play it differently than they did. He didn't skulk. He rode in bold as brass and bought the best. Like McComas and Coaly and the Border Star Hotel.

But, once safely in his room, McComas could not rest. He only paced the floor and peeked continually past the drawn shade down into the sun haze of the main street. It was perhaps half an hour after signing the register that he gave it up and went downstairs for just one drink. Twenty minutes more and he was elbows down on the bar of the Ben-Hur Saloon with the girl.

Well, she was not a girl, really. Not any longer. Young, yes. And nicely shaped. But how long did a girl stay a girl at the Laredo prices? She was like McComas. Short on the calendar count, long on the lines at mouth and eye corners. If he had been there and back, she had made the trip ahead of him. Pretty? Not actually. Yet that face would haunt a man. McComas knew the kind. He had seen them in every town. Sometimes going by in the young dusk on the arm of an overdressed swell — through a dusty train window at the dépôt — passing, perfume-close, in the darkened hall of a cheap hotel. Not pretty. No, not ever pretty. But always exciting, sensuous, female, and available, yours for the night, if you could beat the other fellow to them.

Billie Blossom was that kind.

Her real name? McComas did not care. She accepted McComas; he did not argue Billie Blossom.

She came swinging up to him at the bar, out of the nowhere of blue cigar smoke which hid the poker tables and the dance floor and the doleful piano player with his two-fingered, tinkly, sad chorus of "Jeannie with the Light Brown Hair." She held his eyes a long, slow moment, then smiled: "Hello, cowboy, you want to buy me a drink before you swim the river?"

He stared back at her an equal long, slow moment, and said: "Lady, for a smile like that I might even get an honest job and go to work."

That was the start of it.

They got a bottle and glasses from the barman, moved off through the smoke, McComas following her. She had her own table, a good one, in the rear corner with no windows and facing the street doors. They sat down, McComas pouring. She put her fingers on his hand, when he had gotten her glass no more than damp. And, again, there was that smile shaking him to his boot tops.

"A short drink for a long road, cowboy," she said.

He glanced at her with quick suspicion, but she had meant nothing by it.

"Yes," he nodded, "I reckon that's right," and poured his own drink to match hers. "Here's to us," he said, lifting the glass. "Been everywhere but hell, and not wanting to rush that."

She smiled, and they drank the whiskey, neither of them reacting to its raw bite. They sat there, then, McComas looking at her.

She was an ash blonde with smoky gray eyes. She had high cheekbones, a wide mouth, wore entirely too much paint and powder. But always there was that half curve of a smile to soften everything. Everything except the cough. McComas knew that hollow sound. The girl had consumption, and badly. He could see where the sickness had cut the flesh from her, leaving its pale hollows where the lush curves had been. Yet, despite the pallor and the wasted form, she seemed lovely to McComas.

He did not think to touch her, or to invite her to go upstairs, and she thanked him with her eyes. They were like a young boy and girl — he not seeing her, she not seeing him, but each seeing what used to be, or might have been, or, luck willing, still might be.

McComas would not have believed that it could happen. Not to him. But it did. To him and Billie Blossom in the Ben-Hur Saloon in Laredo, Texas. They had the bottle and they had the sheltered corner and they were both weary of dodging and turning away and of not being able to look straight back at honest men and women or to close their eyes and sleep nights, when they lay down and tried to do so. No-name McComas and faded Billie Blossom. Outlawed killer, dance-hall trollop. In love at first sight and trying desperately hard to find the words to tell each other so. Two hunted people locking tired eyes and trembling hands over a bareboard table and two unwashed whiskey tumblers in a flyblown *cantina* at sundown of a hell's hot summer day, two miles and ten minutes easy lope from freedom and safety and a second beckoning chance in old Mexico, across the shallow Río Grande.

Fools they were, and lost sheep.

But, oh! that stolen hour at sunset in that smoke-filled, evil-smelling room. What things they said, what vows they made, what wild sweet promises they swore! It was not the whiskey. After the first, small drink, the second went untasted. McComas and Billie Blossom talked on, not heeding the noise and coarseness about them, forgetting who they were, and where. Others, telling of their loves, might remember scented dark parlors. Or a gilding of moonlight on flowered verandahs. Or the fragrance of new-mown hay by the riverside. Or the fireflies in the loamy stardust of the summer lane. For McComas and Billie Blossom it was the rank odor of charcoal whiskey, the choke of stogie cigars, the reek of bathless men, and perspiring, sacheted women.

McComas did not begrudge the lack. He had Billie's blue eyes for his starry lane, her smile for his summer night. He needed no dark parlors, no willow-shaded streams. He and Billie had each other. And they had their plans.

The piano played on. It was the same tune about Jeannie and her light brown hair. McComas feared for a moment that he might show a tear, or a tremble in his voice. The song was that beautiful, and that close to what he and Billie were feeling, that neither could speak, but only sit with their hands clasped across that old beer-stained table in the Ben-Hur Saloon, making their silence count more than any words. Then, McComas found his voice. As he talked, Billie nodded, yes, to everything he said, the tears glistening beneath the long, black lashes which swept so low and thickly curled across her slanted cheekbones. She was crying because of her happiness, McComas knew, and his words rushed on, deeply, recklessly excited.

He did not remember all that he told her, only the salient, pressing features of it: that they would meet beyond the river, when darkness fell; that they would go down into Nuevo León, to a place McComas knew, where the grass grew long and the water ran sweet and a man could raise the finest cattle in all Mexico; that there they would find their journeys' end, rearing a family of honest, God-fearing children to give the ranch over to when McComas was too aged and saddle-bent to run it himself, and when he and Billie Blossom had earned their wicker chairs and quiet hours in the cool shadows of the ranch house *galería,* somewhere down there in Nuevo León.

It went like that, so swift and tumbling and stirring to the imagination, that McComas began to wonder if it were not all a dream. If he would not awaken on that uneasy bed upstairs in the Border Star Hotel. Awaken with the sound of the sheriff's step in the hallway outside. And his voice calling low and urgent through the door: "Open up, McComas. It's me, and I've come for you at last."

But it was no dream.

Billie proved that to McComas, when she led him from the table and pulled him in under the shadows of the stairwell and gave him the longest, hardest kiss he had ever been given in his life. And when she whispered to him: "Hurry and get the horses, McComas. I will pack and meet you in the alley out back."

McComas pushed across the crowded room, the happiest he had been in his lifetime memory. But he did not allow the new feeling to narrow the sweep of his restless eyes. Or slow his crouching, wolf-like step. Or let his right hand stray too far from the worn wooden grip of his .44. He still knew his name was McComas, and that he was worth $500, alive or dead, to the Encinal sheriff and his La Salle County posse. It was the price of staying alive in his profession, this unthinking wariness, this perpetual attitude of *qui vive*. Especially in a strange town at sundown. With the hanging tree waiting in the next county north. And a long life and new love beckoning from across the river, from two miles south, from ten minutes away.

He went out of the batwing saloon doors, glidingly, silently, as he always went out of strange doors, anywhere.

He saw Anson Starett a half instant before the latter saw him. He could have killed him then, and he ought to have. But men like McComas did not dry-gulch men like Anson Starett. Not even when they wear the pewter star and come up on your heels hungry and hard-eyed and far too swiftly for your mind to realize and to grasp and to believe that they have cut you off at last. You do not let them live because they are gallant and tough and full of cold nerve. You do it for a far simpler reason. And a deadlier one. You do it for blind, stupid pride. You do it because you will not have it said that McComas needed the edge on any man. And while you do not, ever, willingly, give that edge away, neither do you use it to blindside a brave man like Sheriff Anson Starett of Encinal.

What you do, instead, is to keep just enough of the edge to be safe. And to give just enough of it away to be legally and morally absolved of murder. It was a fine line, but very clear to McComas. It wasn't being noble. Just practical. Every man is his own jury, when he wears a gun for money. No man wants to judge himself a coward. All that has been gone through when he put on the gun to begin with. Perhaps, it was even what made him put on the gun to begin with. What did it matter now? Little, oh, very, very little. Almost nothing at all.

"Over here, Anse," said McComas quietly, and the guns went off.

McComas was late. Only a little, but he was late. He knew and damned himself, even as he spun to the drive of Starett's bullet, back against the front wall of the Ben-Hur, then sliding down it to the boardwalk at its base.

But he had gotten Starett. He knew that. The Encinal sheriff was still standing, swaying out there in the street, but

McComas had gotten him. And, he told himself, he would get him again — now — just to make sure.

It took all his will to force himself up from the rough boards beneath him. He saw the great pool of blood, where he had fallen, but it did not frighten him. Blood and the terrible shock of gunshot wounds were a part of his trade. Somehow, it was different this time, though. This time he felt extremely light and queer in the head. It was a feeling he had never had before. It was as though he were watching himself. As though he were standing to one side, saying: "Come on, McComas, get up . . . get up and put the rest of your shots into him before he falls . . . drive them into him while he is still anchored by the shock of that first hit. . . ."

But McComas knew that he had him. He knew, as he steadied himself and emptied the .44 into Starett, that he had him, and that everything was still all right. But he would have to hurry. He could not stay there to wait for Starett to go down. He had to get out of there, while there was yet time. Before the scared sheep in the saloon got their nerve back and came pouring out into the street. Before the sound of the gunfire brought the local law, running up the street, to help out the sheriff from Encinal.

He thought of Billie Blossom. . . . The good Lord knew he did. But she couldn't do anything for him now. It was too late for Billie Blossom and gunfighter McComas. They had waited and talked too long. . . . Now he must get out. . . . He must not let the girl see him hurt and bleeding. . . . She must not know. . . . He had to get to his horse at the hitching rail. . . . Had to find Coaly and swing up on him and give him his sleek black head and let him go away up the main street and out of Laredo. . . . Yes, he must find Coaly at the rail . . . find him and get up on him and run! run! run! for the river . . . just he and Coaly, all alone and through the gathering dusk. . . .

He could not find Coaly, then. When he turned to the hitching rail in front of the Ben-Hur, his trim, black racer was not there. He was not where he had left him, all saddled and loose-tied and ready to run. McComas was feeling light and queer again. Yet he knew he was not feeling that queer. Somebody had moved his horse. Somebody had untied him and taken him, while McComas was on the boardwalk from Starett's bullet. Somebody had stolen Coaly, and McComas was trapped.

Trapped and very badly hurt. And left all alone to fight or die in the streets of Laredo.

It was then that he heard the whisper. Then that he whirled, white-faced, and saw her standing at the corner of the saloon, in the alley leading to the back. Standing there with a black Mexican *rebozo* drawn tightly over her ash-blonde hair, shadowing and hiding her hollow cheeks and great gray eyes. McComas could not distinctly see her face. Not under the twilight masking of that dark shawl. But he knew it was she. And he went running and stumbling toward her, her soft voice beckoning as though from some distant hill, yet clear as the still air of sundown — *"Here, McComas, here! Come to my arms, come to my heart, come with me . . . ."*

He lunged on. Stumbled once. Went down. Staggered back up and made it to her side before the first of the murmuring crowd surged out of the Ben-Hur to halt and stare at the great stain of blood, spreading from the front wall of the saloon. The moment her white, cool hands touched him, took hold of him and held him up, he felt the strength flow into him again. The strength flow in and the queer, cold feeling disappear from his belly and

365

the cottony mist dissolve from before his straining eyes. Now he was all right.

He remembered clearly, as she helped him along the side of the *cantina*, looking down at his shirtfront and seeing the pump of the blood jumping, with each pulse, from the big hole torn midway between breastbone and navel. He remembered, thinking clearly: *Dear Lord, he got me dead center! How could it have missed the heart?* Yet, he remembered, even as he heard his thought-voice ask the question, that these crazy things did happen with gun wounds. A shot could miss a vital by half a hair's width, and do no more harm than a fleshy scrape. There was only the shock and the weakness of the first smash, and no real danger at all unless the bleeding did not stop. And McComas knew that it would stop. It was already slowing. All he had to worry about was staying with Billie Blossom until she could get him to a horse. Then he would be able to make it away. He could ride. He had ridden with worse holes through him. He would make it. He would get across the river, and he and Billie would still meet on the far side.

She had a horse waiting for him. He ought to have known she would, a girl like that, old to the ways of Texas strays and their traffic through the border towns. He should even have known that it would be his own horse, saddled and rested and ready to run through the night and for the river.

Yes, she had slipped out of the Ben-Hur before the others. She had seen how it was with McComas and Anson Starett. And she had untied Coaly and led him down the alley, to the back, where McComas could swing up on him, now, and sweep away to the river and over it to the life that waited beyond. To the life that he and Billie Blossom had planned and that Anson Starett had thought he could stop with one bullet from his swift gun. Ah, no! Anson Starett! Not today. Not this day. Not with one bullet. Not McComas.

There was no kiss at Coaly's side, and no time for one.

But McComas was all right again. Feeling strong as a yearling bull. Smiling, even laughing, as he leaned down from the saddle to take her pale hand and promise her that he would be waiting beyond the river.

Yet, strangely, when he said it, she was not made happy. She shook her head quickly, looking white and frightened and talking hurriedly and low, as she pressed his hand and held it to her wasted cheek.

And the tears which washed down over McComas's hand were not warm; they were cold as the lifeless clay, and McComas heard her speak with a sudden chill which went through him like an icy knife.

"No, McComas, no! Not the river! Not while there is yet daylight. You cannot cross the river until the night is down. Go back, McComas. Go back the other way. The way that you came in this afternoon, McComas. Do you remember? Back toward the cemetery on the hill. You will be safe there, McComas. No one will think to look for you there. Do you hear me, McComas? Wait there for me. High on the hill, where you saw the open grave. You can watch the Laredo road from there. You can see the river. You can see the sheriff and his posse ride out. You can see when they are gone and when it is safe for you to ride out. Then we can go, McComas. I will meet you there, on the hill, by that new grave. We will go over the river together, when it is dark and quiet and all is at peace, and we know no fear. Do you understand, McComas? Oh, dear God, do you hear and understand what I am telling you, my love . . . ?"

McComas laughed again, trying to reassure her, and to reassure himself. Of course, he understood her, he said. And she was thinking smart. A sight smarter than McComas had been thinking since Starett's bullet had smashed him into that front wall and down onto the boardwalk. He got her calmed and quieted, he thought, before turning away. He was absolutely sure of it. And when he left her, turning in the saddle to look back as Coaly took him out and away from the filthy hovels of Laredo into the clean, sweet smell of the mesquite and catclaw chaparral, he could still see her, smiling and waving to him, slender and graceful as a willow wand moving against the long purple shadows of the sunset.

It was only a few minutes to the cemetery. McComas cut back into the main road and followed along it, unafraid. He was only a mile beyond the town, but in some way he knew he would not be seen. And he was not. Two cowboys came along, loping toward Laredo, and did not give him a second glance. They did not even nod or touch their hat brims going by, and McComas smiled and told himself that it always paid to wear dark clothes and ride a black horse in his hard business — especially just at sundown in a strange town.

The rusted gates of the cemetery loomed ahead.

Just short of them, McComas decided he would take cover for a moment. There was no use abusing good luck. Down the hill, from the new grave on the rise, were coming some familiar figures. They were the long-jawed preacher and square-built deputy sheriff he had passed earlier, on his way into Laredo. They might remember him, where two passing cowboys had shown no interest.

Up on the rise, itself, beyond the deputy and the parson's lurching buggy, McComas could see the two Mexican gravediggers putting in the last full shovels of flinty earth to fill the fresh hole where they had lowered the long black coffin from the flatbed wagon. And he could see, up there, standing alone and slightly apart, the weeping figure of the young girl in the black *rebozo*.

McComas thought that was a kind, loyal thing for her to do. To stay to say good bye to her lover. To wait until the preacher and the deputy and the gravediggers and the wagon driver had gone away, so that she might be alone with him. Just herself and God and the dead boy up there on that lonely, rocky rise.

Then, McComas shivered. It was the same shiver he had experienced on this same road, in this same place, earlier that afternoon. Angered, he forced himself to be calm. It was crazy to think that he knew this girl. That he had seen her before. He knew it was crazy. And, yet. . . .

The deputy and the preacher were drawing near. McComas pulled Coaly deeper into the roadside brush, beyond the sagging gates. The deputy kneed his mount into a trot. He appeared nervous. Behind him, the preacher whipped up his bony plug. The rattle of the buggy wheels on the hard ruts of the road clattered past McComas, and were gone. The latter turned his eyes once more toward the hilltop and the head-bowed girl.

He did not want to disturb her in her grief, but she was standing by the very grave where Billie Blossom had told him to meet her. And it was growing dark, and Billie had wanted him to be up there so that he could see her coming from town to be with him.

He left Coaly tied in the brush and went up the hill on foot. He went quietly and carefully, so as not to bother the girl, not to violate her faithful sorrow. Fortunately, he was able to succeed. There was another grave nearby. It had a rough boulder for a headstone, and a small square of sun-bleached pickets around it. McComas got up to this plot without being seen by the girl. He hid behind its rugged marker and tottering fence, watching to be sure the slender mourner had not marked his ascent.

Satisfied that she had not, he was about to turn and search the Laredo road for Billie Blossom, when he was again taken with the strange, unsettling chill of recognition for the girl in the black *rebozo*. This time, the chill froze his glance. He could not remove his eyes from her. And, as he stared at her, she reached into a traveling bag which sat upon the ground beside her. The bag was packed, as though for a hurried journey, its contents disordered and piled in without consideration. From among them, as McComas continued to watch, fascinated, the girl drew out a heavy .41-caliber Derringer. Before McComas could move, or even cry out, she raised the weapon to her temple.

He leaped up, then, and ran toward her. But he was too late. The Derringer discharged once, the blast of its orange flame searing the *rebozo*. McComas knew, from the delayed, hesitating straightness with which she stood before she fell, that it had been a death shot. When he got to her, she had slumped across the newly mounded grave, her white arms reaching out from beneath the shroud of the *rebozo* in a futile effort to reach and embrace the plain pine headboard of the grave. McComas gave the headboard but a swift side glance. It was a weathered, knotty, poor piece of wood, whipsawed in careless haste. The barn paint used to dab the deceased's name upon it had not even set dry yet. McComas did not give it a second look.

He was down on the ground beside the fallen girl, holding her gently to his breast, so that he might not harm her should life, by any glad chance, be in her still.

But it was not.

McComas felt that in the limp, soft way that she lay in his arms. Then, even in the moment of touching her, the chill was in him again. He *did* know this girl. He knew her well. And more. He knew for whom she mourned, and he knew whose name was on that headboard.

It was then he shifted her slim form and slowly pulled the black *rebozo* away from the wasted, oval face. The gray eyes were closed, thick lashes downswept. The ash-blonde hair lay in a soft wave over the bruised hole in the pale temple. It was she,

Billie Blossom. The girl from the streets of Laredo.

McComas came to his feet. He did not want to look at that weathered headboard. But he had to.

There was only a single word upon it. No first name. No birth date. No line of love or sad farewell.

Just the one word:

McComas

He went down the hill, stumbling in his haste. He took Coaly out of the brush and swung up on him and sent him outward through the night and toward the river. It was a quiet night, with an infinite field of gleaming stars and a sweet, warm rush of prairie wind to still his nameless fears. He had never known Coaly to fly with such a fleet, sure gait. Yet, swiftly as he went, and clearly as the starlight revealed the silvered current of the river ahead, they did not draw up to the crossing. He frowned and spoke to Coaly, and the black whickered softly in reply and sprang forward silently and with coursing, endless speed through the summer night.

That was the way that McComas remembered it.

The blackness and the silence and the stars and the rush of the warm, sweetly scented wind over the darkened prairie.

He forgot if they ever came to the river.

About the Author

Henry Wilson Allen wrote under both the Clay Fisher and Will Henry bylines and was a five-time winner of the Spur Award from the Western Writers of America. He was born in Kansas City, Missouri. His early work was in short subject departments with various Hollywood studios, and he was working at M-G-M when his first Western novel, NO SURVIVORS (1950), was published. While numerous Western authors before Allen provided sympathetic and intelligent portraits of Indian characters, Allen from the start set out to characterize Indians in such a way as to make their viewpoints an integral part of his stories. RED BLIZZARD (1951) was his first Western novel under the Clay Fisher byline and remains one of his best. Some of Allen's images of Indians are of the romantic variety, to be sure, but his theme often is the failure of the American frontier experience and the romance is used to treat his tragic themes with sympathy and humanity. On the whole, the Will Henry novels tend to be based more deeply in actual historical events, whereas in the Clay Fisher titles he was more intent on a story filled with action that moves rapidly. However, this dichotomy can be misleading, since MacKENNA'S GOLD (1963), a Will Henry Western about gold-seekers, reads much as one of the finest Clay Fisher titles, THE TALL MEN (1954). His novels, I, TOM HORN (1975), ONE MORE RIVER TO CROSS (1967), JOURNEY TO SHILOH (1960), CHIRICAHUA (1972), and FROM WHERE THE SUN NOW STANDS (1960) in particular, remain imperishable classics of Western fiction. Over a dozen films have been made based on his work.

"I am but a solitary horseman of the plains, born a century too late and far away," Allen once wrote about himself. He felt out of joint with his time, and what alone may ultimately unify his work is the vividness of his imagination, the tremendous emotion with which he invested his characters and fashioned his Western stories. At his best, he wove an almost incomparable spell that involves a reader deeply in his narratives, informed always by his profound empathy for so many of the casualties of the historical process.

"The Skinning of Black Coyote" under the byline Clay Fisher first appeared in *Esquire Magazine* (11/51). Copyright © 1951 by Esquire Magazine, Inc. Copyright © renewed 1979 by Henry Wilson Allen. Copyright © 1999 by Dorothy H. Allen for restored material.

"Not Wanted Dead or Alive" under the byline Will Henry first appeared in WILL HENRY'S WEST (Texas Western Press, 1984) edited by Dale L. Walker. Copyright © 1984 by Henry Wilson Allen.

"The Streets of Laredo" under the byline Will Henry first appeared in WESTERN ROUNDUP (Macmillan, 1961) edited by Nelson Nye. Copyright © 1961 by Henry Wilson Allen. Copyright © renewed 1989 by Henry Wilson Allen.

"Comanche Passport" under the byline Will Henry first appeared in *Zane Grey's Western Magazine* (9/51). Copyright © 1951 by The Hawley Publications, Inc. Copyright © renewed 1979 by Henry Wilson Allen. Copyright © 1999 by Dorothy H. Allen for restored material.

"The Tallest Indian in Toltepec" under the byline Will Henry first appeared in SONS OF THE WESTERN FRONTIER (Chilton Book Company, 1966). Copyright © 1966 by Henry Wilson Allen. Copyright © renewed 1994 by Dorothy H. Allen.

The employees of Thorndike Press hope you have enjoyed this Large Print book. All our Large Print titles are designed for easy reading, and all our books are made to last. Other Thorndike Press Large Print books are available at your library, through selected bookstores, or directly from the publishers.

For more information about titles, please call:

(800) 257-5157

To share your comments, please write:

Publisher
Thorndike Press
P.O. Box 159
Thorndike, Maine 04986

Grant Public Library
Grant, NE 69140

Grant Public Library
Grant, NE 69140

WITHDRAWN